The Beauty's Beast

THE FAIRY TALES OF LYOND SERIES

ELI DONOVAN, E.D. WALKER

Cover designed by Najla Qamber Designs www.qamberdesignsmedia.com

Edited by Jill Noble

Copy edited by the Formatting Fairies

Formatting by Eli Donovan with Atticus Software

Contact the author: writerelidonovan@gmail.com

Eli Donovan Website: www.elidonovan.wordpress.com

PRINT ISBN: 9780996009911

Dedication

To *Marie de France*, for providing the inspiration for this story.

And to the marvelous *Chris Juzwiak*. I can declare, in all sincerity, that this book would never have happened without him.

Contents

Epigraph

"I don't want to forget Bisclavret;
...the Normans call it Garwaf [the Werewolf]
In the old days, people used to say—
And it often actually happened—
That some men turned into werewolves
And lived in the woods.
A werewolf is a savage beast;
While his fury is on him
He eats men, does much harm,
Goes deep in the forest to live.
But that's enough of this for now:
I want to tell you about the Bisclavret..."

—From "Bisclavret" by Marie de France
(As translated by Robert Hanning and Joan Ferrante)

Prologue

O nce upon a time...

Is that how all the stories used to start? After all this time, all this solitude, I'm not sure what I remember anymore. What is real?

Once upon a time I was a man. I remember that much. Not just a man, but a knight.

Remember that. Hold to that.

A knight I was, cherished by the king himself. Respected. Renowned. The most beloved knight in all the land. A hero.

But now I am a beast. What honor I possessed has disappeared along with my fine clothes and gold-etched armor. Along with my titles and honors and lands. Along with her...

All lost, all gone, and now...

The wolf's upper lip curled back over his fangs, and a low rumble escaped his throat. Were it still a human throat, the growl might have passed for a rueful chuckle. From the throat of a wolf, the sound was little better than a deep snarling.

And now? And now what? He bounded out of the cool shade of his den. His paws sank into the wet, spongy ground beneath him as he ran through the forest, fighting to outpace his thoughts. Normally, he hid himself from the light of the day. The sunshine brought back too many memories of what he'd been—and hammered home all too forcefully what he was *now*.

Today he found no rest wherever he went. All his soul searching only stirred up a restless, painful energy inside him. When you are a beast, what good is there in trying to think like a man?

Echoing growls from his ribcage reminded him of what his human thoughts had distracted him from for too long: wolf, man, or otherwise—he was *hungry*.

Chapter One

L ady Kathryn understood where her duty lay. She truly did. The hitch, though, the tricky part, the twisty trouble was...well, she was having a difficult time convincing herself that her duty was to do her duty.

The royal court of Lyond had not taken part in a hunt since the marriage of the Princess Aliénor from Jerdun to their King Thomas a month previous. Kathryn had been one of the queen's ladies only since Aliénor's marriage, but in one short month Kathryn had grown very fond of her queen. She would do almost anything for her, but...did it have to be hunting?

Riding had never been one of Kathryn's favorite pastimes. When her father had gambled away the funds necessary to keep their horses, the loss of her late mother's mare had caused Kathryn only a small touch of regret. She certainly liked horses, and riding could be pleasant, but *this*—this neck-or-nothing tear through the woods, the bouncing and jostling, that she could *not* like.

Meanwhile, the great brute of a horse below her kept ignoring all her most urgent instructions. Clearly, the horse recognized who was master, and it certainly was *not* the featherweight astride his back, pulling at his reins. He had his head now and would not have slowed for a rider twice as skillful as Kathryn. With an angry whinny, the horse broke from the group of hunters and careened wildly off into the forest.

Teeth jarring together, branches whipping her face, Kathryn clenched her legs around the horse's sides and fought to hold on. Unfortunately, a bare moment later, she tumbled forward off her horse's neck, the ground rising up to meet her. "*Oof.*" She lay stunned in the damp leaves, the musty smell of the dirt thick in her nostrils.

Meanwhile, the careless beast who'd tossed her galloped gleefully back to his stable for some oats and a good brushing down.

Kathryn pushed upright with a groan. "Oh dear." The hunt was on, and her companions would probably not miss her for some time. When the world stopped spinning, she stood with the aid of an obliging tree trunk and took in her surroundings. The lush forest possessed a heavy covering of brush on the ground, clustering around the roots of the tall trees.

"Help!" She put a hand to her chest, trying to calm her still-hammering heart. "Anyone? Hello?"

The forest swallowed her cries. The only sounds around her were the gentle rustlings of wind in the trees. She swallowed her fear, stifling it, and started walking, hoping someone had noticed her difficulties and come looking. She would be having a very long day if they hadn't.

A strange noise caught her attention, and she tilted her head to listen. Barking, horses, and—the high-pitched howl of a wolf? She froze. *I thought we hunted the hart this day.* This thought was swiftly chased away by another and rather more alarming one: *They're coming this way.*

The crashing of hooves through the underbrush filled her ears, along with the bloodthirsty cries of the hunting dogs and the triumphant shouts of men.

She stood at the edge of a small clearing. A hoyden in her youth, Kathryn was out of practice now and had a little difficulty maneuvering with her hampering skirts. Nevertheless, she swung herself up quickly enough onto the first branch of the nearest tree.

Just in time too. The king and his entourage, having trapped their quarry at last, thundered into the clearing, their giant horses trampling over the place where she had been standing.

The wolf smelled the dogs before he heard the sounds of the hunt echoing in his forest. The hounds scented him before they gave chase, howling and baying while they tracked his progress through the woods. His werewolf's scent, and the stench of magic about him, always drove poor beasts like hunting dogs mad.

Ah, well. The wolf believed himself rather smarter than even the wiliest hunting dog and had tricks enough to bring himself safely home. He stretched his muscles and broke into a run, shoulders flexing, muscles singing at the exercise.

He caught a hint of smell then—the merest breath to fill his nostrils. But it was enough. A spasm of grief choked him, and a whine broke from his throat. The wolf stopped. He could not have moved if he'd wanted to—and he did not want to.

My king, he thought, just before the hounds caught up to him. He ran then, cursing himself as he darted between the trees and slogged through the tangles of underbrush. *Idiot. You let one smell on the air distract you long enough for the dogs to get your scent. Now what are you going to do?*

Befuddled and at war with himself, he fumbled through his escape, stumbling, taking wrong turns. His baser instincts pulled with every fiber of muscle for him to slip away and lose himself in the forest, foiling this hunt as he had so many others. Yet his human heart, and what parts of his head it still had sway over, urged him in the other direction—back to the humans. Back to the king.

His hesitation, his dreadful indecision, gave the hunting dogs the edge. The wolf wore himself out running from them *and* from himself. If he didn't focus—and soon—the dogs would get him.

The swift hounds chased him for hours, wearing the wolf down, tiring him out so he would be too weak to give more than a token fight at the end. He remembered this tactic well from when *he* had been the hunter on the horse. He winced remembering all the poor beasts his prized hounds had chased down for him and the terrified, fatigued animals he had put to death as a man and ceremoniously carved up to feed to his hunting dogs.

At least I know what happens next.

The largest of the hounds caught up with the werewolf, pacing along beside him. The hound's rasping breaths rang loud in the wolf's ears. Dog and wolf were of similar height, though the wolf's body had more weight to it, larger muscles.

The hound, a whipcord of wiry strength with jaws of iron, pounced on the wolf. The werewolf dodged, and the deathblow meant for his neck fell instead to his shoulder. Searing heat erupted along the wolf's side, and he snarled. The hound thrashed and bit down again with bruising strength.

With true remorse as the wolf remembered how fond he had been of his own hounds, he savagely locked onto the dog's neck. With a bone-shattering crunch, the wolf snapped the dog's neck and ripped its throat open.

Gurgling, eyes rolling back, the dog fell dead to the soft turf of the forest. Even as the wolf mourned the beast, he reveled in the metallic stench of the dog's blood and savored the hot broth. Yet he did not linger long over his kill as the other dogs caught up to their dead leader. The thunder of hooves and the jeering calls of men echoing among the trees meant their masters weren't far behind.

With a whimper, he leapt into motion again, his long strides making his injured shoulder flare with pain. The wolf's stomach rumbled from hunger. He could still taste the hound's blood in his mouth, mingling with some of his own. His body ached from fatigue.

His wounded shoulder betrayed him, and he stumbled. Falling, he rolled across the spongy earth, kicking up the rich scent of mud and the sharp tang of broken greenery.

Wet and sticky with blood, the wolf rolled to his feet with a snarl. He blinked bleary eyes to focus on his surroundings. The dogs closed in around him, pressing him back to a tight knot of trees. He faced the pack of snarling hounds as their masters rode into sight just through the trees. He tried to stagger out of the clearing, to shelter, to safety, but a hound snapped at him and, growling low, forced the wolf back.

The hunt thundered into the clearing, and the ground vibrated beneath his paws from the force of so many horses. Riders stalked the wolf on all sides, cornering him. Slowly the dogs crept nearer to tear him limb from limb for the delectation of their keepers.

Let them come. He snapped at the nearest hound, growling loud enough that his whole body seemed to vibrate with the sound. *I am not a knight anymore, but I can still fight. This I will do to the end. To the death.*

Through his haze of fatigue, he wondered idly why the dogs had not finished him yet. His human memory cheerfully supplied the answer to the wolf's addled wits: in a hunt like this, the actual kill was saved for the highest-ranking member. In this case: King Thomas.

The king was going to kill him. Then the nobles and other worthies would hack him to bits. Very ceremoniously and reverently, of course, but all the same, there would not be much left of the wolf at the end. Then, last, in reward for a job well done, the dogs might get to eat some of his mangled carcass. As far as an ugly death went, it was hard to top that.

But oh, his body ached and his heart hurt, and if he got to see his king again...*Fool that I am, that might almost be worth it.*

———◆———

The hunters' prey was a wolf. The largest wolf Kathryn had ever seen or heard tell of. As large as a man. Ugly wounds spotted the beast's black coat, and a deep bite mark on its shoulder glistened with blood. The wolf growled at the group, almost as if he realized what was coming.

She had never seen a wolf so close before, and she studied it in fascination from her vantage point. It had a rather luxurious black pelt and a long snout.

She jumped as the wolf raised its head and hurled a defiant snarl at its tormentors. *Those eyes.* No wolf's eyes ever looked like that. She had seen wolves from a distance at night near her home and, true, all wolves had uncanny eyes. She had always half believed they could see to your soul and back again. Their eyes held knowing, but not like this. This wolf's eyes, they were *human*. The dark blue, round-pupiled eyes of a human.

She gasped, and the rider below her tree glanced up. Stomach churning, Kathryn found herself staring down into the amused face of King Thomas.

Oh dear.

The king laughed. "What have we here? A tree dryad? A nymph, mayhap?" His mouth turned up in mild amusement. "Lady Kathryn, is it not?"

She had never before spoken to King Thomas in her time at court. For a long, shocked moment, she studied her ruler in mute fascination. Broad shouldered and vigorous despite being in his mid-forties, the king had a quiet dignity, an inborn strength. His face was lined but had a rugged appeal, the fascination of a face well lived in. His features had a certain leonine cast to them, with a graceful appeal and refinement of line. The king's gray-blue eyes were kind, though dimmed from within by some terrible sadness.

She realized she'd been staring and hastily executed the most graceful bow she could manage while clinging to her tree. "The wolf, my lord—"

"A magnificent beast. Too large and certainly too wily to be anything but magical. His pelt will be a fine prize."

"*No.*" The syllable tore itself from her throat before she could think the better of speaking.

The king's eyes blazed with anger. She lowered her gaze, and embarrassed heat bloomed across her face as the rest of the hunting party craned to look at her.

———◆———

"No." A voice broke through the weariness pounding at him. The wolf glanced into the canopy of trees and saw a face, sweet and sympathetic, hanging above him. A face with rosy cheeks and kind, light-green eyes. The first human face he

had really looked at, really seen, in two years. *Well, if I am to die today in this accursed form, at least I have seen the face of human compassion one last time.*

The green eyes lowered, and his own gaze followed them. His breath caught as he saw the king—a face as well known to him as his own human face had once been. A sight more beloved than any other. He looked into the face of the king, his lord, his family, and the wolf's heart clenched with pain.

Not quite knowing what he did, the werewolf gathered what remained of his strength. With a grunt of pain at the tearing hurt from his shoulder, the wolf leapt over the ring of dogs separating him from his liege.

He landed by the hooves of King Thomas's horse and, before the animal could shy away, the wolf had caught the stirrup of the saddle with his paws. As best he could manage with his lupine snout, the wolf humbled himself before his lord and licked the great man's boot.

— ◆ —

King Thomas stared at this marvel for a full minute and might have stared still longer but for Kathryn's intervention as she screamed, "My lord, *the dogs!*"

The king finally noticed that not only the dogs but also their keepers had advanced on the wolf with deadly intent. "*My lords.*" The king raised one leather-gloved hand. All action in the clearing halted at this slight gesture. The dogs' keepers brought them to heel, and the men waited, holding their collective breath. The rasping of the injured wolf became the loudest noise about. Even the accustomed rustlings and murmurs of the wild things in the woods seemed to have stilled themselves to hear the king's announcement.

"Behold this marvel." King Thomas signaled to the wolf on the ground. "A humble beast begs for his king's mercy. Truly—" He paused and looked more closely at the wolf. "I think this beast has the mind of a man. Take my dogs away."

Because he was their liege, the meadow soon emptied of all save the king, his most trusted retainers, the queen, Kathryn—still in the tree—and the wolf.

"Do you require assistance to descend, my lady?" the king asked Kathryn, his mouth twitching in a grin.

Kathryn composed her face and shook her head. She leapt down from her sanctuary, landing a few feet away from the wolf. Pity stabbed at her heart as she stared at the disheveled creature, the labored heaving of its sides, the bloody patches on its hide. "What will you do with the beast, my lord?"

King Thomas alighted from his horse, offering her his arm. As she stepped forward, he covered her hand where it rested on his elbow. A quick wink came and went so fast she could not be sure she'd seen the movement at all.

The king turned from her and addressed his courtiers. "As I am king, hear me and obey. I do here and now extend the hand of mercy to this creature. He is rational. He has a mind. No one is to harm him. Ever." King Thomas sighed with great weariness. "I shall hunt no more today. Let us return."

One of the knights surrendered his own mount to Kathryn and led the great stallion by the reins as she rode. The knight, Sir Edric, grinned over his shoulder at her as he led the horse, but Kathryn gave him only a wan smile in return. She closed her eyes, the swaying gait of the animal soothing as she drooped with fatigue in the saddle.

"My lady."

She blinked her eyes open and looked to her escort.

"The king requests that you attend him," Sir Edric said.

Kathryn stifled a sigh and nodded, taking the reins from the knight's outstretched hand. She trotted the horse to the front of the column to ride beside the king as requested. On the king's other side, Queen Aliénor frowned at the king. "But, husband, isn't it possible this could be a trap? Some magical mischief sent from Jerdun."

Kathryn froze, feeling her eyes go wide.

The king glanced over and noticed her at last. He smiled. "Lady Kathryn, what think you of this?" He motioned to the ground on his right side.

Kathryn craned to see past his horse and gasped to see the wolf limping quite determinedly in step with the king's horse. Kathryn had believed the wolf all but dead back in the clearing. Truly, she thought they had left him there. A misapprehension, apparently.

Queen Aliénor shook her head. "I don't think this is a good idea. The beast could be dangerous."

King Thomas made a small gesture of negation with his hand. "I disagree. I trust the wolf. He feels...familiar somehow. Noble."

His wife made a small, dissatisfied *hmph* noise and looked behind. "Well, I do not trust the beast."

King Thomas caught her hand and dropped a quick kiss. "Trust me then." He scratched the line of his bearded jaw and addressed Kathryn again, "While you were being helped to a mount, a few of my men tried to deter the wolf from this course of action. They were, shall we say, disabused of the notion that he would be parted from me."

Kathryn grimaced. She hated to think they had been wrong about a noble, knowledgeable beast, after all. Maybe Queen Aliénor was right to be afraid.

"Oh, nothing serious," the king explained, perhaps noticing Kathryn's discomfort. "Just some light scratches and bruising."

Kathryn snorted to find the king so nonplussed at the threat of his best men being mauled by a mystical animal.

"What shall I do with the creature, Lady Kathryn? Any suggestions?"

The queen opened her mouth but pinched it closed, swallowing whatever she'd been about to say. She creased her brows, watching Kathryn.

Kathryn shifted uneasily, feeling torn between the two royals. Her loyalty was to the queen, and clearly Queen Aliénor disliked the beast. But, after saving the wolf in the clearing, it seemed wrong to leave him behind to bleed to death in the forest. Kathryn couldn't bring herself to say anything to either monarch and simply stared hard at the back of her horse's neck. *Coward.* The slightest misstep could see her banished from court, though. Her father would be furious with her if she were cast out. She dare not risk that.

She darted a sideways glance at the king. A corner of his mouth tipped up as if he sensed some of her inner turmoil. "Perhaps inspiration will strike when we reach my castle."

———◆———

My king. The werewolf trotted—well, limped eagerly—along at the heels of Samson, the king's horse. The werewolf, despite his still-blighted life, basked in the glow of not only his king's mercy but also his generosity in taking along an injured wolf.

What good have I done in the world to deserve so great a boon? Not only to behold the face of my king but also to be with him, ride with him again. Beast or no beast, what does my form matter if I am to have a chance to serve my lord again?

He smiled to himself, happily padding along in step with the king's horse. Yet the wolf's happiness wavered as the maiden from the tree craned around in her saddle to look at him. Her hair was disheveled. Mud had splashed the front of her gown and spotted the line of her jaw. She seemed very vulnerable to him, innocent even, but the wolf had learned his lesson about women. *Never again.*

He pushed aside this gloomy thought and stared again at King Thomas. No, the wolf would allow nothing to tarnish his joy at this reunion. *I have my king again, and nothing and no one else matters.*

Chapter Two

When they reunited with the rest of the hunting party in a clearing, the wolf caused much comment among the queen's other ladies. A few shrieked and sank into the arms of the nearest men. The queen merely stood with her fists clenched and a pleat of worry between her brows.

King Thomas knelt before the beast, gently rubbing its ears, and the wolf's tongue lolled out from happiness. "I think the beast has walked far enough this day. I will carry him before me on my saddle."

Queen Aliénor hissed a breath out through her teeth. "Stubborn—" She shook her head. "You will do no such fool thing. I will give up my coach to the creature, which will be entirely more comfortable for him. My ladies and I can ride."

King Thomas grinned at his wife, looking happy, looking much younger than his forty odd years. Kathryn restrained a wistful sigh as she watched the two of them.

The king stood and brushed wolf hair off his hose. "Someone will have to ride with the beast, my queen, to see that he doesn't hurt himself worse before we reach the castle." King Thomas looked expectantly at his master of the hounds.

The groom spat and crossed his arms. "I'll ne'er touch the filthy beast, an' you can do your worst, sire, but that won't change me mind."

King Thomas, perhaps recalling with sympathy the death of the kennel keeper's favorite hound, shook his head. "I understand." Pacing beside the carriage, the king rubbed thoughtfully at his lips. "Now what's to do for the animal? None of my men will touch him."

Chewing her lip in indecision, Kathryn looked again to the wounded beast, which had collapsed inside the queen's ornate carriage. The wolf's breathing came in ragged pants, and blood spilled down his shoulder to his leg.

Whomever her actions might anger, she had to help him. She stepped forward and gently touched the king's arm to claim his attention. King Thomas looked down at her, his expression politely inquiring.

"Your Highness, I kept dogs at home. They would get into mischief all the time. I have never had to deal with anything as severe as this, but I did learn a little leechcraft from my uncle before his death. I might be able to do something for the beast. If there truly is no one else."

The king patted her hand and addressed the rest of his entourage. "*Is* there anyone else?"

The crowd visibly recoiled at the request, clumping together into tight groups of three or four. The queen's face scrunched with worry again. "You don't have to, Lady Kathryn."

"I...I want to, my lady."

Queen Aliénor blinked and shook her head, looking uneasily at the wolf again.

King Thomas looked to Kathryn, smiling again. "Well, what say you, my lady? Will you stay with the wolf, help him, and care for him in his sickness?"

Kathryn stifled her disquiet and nodded. "I will heal him as best I can and, when he is well, I shall do whatever else is required of me to aid him."

"And you, my fine beast?" said the king to his newest vassal.

The wolf gazed at King Thomas with a look of such naked fidelity and fondness, Kathryn almost turned away. The idea that an outsider should behold such raw and wild emotions seemed indecent.

The king scratched the wolf's head, still speaking to the animal as if it could understand. "How will you repay your debt of honor to the lady for this generous service? Will you attend the Lady Kathryn, guard her, and care for her? Be her champion should she ever have need of one?"

The wolf sniffed at the carriage floor, obviously stalling, before he looked back at the king and inclined his head ever so slightly.

King Thomas beamed at this further display of intelligence. "Remarkable. Truly a remarkable creature."

"He is at that." Kathryn bent to caress the wolf's head, but the animal ducked away from her touch, dropping his head to his paws again and shutting his eyes. She curled her fingers back, stung by the rejection.

Prickling with nervousness, Kathryn allowed the king to help her into the carriage. The door swung tightly closed, shutting her up in the dimness with the wounded wolf.

Kathryn and the wolf had been among the first to arrive at the castle, but upon the wolf stepping down from the carriage, he froze and stood stationary before the great doors of the stronghold. She watched the rest of the court pour by her. Fine ladies, gentle knights, grooms, servants, horses, carriages, and dogs all went into the king's castle. Still the wolf remained immobile before the doors. Something like fear or grief—possibly both—shone out of his peculiar blue eyes.

She studied the wolf and waited. She had time. All the time in the world, in fact, since the king had expressly said her first duties now lay in tending to the wolf. A tirewoman who had been called to assist Kathryn arrived. The servant worriedly shifted from foot to foot, chafing her hands as she eyed the wolf with misgiving.

Kathryn, however, did not mind waiting on the wolf's pleasure. Some significant struggle occurred now within the beast. His body had tensed, and he stared at the castle, taking in the high walls, the square battlements, his dark eyes flicking all over the place as he panted and shook. Kathryn did not coax him. Better to let him fight it out on his own rather than force him forward when he was not ready.

While they lingered on the threshold, the castle steward found them. "King Thomas has instructed me to secure you the necessary implements for tending the beast." The steward huffed and glanced with disfavor at the still immobile animal.

Ignoring his tone, Kathryn gave the servant a list of the necessary tools to tend the wolf's injuries, most especially the bite on his shoulder.

"And further," the steward said, making a note of all the items she had listed, "I am to show you to Master Llewellyn's workshop—"

"Master Llewellyn?"

"The king's wise man and Court Magician."

"I know who he is." Kathryn bit her cheek as her nerves jolted inside her. Master Llewellyn was the king's right-hand man, one of the most important officials in the kingdom. Surely he wouldn't appreciate some woman using his workspace to tend a wild animal.

The steward cleared his throat with thinly veiled annoyance. "The *king* has granted you use of Master Llewellyn's workshop to house the beast and care for him tonight."

"Will Master Llewellyn mind?"

"He is currently away gathering herbs in the mountains and is not expected back for a few more days."

Which didn't exactly answer her question, but it seemed the steward had no wish to be helpful, and Kathryn had a wounded wolf to care for. "Oh. Well, all right. Thank you." She dipped her head in acknowledgment, and the steward bowed as if she owed him something. The man left to fetch her tools and helpers. The scrawny maidservant would not be enough, and Kathryn supposed the woman was only there as chaperone to herself anyway, to preserve Kathryn's chastity and honor.

After a few steps, the steward turned back. "Oh yes, and is there anyone particularly suited to sitting the night out with the wolf?"

"Yes," Kathryn said. "I shall, of course."

This snapped the wolf out of his reverie, and he growled at her, more warning than menace.

Startled, Kathryn frowned and then, guessing the problem, she smiled. She knelt so only the wolf would hear her. "I'm sure staying in the quarters of a gentleman wolf is not exactly proper. But I think you are too fragile to watch the night out alone. We cannot have your condition worsen. Not if you are to be a member of the court, at any rate."

———◦◦◦———

A member of the court, the werewolf thought, much struck. *So I am. The lowliest member to be sure, but here I am. What other miracles might occur now that this first is past?*

The girl gazed at him expectantly, still patient, though she shivered as the evening air blew through the king's courtyard with the setting of the sun. The wolf looked to the trembling girl, and a quite human guilt shuddered through him, entirely alien to his wolfish body.

While inhabiting a wolf's body in a wolf's world, his life had been easier. Here and now, the hunger rushing in veins that had once pumped human blood almost overwhelmed *all* aspects of him. To enter this castle, this hallowed place, to experience even a reflected shadow of the old chivalry by which he had lived his life—he almost couldn't bear the aching in his heart.

A large part of him wanted to turn tail and run back to his isolated forest as fast as his lupine legs could carry him. Yet his human heart and his rational mind decided that nothing—not wicked fairies or a cruel goddess, enemy warriors or even another werewolf—would drag him from his home again. Finally, hesitantly, painfully, the wolf put one paw through the castle doors.

The girl watched him. "You might not have heard, but the steward has given me use of Master Llewellyn's workshop to treat you. In the garden, I believe."

The wolf cut through the main corridor of the castle, then exited out the back, turning toward a small shed snuggled up cozily against the stone walls of the castle. He led the girl without hesitation to the right building. When he glanced back, the girl was smiling to herself.

He pushed the workshop door open with one paw and waited for her to precede him. The maiden did and, keeping her face averted and her voice bland, she said, "Have you been to the castle before, Sir Wolf?"

He looked up at her sharply and huffed in a fair approximation of a human sigh. He had not meant to reveal he knew the castle, but in his present state of pain and abstraction, he had fumbled. Shaking his head, he walked into the old workshop with as much dignity as he could muster while limping on stiff legs.

The steward fulfilled all of Kathryn's wishes with precision and speed. The proper implements were there and waiting, as well as three strapping young lads from the stables who were used to violent animals and dirty work.

As the wolf wriggled his way onto the worktable, he eyed these helpers with disfavor.

"Do I need them to make you behave yourself, d'you think?" Kathryn whispered.

The wolf gave her a sharp look and then, ever so slightly, shook his head. *No.*

Smiling, Kathryn turned to the stable hands. "Just one of you, for now, to hold him steady for the first part, and the other two can step in if necessary." She gave the wolf a look from under her lashes. "Which I sincerely hope will not be necessary."

The grooms exchanged uneasy glances amongst themselves but did not speak.

Kathryn breathed deeply to steel herself and bent to examine the wolf's injuries. She had seen a few dogfights in the kennels at home, and these wounds were rather typical of a death fight. Large, deep lacerations covered his shoulder where the hound had grabbed him, and smaller cuts on the wolf's face showed where the hound had scratched at him before being killed. Mud and blood—some of which even belonged to the wolf—matted the wolf's coat.

"I'll have to use the iron to cauterize the deepest wound, I'm afraid, to prevent infection," she said absently to the wolf. Rolling up her sleeves, she patted his side gently. "I'm going to have one of my helpers here wash your wounds with wine while I get the bellows going and heat the iron."

One of the stable lads stepped forward. "I can do that, m'lady. I've practice enough with the iron from tending the dogs and horses."

She nodded. "All right. Make sure to use charcoal, not coal. And don't let the iron get so hot that flame leaps from it." Her helper nodded and went to heat the iron.

As she made everything ready, the other two grooms skirted wide around the wolf, apparently loath to touch him. She sent one to get honey and brandy from the kitchen and the other to heat water on one of the workshop's impressively efficient little braziers. She herself set about cleaning the wolf's filthy coat, rinsing the dirt and detritus from the scratches on his face and body.

He settled in comfortably to her handling. When she dabbed at the scratches with the wine, he did not flinch, snap, or otherwise make any overtures of violence toward her, even though her ministrations must have hurt him. She smiled. "You are indeed a mild-mannered wolf."

The wolf winced as she touched some tender spot. Had he been only a brutish animal, he might have whined from the pain in his shoulder. He certainly would have snapped at her, but instead he remained passive and patient. As she continued their one-sided discourse, chattering amicably about random odds and ends, the wolf looked at her rather sardonically, his eyes narrowed. The back of her neck tingled with awareness. *He understands me. Every word.* This wolf was obviously more than he seemed.

But how much more?

The girl's restful stream of prattle flowed over the wolf in a warm haze, and he closed his eyes, leaning his head against a soft cushion. Memories prickled on the edge of his senses, unwelcome and painful.

"My sweet lord." Unshed tears rimmed the corners of his wife Alisoun's pale brown eyes. "My love, please, I beg you, tell me where you go. Where do you stay when you leave me at the end of every month? You are so good a knight, so honorable, so forthright and true, and yet I fear you have a lover. Tell me the truth at once, else I shall die in not knowing." She collapsed into hysterical sobs, and he gathered her in his arms, comforting her and kissing her tears away.

Assurances that she was his only love fell on deaf ears. Alisoun would not be comforted.

"Have mercy, my love." He feathered kisses over the soft gold of her hair. "If I tell you my secret, I shall lose your love. I shall lose all I have, even my very self..."

In the end, because he loved her, he kept nothing from her. Truth be told, she'd given him little peace. When the day of his accustomed departure had neared, she'd threatened to follow him if he would not tell her where he went. So he told her, and in so doing he lost everything because of his trust in her—

The wolf flinched, returning to the present as one of the grooms yelled that the iron was heated. As carefully and quickly as the wolf could without harming himself, he eased away from the maiden's lap, where he had been half dozing.

The girl slid off the table, smoothing the front of her dress down and brushing away the black hairs he'd shed on her. His face heated, and for once he was grateful to have fur to hide his embarrassment.

The other grooms had returned from their previous errands, and all was ready. Except the girl's nerves, it seemed. She straightened her shoulders, obviously bracing herself. The blood had drained from her face, and her hands shook.

I suppose I should be glad she's not enjoying this, but I wish she looked more confident.

"Hold the wolf, please." She leaned close to him, her voice steady. "I am sorry. It is undignified, but even humans are restrained when the iron is applied."

Even humans, the wolf thought with distaste, but he nodded.

"I will see they do not hurt you." She stroked his muzzle so quickly he did not have time to flinch away.

Years had passed since a human had touched him, and he shivered at the light contact, suddenly craving more. All in one day he felt more human than he had in two years. All because of this girl.

He studied her as she made her preparations. A young woman certainly, her face unlined, her body strong and supple. No more than nineteen perhaps, medium height for a woman. Slim hips and a dainty bust gave her a trim figure, pleasing enough, but not so fine as to make a man's eyes follow the swish of her skirts as she walked past. The girl's hair shone becomingly, but her thick braid was of that troublesome shade between brown and blond, a golden sheen that caught the light but still lacked something of the dash true blond hair has.

With skin rather tanner than the fashion, she coupled that defect with, of all the most unfortunate afflictions, freckles on her nose. But the animation of her countenance, the lively joy behind her features, made a person forget she was not—strictly speaking—beautiful. Her eyes were unarguably her best feature: pale green, lushly lashed, and lovely beyond compare.

Once an expert judge of these matters, the wolf decided the girl was pretty, pert, and certainly intriguing in her own way, but she definitely was not the beauty his wife had been.

Another face flashed across his mind's eye, another woman, blond with brown eyes, and more attractive than any mortal maid had a right to be. He shivered at the memory of his wife's delicate fingers running through his hair. The girl dropped another careless caress on his head, and he ducked away from her. *This is too much.* He averted his gaze so he would not have to see the hurt on the maiden's face.

Grabbing a clean-looking rag, the girl gently bound his muzzle, tying the knot tight enough so he could not open his mouth. She scratched at his ears. "So you don't bite your tongue off." She sighed. "We're going to tie your feet as well."

He gazed at the low ceiling but did not struggle or flinch as she tied his feet to the table.

One of the burly grooms came forward to hold the wolf's shoulder still so he could not move and cause the hot brand to slip. The other stable hand moved to hold his legs steady where the rope was tied. The tirewoman, who had kept herself apart from the proceedings until now, came forward with the mixture of brandy and honey that had been prepared, at the ready to slather on the burn afterward. The third stable hand pulled the iron from the brazier and addressed himself to the girl. "Here, m'lady, let me do this. S'not proper for you."

The green-eyed girl gently lifted the hot iron from the stable hand's grip, a wisp of hair falling over her forehead as she shook her head. "I have experience in this, I promise you." She glanced at the wolf, gently stroking his head, her voice soft, soothing. "Ready, Sir Wolf?"

<hr />

The wolf caught Kathryn's eye and blinked. She understood that to be *yes*, and so, hand steady even as her nerves frayed to the breaking point, she applied the iron to his skin. All the while she cycled through her memories of her uncle showing her how to do this many years ago on one of their injured horses.

She could hear Uncle Flavio's evenly measured tones as clearly as if he were in the room with her. She allowed the memory of him to wash over her, guiding her actions. *"Little niece, be careful. You want to make sure when you apply the iron, like this—"* he'd demonstrated, his hand as firm while he held a sizzling iron against quivering flesh as when he held his cup at dinner. *"You leave the iron on long enough to create a small red spot, just so."* He had indicated the livid red mark on the horse's creamy yellow flank. *"And not just merely singe the animal's fur, which will do nothing. Take care."* This as he handed the iron off to one of his helpers. *"You do not want to leave the iron on too long and puncture the skin. Yes, good?"*

Kathryn swore as she finished her operation and hurriedly pulled the iron away, passing the long rod off to someone else, she saw not who. She wiped sweat from her brow with her sleeve and held her other hand out at once for the honey salve. The wolf, who had behaved like a prince throughout the whole agonizing operation, closed his eyes, clenching them tightly in pain, panting through the gag around his mouth.

She dosed his burn liberally with the honey-and-brandy salve and left the wound open to the air. The tension in his body eased, and the wolf at last opened his uncanny blue eyes to stare at the ceiling again.

She smiled, giving a breathless, giddy laugh. There would be swelling and bruising, and the poor beast would be rather sore and miserable for days, but now, at least, he would probably recover completely. She untied his muzzle and stroked the fur there back into place. Still groggy with pain, the wolf did not avoid her hands this time.

"If that's all, m'lady, you can leave him to us for the night and return to the queen," one of her helpers piped up.

"No, no." The king had given Kathryn permission to take as long as she needed, and she did not wish to leave the job only half done. She would see the night through with her patient. If he did well, then in the morning—and *only* then—would she surrender him to other hands. "You can return to your duties, kind sirs. My maid and I will stay here tonight and tend the wolf." Truly, Kathryn would not miss the other ladies-in-waiting to the queen. A night away from their scheming and maneuvering for position would be a welcome respite.

With obvious reluctance, the grooms obeyed Kathryn's orders. After carrying the wolf to the bed as she'd asked, the men filed out the door. She and the maidservant were left alone together.

"The beast gets the bed, my lady?" The tirewoman's voice held a note of disapproval.

"I—I do not wish to face the king tomorrow if the beast dies." It was more complicated than that, a half-crazy feeling Kathryn barely wanted to acknowledge in herself, let alone explain to a near-stranger. She wouldn't make a human patient sleep on the ground, and somehow she couldn't do that to the wolf either.

Still looking dubious, the maid nodded. "I'll fetch some extra bedding."

Kathryn escorted the maid to the door and blinked in surprise to find a guard outside the workshop's entrance.

"Are you here for me or the wolf?" she asked.

"For your honor and safety, my lady," the guard replied, voice flat.

Too exhausted to argue, Kathryn went back inside, only to discover the wolf awake and stubbornly trying to pull himself off the bed.

Chapter Three

During the daytime in the woods, when the wolf slept, he would dream human dreams of torment. Nightmares, he supposed they were. The look in his wife's eyes, eyes that he had loved so well, often filled his mind. She had only looked so for a moment. One flickering spark of…what? Revulsion? Fear? Anger? And then his wife had glanced away and spoken the same loving words of old, so he had forgotten the flicker of disgust he'd seen. He'd pushed his doubts away and pretended he still had her love. Pretended he could still trust her.

He had left his hall and rode alone to his favorite haunt that fateful day. He loved the beautiful King's Forest because if he rode to the depths of the woods, no man would disturb him, and every farmer's chickens would be safe from his insatiable appetite. The nearby shrine also possessed a hollow rock he found convenient for storing his clothes. Fool that he was, he had even told Alisoun about the rock.

"You stubborn beast," the girl scolded him.

He blinked and focused on the girl as she shooed him toward the bed. *Not "the girl." Lady Kathryn.* She had saved his life. Learning her name was surely the least he could do.

"Back to bed, Sir Wolf. What are you doing?"

Startled, he searched her face. *Does she really think I understand her? Or is she only joking with herself?* As he had no wish to be revealed as a werewolf, her behavior worried him. He looked at her, pain fogging his vision, and shook his head.

"Oh, don't play the dumb mutt with me either. If you're smart enough to beg the king for mercy, you're smart enough to know what I mean when I say get your fluffy tail back in bed." She pointed, her delicate face set in a comically severe expression.

He did not move.

Lady Kathryn pouted, an expression oddly unsuited to the practical good sense she'd demonstrated thus far. "You will not oblige me by getting on the bed?"

The wolf gave her a stern look. *I take the bed while you—what? Sleep on the floor? Unthinkable.*

"All right, my Lord the Stubborn, will you share the bed with me?"

His wound stung and throbbed, and his limbs dragged with fatigue when he moved them. Still, though he was a wolf, some part of him had been and still was a man—sort of. He would no sooner jump in an honorable maiden's bed out of wedlock than he would piss on the king's leg. The bench seemed an acceptable compromise. He jerked his snout toward the hard, flat board.

Lady Kathryn rolled her eyes and shrugged. "You win, my lord. I, bed. You, bench."

Satisfied, the wolf rose with difficulty, jumping off the high table and crossing the room. He pawed at the flat top of the bench for a moment before he at last managed to pull himself up. He settled his limbs as comfortably as he could on the hard wooden bench.

———— •◇• ————

The tirewoman returned, smiling her approval when she found Kathryn snug in the bed, sans wolf. The maid deposited her own bed for the night—a hard pallet and thin blanket—on the floor next to the mattress. "I sent word to the queen you would be spending the night here."

"Thank you." Kathryn pillowed her head on her arms and watched the lone candle flame dance, caught by a small breeze through the open window. *It has truly been a very long day. And a strange one.*

The tirewoman bedded down with a small sigh to Kathryn's side. Perhaps she had had a long day too.

Kathryn rolled over. "Shall I tell you a story, Sir Wolf?" she asked, expecting no answer and needing none. "I am said to be well versed and not entirely without skill in the telling." She looked into the wolf's eyes for the answer. He blinked owlishly, which she guessed to be his way of saying yes.

She settled against the pillows of the healer's humble cot as she told the wolf tales of a clever fox and his exploits with other members of a fictional animal court. The lordly lion king, the cowardly rabbit, the poor friar-bear, and many others besides in a myriad collection of intricate and hilarious encounters.

Kathryn did leave out the bawdier tales, and the sex-crazed she-wolf, in deference to her audience. Those tales were fine among the highborn ladies, but men had funny ideas about how women should speak.

Gradually, her audience's attention seemed to slacken, and the tirewoman began to snore softly. The wolf, too, seemed to have drifted off somewhere between the tale of the lion-king's court and the beating of Bruin the Bear.

The poor wolf had many scars. There were various old nicks and cuts taken out of his hide, and the bite on his shoulder would leave another lasting mark on the landscape of his body. A long, deep line was cut over the side of his face, crossing just shy of his right eye. She did not think an average wolf could come by such a scar in the normal way of things. A scar from his old life, mayhap?

Was he a werewolf as she suspected? Had he perhaps been a soldier or a man-at-arms as a human? A knight, even? That would explain his familiarity with the castle and the intense fealty he displayed toward the king. *Who are you, Sir Wolf?*

He went back home when he found the clothes missing—well, no, he went back after he tore the shrine's grounds apart to see if his clothes had been moved anywhere nearby. His lupine nose should have been a boon as he tried to scent the clothes. Yet after a week of frenzied searching, there was never a trace to be found.

Finally, defeated and afraid, he went back to his manor to see if Alisoun had, for some reason, taken his things. Maybe she had thought he would like them laundered before returning to his human state?

He arrived at his manor just as Lord Reynard, the Earl of Troumper, rode through his gate. Reynard was another knight in service to the king. Red haired, broad chested, fiery tempered, and wicked, Reynard had always greeted him with thinly veiled loathing.

In his wolf form, he paused, not wishing the fellow knight to suspect aught amiss. The wolf circled back, hiding in the line of trees to watch and learn why Reynard visited his home while the lord of the castle was away.

A servant met Reynard and led the big knight's horse to the stable. Another servant escorted Reynard around the back of the castle to the ornamental garden the werewolf had planted for Alisoun as a wedding gift.

Alisoun sat there waiting for Reynard. Her lovely golden hair hung unbound down to her waist, and in the soft light of many torches, she seemed blessed with an angelic halo. She dismissed the servant, and Reynard and Alisoun sat alone together.

She did not rise from her stone bench, only looked up at Reynard with flushed cheeks and the glow of anticipation about her eyes. "Well?"

"I found the clothes. They are safe hid where the monster shall not unearth them." Reynard licked his lips and stepped toward her. His gaze roamed hungrily over her figure in its tightly laced, cream-colored gown. "Your husband will plague you no more with his malignancy. I have done as you told me. Honor your oath to me."

Alisoun smiled then. A smile that had once been for her husband alone—or so the wolf had believed. She rose from the bench and enfolded Reynard in her arms. She stared into the knight's eyes with a sensuous smile. "I promised you my body and my love. You shall have both tonight. And when the quest for my husband has cooled, you shall have my hand." She stroked Reynard's dirty, travel-stained cheek with one hand and purred into his face. *"And all the werewolf's lands into the bargain."*

Reynard stopped her mouth with a lusty kiss. He hauled her into his arms, pawing at her clothes, obviously anxious to consummate their affair before Alisoun could refuse or turn him away.

The wolf ran back to the woods. Reynard had hounded Alisoun for months, but the wolf had tolerated the knight's lechery because Alisoun had treated the man with open disgust. Until now.

Until her husband had told her of his condition. His *"malignancy."*

The wolf did not rest until he was safely back in the center of his forest. He did not leave the woods again until his king reclaimed him, taking him, however unwittingly, back into the world he had been born to.

A beam of moonlight fell on his eyes. He had been dreaming but could not remember of what. He scratched his nose idly with one large paw then sneezed. In his drowsiness he forgot where he was, what he was. His bed was a hard wooden bench, and his limbs moved stiffly as he unfolded his body from a curled position. Someone stirred beside him, and moonlight limned the soft lines of a woman in bed. Without thinking, he jumped from his hard bench and crossed to climb into bed next to her. When he snuggled his body into the warmth at the small of her back, she mumbled something in her sleep but then settled in, snoring softly.

She snores like a mouse. He smiled to himself, and sleep once again claimed him.

When he woke up some hours later alone in the bed, he stared at the rumpled bedding, appalled. *I slept the better part of the night in bed with the maiden—with her...all night...in the bed*—all night. He jumped down at once and sniffed about for the gi—for Lady Kathryn.

When he glanced at the tirewoman from yesterday, she inhaled sharply. He looked away just as quickly, fearful that any prolonged study of the servant would provoke her to scream.

Lady Kathryn opened the door a moment later, dressed in a clean gown and apparently having been awake for hours. Rosy cheeked and fresh faced, she seemed well rested, the trials of the day before showing only in the deep shadows under her kind green eyes.

She carried a tray. "Breakfast, Sir Wolf." Instead of setting the food on the floor, as most people would have done, she set his meal on the small worktable.

He would have more difficulty eating that way, but this girl seemed unwilling to let him pretend to be a simple beast. So, to oblige her, he stretched and stood on his hind legs to eat breakfast.

Kathryn watched the wolf for a moment before she spoke. "You pushed me out of bed with your great hulking body last night, you know." If the wolf blushed, Kathryn could not see the reddening through all that black fur, but he did pause in his eating and seemed almost to grimace. "We are supposed to see the king as soon as you have supped."

The wolf swallowed what he had been chewing and dropped to all fours at once. *I'm ready* was writ plainly across his furry face.

"King Thomas will wait. He is not impatient." But the wolf refused to return to his breakfast, so Kathryn gave in. "I'm checking the wound first." She motioned toward the bed.

The wolf hesitated but then, apparently realizing it would be more expedient to yield to the tyrant in this case, he jumped onto the bed. She checked his wound and applied more of the soothing honey salve. As she slicked her finger over his wound, he met her gaze. Kathryn stared back, transfixed. His eyes were even stranger seen close up, deep cobalt irises with the palest of blues fanning out in slivers and waves from his pupils, piercing through the darker shade of blue.

She had never heard of a wolf with dark blue eyes before. Intelligence stared back at her out of those eyes, uncanny intelligence compared to a normal wolf.

He jerked away from her, denying their connection, which he very obviously did not want.

Her examination done, their need of the workshop at an end, Kathryn shooed the wolf out and shut the building up. She and the wolf, escorted primly by the weary tirewoman, marched to see King Thomas and his knights.

At the training field, the king sparred with a young squire soon to take his vigil and, if he passed that test, to be dubbed. As they fought, the young man flailed a bit against the king's greater expertise.

The wolf watched the sword match with obvious interest, and Kathryn waited. Eventually King Thomas, though slower in his movements, proved to be the more skillful. He knocked the young man down with a well-placed blow from the hilt of his sword. To soften the defeat, King Thomas extended a hand to help the lad up from the dirt.

The wolf barked his approval, and his tail snaked in a temperate wag across the ground. The king wiped the sweat from his brow with the back of one hand and, with an engaging grin, took leave of his opponent to receive his newest guests.

"I thank you, my lady." King Thomas kissed Kathryn's hand. "Thank you for tending his hurts and keeping him for me while I arranged a place for him here among my knights. Is he well?"

Kathryn smiled at the wolf, then back at the king. "He is, sire. I would watch his shoulder and make sure he does not exert himself. Though there's no reason for him to remain coddled since he made it clear last night that he doesn't relish such treatment."

The king swatted playfully at the beast's ears. "You have offended the lady, my wolf?"

Kathryn bowed. "No, sire, he is the most well-mannered wolf I have ever met. It was my pleasure to tend him."

"Truly a remarkable wolf, in point of fact." The sound of a stranger's voice made Kathryn turn to look.

The newcomer dwarfed them all, towering a head above even the king as King Thomas stepped forward to greet the new man. The stranger's skin had been tanned to a nut brown, but his hair was sun-bleached so fair as to be almost white. His face remained lightly lined, though, so he could not have been more than midway through his thirties. His eyes were the color of a hard winter sky, but they warmed in friendly amusement quicker than the sun could warm the flowers of the court in summer. He wore the simple black hooded robes of an occultist who needed neither fancy jewelry nor arcane symbols to do his work or to mark him as one of the Gifted. The man carried his talents about him like a suit of clothing well-worn and accustomed.

The king stepped back from his magician and presented him to Kathryn. "Lady Kathryn, this is my wise man and Court Magician, Master Llewellyn."

Flustered, Kathryn dipped in a small curtsy. "Brother."

"Oh, I'm a magician, not a monk. Please call me Llewellyn." The magician bowed at the waist. "My lady."

"Good harvest?" The king laughed.

The magician bowed and patted a sturdy leather satchel at his side. He turned to Kathryn and gave her a small smile. "Every few months our king grants me leave to wander in the mountains and gather medicine for my potions and such."

Now that he mentioned it, the heavy, brisk tang of herbs and spices clung to the conjurer, wafting over to tickle the back of Kathryn's throat.

"I have heard talk of your newest acquisition, my king." Llewellyn's voice vibrated with excitement. "I came at once to see the beast for myself." At the king's sign, the wise man dropped to one knee before the wolf.

The wolf, while the humans talked, had settled onto his stomach, dropping his chin between his front paws. He appeared very much bored by the proceedings, had even closed his eyes as if napping. Yet the animal breathed too quickly for sleep, and his face seemed tense.

Kathryn pursed her lips, worried and confused. *Why is he avoiding Llewellyn?*

Standing, Llewellyn bowed his head to Kathryn. "I wonder, lady, if you would give me a few moments of conference on your observations of the wolf."

"Gladly, Magician." Kathryn turned to take her leave. King Thomas nudged the wolf with his foot, and the beast stood, patiently looking at Kathryn. She knelt and met the wolf's strange eyes with her own.

The beast gently licked her hand before moving to join his king. *Thank you, maiden, for all you did for me,* the gesture seemed to say.

The magician's glance sharpened at this, and a speculative look fell over his features. When he noticed Kathryn watching him, Llewellyn quickly turned his expression to one of casual indifference. He gestured for her to follow him back toward the gardens.

Kathryn could not have said why, but somehow the wolf's parting gesture had reminded her of the courtly kiss a knight bestows on a lady's hand. She covered her kissed hand with the other and held both tight to her stomach. *You are the noblest knight of this land, are you not, Sir Wolf?* She smiled to herself as she followed Llewellyn away from the training field.

Chapter Four

Llewellyn led Kathryn back to his small workshop off the herb garden and escorted her inside the hut's cozy interior. The tirewoman, who still trailed after Kathryn, opted to sit on a stool in the sun and enjoy the smell of plant life wafting from the flowerbeds while the magician conversed with Kathryn inside his hut.

The daylight illuminated the hut's interior, so Kathryn could make out details of the place she had not been able to see last night. Batches of simple herbs hung from the ceiling, and shelves lined the walls filled with meticulously labeled ceramic jars.

Llewellyn motioned to a bench against one wall and waited for Kathryn to arrange her skirts before seating himself on a sturdy wooden stool across from her.

Pouring them each a tall cup from the bottle of wine she had used to clean the wolf's scratches, Llewellyn looked at her expectantly. "Well, my lady, what do you know of our wolf?" The magician absently picked up mortar and pestle to keep his hands busy while they talked. When Kathryn did not speak at once, he smiled. "Forgive me. I misspoke. I meant to say *were*wolf."

Kathryn gaped, setting her wine down so she would not spill it on herself. "You know what he is?"

"You're not the only one who has seen a bit of the world before, my dear," he chided, though he grinned to take any hint of rebuke from his words.

Kathryn hesitated. What to tell the magician, and what might be better kept to herself? She wasn't even entirely sure how much she actually *knew* about the wolf and how much was just conjecture.

"I'm sure you recognized what the creature is," the magician murmured.

Kathryn swallowed. "Did the king?"

The magician paused in his gentle turning motions of the stone implements. He shrugged. "The king might suspect. But no, I'm not sure he entirely understands what he has in his care. I believe he thinks he has just acquired a rather remarkable animal, perhaps with some magical augmentation. No, I'd wager the thought of the garwaf has not entered his head. Yet."

"Garwaf?"

"Ah, an old word we use in the mountains. It is the same as werewolf."

"Are you going to tell King Thomas about the garwaf?" If the king realized he had invited a werewolf into his castle, things might come out worse for the beast.

Llewellyn shook his head. "I can see no purpose in going to the king with my *suspicions* until I have a firmer grasp of the truth." In a quiet whisper, he said, "Many have a prejudice against the garwaf. I thought perhaps our fur-covered friend should be given a chance to show his quality before we tell the king or anyone else what he really is."

That was good of him and showed a certain depth of understanding. Many of the prejudices against werewolves were not sound. The creatures might take on the shapes of wolves, but on the inside they were still human.

Kathryn fisted her hands in her lap with sudden apprehension, bunching up the fabric of her skirt. "Will someone else discover the truth? Someone less discreet?" She gazed at the magician with fear blooming in her heart. She was loath to see any harm fall on the gentle wolf.

Llewellyn put aside his activity to lay a reassuring hand on her shoulder. "Any with enough wit to spot the clues will also have the wisdom to keep such thoughts to himself until an opportune moment." He took a fortifying and appreciative sip of his own wine. "I don't think we need fret for long, at any rate." He went to take his crushed mixture to a brazier and poured the sticky mess into a pot waiting there. "The wolf has already impressed the king greatly. One so noble as I believe the wolf to be will quickly work his way back to a place of honor beside the king."

Kathryn narrowed her eyes. *Back to?*

Llewellyn chose just that moment to present his back to her, busy stirring his mixture as it came to a boil. "Once the wolf is secure in the king's esteem, no slander nor slur—nor uncomfortable but ultimately harmless truth—will displace him. Once our King Thomas gets to know someone, he will not let the prejudice of others, nor even those prejudices he once held himself, sway his judgment. He is as fair-minded and levelheaded a man as ever I have met." Llewellyn looked away, a small, secret smile on his lips. A gentle softening danced across his face before he smoothed the expression away. He tossed a quick grin over his shoulder. "Fear not, maid. Your wolf is safe for the time being."

"You know who he is." He had to. Llewellyn spoke as if he knew the wolf, his personality, his heart. Perhaps even the circumstances of his transformation.

Llewellyn shook his head. "I have only feelings and guesses to go on, and those will avail us nothing without the means to turn him back to his proper form. The worst kind of shame would be to give him back his true name when he would only be trapped forever as a wolf. Better to let his wolf form remain nameless and let his human half keep his honorable name unsullied by the taint of present circumstances."

"Will you tell me who he is? I should very much like to know." Kathryn did not realize until that moment how the wolf's gentle ways and unassuming manners—*manners* in a *wolf*—had affected her. She had a fondness for the beast already, and she wished no harm to fall on his head. A desire blossomed within her to help him back to his former life if she could, knowing something of repression herself. His persecution, at least, might be curable. Hers, as a woman, certainly was not.

Llewellyn turned to her, empty hands open before him. "I cannot risk slander-ing a noble knight of this realm. He may only have removed to another land, as the

whispers say, and not fallen on such unfortunate circumstances as our wolf has."
He came away from his brazier and sat on the bench beside her. Taking her hands
in his, he gave them a small squeeze. "As I treat with the king, so must I treat with
you. Until I know more, I will not unfold my mind to either of you." He gave her
hands a parting pat and rose briskly to return to his work, their interview at an
end, apparently.

Kathryn jumped to her feet, indignant. "But how am I to help the wolf if you
will not tell me who he is?"

Llewellyn stirred his bubbling mixture and did not glance up from the brew's
surface. "Watch over him. Keep him from harm in the court as best you may.
He needs your friendship. Keep safe the physical half, and I will strive to free the
mind and the spirit." He glanced up at her, his face flushed from the steam and
shining. He must have been thirty-five or so, but in that moment the wise man's
face glowed as eagerly as that of any young lad of ten, ripe for an adventure.

She bit back a sharp retort and, accepting her dismissal, bowed her head to the
king's wise man as she left his workshop. Her foot poised on the threshold, she
stopped as a new thought struck her.

He had given her a hint, after all, a clue to the wolf's identity: *"I cannot risk
slandering a noble knight of this realm..."* Llewellyn had said to her. So the wolf
was a knight? One who had disappeared not long ago, perhaps with no logical
explanation? Not many knights could have vanished so in recent history.

A new spring came into her step as she walked through the garden and back to
the castle, the tirewoman doggedly trailing her steps.

The first day back in the castle passed pleasantly for the wolf. He stayed in
constant company with the king and his men, men who had been his comrades
and friends not so long ago. Unsurprisingly, his days among the king's court did
not seem so far gone when he found himself back among the men and places he
had once known so well.

Had King Thomas not shown such marked favor toward him, the wolf might have had a harder time dealing with the knights. However, because King Thomas had so obviously found a new favorite in him, the other knights treated the wolf with respect. By the end of the first day, they had even begun to like him on his own account. He ran counter to every preconceived notion the knights and men-at-arms had of what a wolf should be. He behaved so well the knights were hard pressed *not* to be fond of him.

The beast kept the king company and, during sparring practice for the knights, he went to roughhouse with some of the young pages. He made sure to keep both his claws and his fangs in line, while the children, in turn, made sure to mind his wounded shoulder.

After a rather pleasant tussle, the young lads were ushered away by one of the trainers. Gratefully, the man gave the wolf a head pat and a smile in thanks. In his earlier days on the training field, when the wolf had been a knight, keeping the young pages in line could weary him near to the bone. Although, as a younger knight, he had usually managed to find someone else whom he could charm or bribe into taking his more onerous duties on for him. He regretted that now. Corralling the restless pages, wrestling with them, playing with them, had been quite fun, though his body ached.

What else did I miss while I was busy being an arrogant young lordling?

A lull began as the men went off to clean and change for the evening meal. The wolf looked at the sky, which had begun to blush with the violent purple hues of sunset.

He had always loved children. *I used to dream about having my own children. Imagine my strong sons, my clever daughters.* They had been shallow, half-formed dreams, but still their memory stung. He would have no children now. He let out a low wolf huff—the closest he could manage to a human sigh.

I have new dreams. Simpler, humbler certainly, but just because part of me is lost forever, that does not mean I should give in and be all wolf. Even a half-life is still a life. I will not waste a moment more of this one.

King Thomas called the wolf from the edge of the tourney field, startling him. His new vow held firmly in his mind, the wolf loped happily off to find his lord.

———— ◆◦◆ ————

As her feet shuffled across the stone of the corridor, Kathryn forced herself to set aside the problem of solving the wolf's identity for the moment. She suspected she would be otherwise occupied for the next few hours dealing with her fellow handmaidens. With a deep breath, she steeled herself for the scene to come in the queen's apartments.

One of the other ladies, Beatrice of Troumper, sister to the current earl of those lands, Lord Reynard, had held a grudge against Kathryn since her arrival at the court. Beatrice had no doubt used Kathryn's misadventure in the forest and her absence last night to make Kathryn look bad before the queen somehow. Lady Beatrice seemed to excel at that.

Queen Aliénor also worried Kathryn. The queen had not seemed pleased by yesterday's events. Kathryn did not wish to anger a patroness who could make her life miserable merely by lifting her finger. Yet she also would not, *could not,* leave a creature in need when she might be able to help. *There is more to that wolf than anyone yet knows.* Until the wolf's shoulder healed and the mystery around him unraveled, Kathryn had no wish to leave court. Nevertheless, she would not have much choice in the matter if the queen sent her away.

As she entered the lavishly furnished solar the queen and her ladies occupied, Kathryn squared her shoulders. The ladies of the court sat all in a circle, picking out bright patterns of embroidery on various pieces of fabric. Kathryn sewed well enough, her stitches small, her needle fast, but she had always preferred tending the animals with her uncle to stitchery work with her maid.

Queen Aliénor reclined by the window, glancing up as Kathryn entered. A few years older than Kathryn, Aliénor still looked barely sixteen. She had an oval-shaped face that could have been carved from the purest of white marble. Her features were as idyllic as the statues of old—and could be as hard and unyielding as those of the stone edifices. Her almond-shaped eyes were pale lashed but of a very dark brown. She was a lovely girl with luxurious titian curls, which gave more than a slight hint as to her temperament.

Kathryn modestly lowered her eyes and bowed before the queen. Queen Aliénor set aside her sewing pattern and clasped Kathryn's hands. "Are you well? Did the wolf hurt you?"

"No, no, my queen. He is a very well-behaved animal. Truly, I'm fine."

Queen Aliénor studied her a moment longer, her eyebrows drawn tight together, then she gave a small nod, dismissing Kathryn. "All right. Although I still don't understand what my husband is thinking." Aliénor returned to her chat with Lady Apolline, another handmaiden sitting next to her. The two of them were apparently conferring over repairs to a hemline.

Another set of eyes close at hand shot daggers at Kathryn, and she turned to face Beatrice, the Mistress of the Robes, senior Maid of Honor to the new queen. Beatrice was a young woman drying on the vine at the ripe age of twenty-five but still very beautiful. She narrowed her hazel eyes at Kathryn. "You have decided to grace us with your presence today, after all?" She kept her voice low, probably trying not to catch the attention of the queen.

Ignoring Beatrice, Kathryn went to one of the cabinets and pulled out her own sewing kit bag. She selected a project and claimed the empty stool in the circle. Letting her hands mindlessly accomplish their work, her mind meanwhile turned over the puzzle of the knight's identity.

"Well?" Beatrice demanded in a low hiss. "Have you nothing to say?"

Kathryn did not look up as she said in her most sickly sweet voice, "As you have oft remarked to me: silence is, of all virtues, the most becoming in a maiden. I am merely trying to take your good advice to heart."

Beatrice snorted in a manner most unbecoming to the chief of all the queen's ladies. "Impertinent hussy," Beatrice said barely under her breath.

The queen looked up and darted an uncertain look between Beatrice and Kathryn. Kathryn met her queen's gaze squarely, keeping her posture open, inviting, and wondered what mysteries the queen searched for so fiercely in her face. The queen sighed and looked away, sewing more slowly than usual.

Ill at ease, Kathryn returned to her own sewing. Acute pity for the queen stabbed through her. Queen Aliénor and King Thomas clearly doted on each other, but it must be lonely for Aliénor to be so far from her own homeland. None of the queen's own women had been able or willing to accompany her to her new country when she'd married. Strangers had surrounded Queen Aliénor ever since she'd arrived in Lyond. Kathryn understood how a solitary girl far from home could long for a friend. Any friend. *Although some friends are better than others.*

She darted a glance at Beatrice under her brows. Kathryn often wondered what political machinations had led to the appointment of the domineering Beatrice as senior handmaiden to the new queen. It seemed sometimes as if even Aliénor worried over that too.

Beatrice was full figured, with a deep bosom and a narrow waist falling to wide hips. The earl's daughter stood taller than all the rest of the ladies and a few of the knights, even. She had, Kathryn reflected ruefully, just the sort of figure men dreamed about. Beatrice's hair shone a dark, rich auburn to fall in perfect ringlets and frame her charming heart-shaped face. She was strikingly pretty, with a large, sensual mouth and dark hazel eyes.

Beatrice glanced up and cocked one perfectly shaped eyebrow. "Well, Lady Kathryn?"

Kathryn tilted her head and smiled. "Just admiring your beauty, Lady Beatrice. So hard to believe one as lovely and charming as yourself has been questing for a husband for—how long now? Ten years? Twelve?" Kathryn arranged her face into the picture of innocent curiosity.

Beatrice's jaw clenched, and then she yelped and dug her needle out of her palm. Blotting the blood away with a kerchief, she said, "I was affianced to a worthy baron from Escarcelle as a young child, but he died on a mission to the southern colonies when I was sixteen." Beatrice sniffed and dabbed at the corner of her eye with her kerchief. "My father passed away that same year, and my brother, Lord Reynard, was quite taken up with managing his own affairs for some time before he could make suitable provision for me. I am, however, in daily anticipation of my brother arranging an advantageous alliance."

"Hmm." Kathryn turned back to her sewing.

"And you, Lady Kathryn?" Beatrice's voice was also cloyingly sweet. "You are nineteen, are you not? More than ready for the marriage bed, I should say."

Kathryn pursed her lips but kept her voice light. "Like your brother, Lady Beatrice, my dear father has been taken up with his own affairs and so sent me to court." Not entirely true, but Kathryn wasn't about to relate her whole sad history. The queen was familiar with some of Kathryn's past, but only Kathryn knew all the reasons she had not, and probably never would be, married: *too clever. Too plain. And much, much too poor.*

"Kathryn," the queen said. "Would you fetch my green cloak out of the chest in my chamber please? This room is drafty."

"Of course." Kathryn set aside her sewing and rose.

As the newest and lowest-ranked of all the ladies, Kathryn had to know her place or the rest of the women would cheerfully remind her. Lady Beatrice, as Mistress of the Robes, would hand the queen her chemises when they were dressing her. Lady Avice dressed the queen's hair. The other two, Apolline and Agathe, chose the queen's slippers and stockings. If luck favored Kathryn, she might be allowed to choose one of the ribbons for the queen's hair. To be allowed to fetch something was an uncommon honor for Kathryn. Perhaps the queen was annoyed with her about yesterday and was using this errand as an excuse to get her out of the room. That would give Beatrice and the queen a few moments to gossip about Kathryn unhindered.

Or maybe I'm being paranoid. She slipped through the door joining the queen's solar to her private apartments. The chest sat under a portrait to the right of the bed. A little digging amongst lush velvets and sturdy woolen things produced the desired forest-green wool cloak. Kathryn folded the garment carefully over her arm and straightened.

She found herself staring into the face of a handsome young man. The lifelike portrait hung nearly eye level over the chest of clothing. The subject of the painting had been about Kathryn's age, maybe a year or two older, at the time of the portrait. The young man was *very* handsome with dark hair, warm brown skin, and deep blue eyes as well as the same long, distinctively aquiline nose as the king. He reminded Kathryn of someone—besides King Thomas—but the image was elusive. Perhaps this was just one of the king's long-dead brothers.

Then she looked again at his eyes. She frowned. *Surely not.* Impossible for her to have found her werewolf hanging in the queen's bedroom. She shook her head and realized she had been too long about her errand. She hurried back.

As she helped the queen into her cloak, she said with careful indifference, "My lady, who is the man in that portrait in your bedroom? The one that hangs over your clothing chest."

Queen Aliénor frowned. "The king's nephew. Gabriel fitz Michael. The Duke of Dorré."

A little frisson of excitement zipped through Kathryn. *The missing heir.*

Beatrice bit off the end of her thread. "The king disinherited Lord Gabriel. My brother holds the Dorré title now."

The queen hesitated, then said, "King Thomas *did* disinherit Gabriel but he—well—he could not bring himself to destroy that portrait. The portrait is all he has left of his nephew now the man has disappeared."

The missing heir. Lord Gabriel, of course. Kathryn pressed her feet firmly to the floor to keep from bouncing with excitement.

Aliénor dropped her gaze to her sewing, her face sad. "I never met the duke, but I have heard he was a very embodiment of virtues. So handsome, so brave, so noble and good. Gabriel became the king's heir once my husband's first wife died in childbirth. The boy was my lord's favorite knight as well. My king's heart broke when Gabriel disappeared. As I understand the case, Gabriel left lands, title, wife, and all without so much as a word?" Aliénor had not been married to the king when this scandal had broken.

"Did he just disappear?" Kathryn asked. "Or did he leave some word?" The whole kingdom had heard the story of the lost heir, of course, but tales had sprung up like so many weeds around the truth. Kathryn burned with sudden curiosity to learn the facts of the case.

"Some said he left to retake our colonies in the south," Apolline murmured.

The queen thought for a moment. "As I understand it, Lord Gabriel often left his home without telling anyone, not even his lady, where he went. When he disappeared for good, his friends generally assumed he had decided to leave permanently. My lord valued Gabriel, however, and searched for him, made inquiries—but no information was forthcoming. The duke is presumed to be lost forever to our court. A man's business is his own, I suppose."

"I think it was shameful." Beatrice shook her head. "My brother Reynard, Earl of Troumper, married the good Lady Alisoun after her husband abandoned her." Beatrice's massive bosom swelled with pride. "Gabriel's old lands and duties at Dorré are overseen by Reynard now, by order of the king."

The queen nodded, her hand going to her throat, absently fingering the bow Kathryn had tied. "I think my husband was very angry. Gabriel left without sending word to him, and one cannot help but feel the injustice to Lady Alisoun. The king made what decisions he thought right after Gabriel left."

How strange. Although Kathryn supposed a man who seemingly abandoned his honor and his oaths would not be much missed, whatever his former prominence had been. Yet the facts certainly fit. Especially that the duke had disappeared periodically, even before his final absence. A werewolf would probably absent himself in such a way if he wished to prevent his loved ones from discovering his secret. *Poor man.* A knot of tension clotted beneath Kathryn's sternum. *Poor wolf.* What could have happened to trap him as an animal?

She decided she wouldn't discuss with anyone but Llewellyn what she suspected. The magician was right that to reveal the wolf's identity while he remained a beast would be monstrously unfair.

Beatrice glanced out the window and set down her sewing. "Time to dress for dinner, my queen." She stepped toward Aliénor.

Their liege lady looked to Kathryn instead. "Would you help me dress tonight?"

A hastily stifled gasp went around the room of ladies. Beatrice's will had not been flouted in recent memory.

Kathryn opened her mouth to accept the honor, but Beatrice cut her off. "The steward sent me a note this morning. Her services"—Beatrice gave the word the worst kind of implications— "are requested for the king's new pet. Master Llewellyn is busy, so she's to see to the beast's shoulder again, I was commanded to tell her. He's being brought to our chambers as I speak." Beatrice grimaced, apparently not relishing the thought of a wild beast in her apartments.

Kathryn formed the intention at once of using Beatrice's bed as an examination table.

Aliénor wilted but patted Kathryn's hand. "Go with all haste, Lady Kathryn, but sit by me at dinner if you will. Lady Avice." The queen turned at once to another of her ladies. "You will help me to dress."

With that second outright snub of Beatrice, the queen regally swept from the room with her train. Beatrice brought up the rear, glowering at Kathryn as she slammed the queen's bedroom door.

Kathryn was free. For now. She hurried to her room, anxious to see the wolf.

He perched on his hind legs, resting his front paw on the windowsill, looking at the courtyard and stables below, watching the comings and goings of the grooms with apparent contentment. She bobbed him a curtsy. "Evening, Sir Wolf." *Or should I say: my lord Duke?*

He looked at her and docilely climbed onto the bed she indicated—Beatrice and Apolline's bed. Kathryn grinned as she went to him, glad to see the servant had made all ready in the form of bandages and healing poultices. "I hope you didn't overdo your training today with King Thomas, my lord."

The wolf snorted but, as she touched a sore spot when prodding his wounds, he let out an involuntary growl.

"Apologies."

He pressed his wet nose to the back of her hand, and she guessed that he understood she was doing her best not to hurt him.

Kathryn reached up and stroked the side of his face in a friendly caress, tracing the line of his scar. There had been no such scar on the portrait. She wished she'd remembered to ask the others if the Lord Gabriel had borne a scar. No, she wished she'd *dared* to ask.

She paused and studied the wolf when she realized he was not shying away from her touch as he had yesterday. He blinked at her, his eyes soft, and warmth stole into her heart as she smiled at him.

———◦———

She's lovely. The wolf had not quite appreciated how pretty those large green eyes of hers were, nor the soft, golden brown of her hair where her thick braid lay across the shoulder of her gown. She was not a beauty and never would be. Yet something in the animation of her features and the compassion of her face made her looks more appealing than mere beauty, and both would certainly stand the test of time and trial better.

Did Alisoun ever have kindness in her eyes? Love, yes. But compassion? Empathy? Did I ever see true benevolence in her? He huffed with self-disgust. *Did I ever bother to look? To see past Alisoun's beautiful face and fair hair? Her fine manners and the grace of her figure? I knew Alisoun as a woman and wife, but did I ever bother to find out what kind of person she might be?*

The answer was plain. *No.* Sharp regret slashed at his gut, painful and profound.

He had looked forward to this all day, to maybe seeing Kathryn again. Llewellyn often kept busy mixing his medicines and tending his garden and would not spare time to tend an animal with only trivial hurts. Guilt prickled in the wolf's shoulders that he had held himself so aloof from the girl before when she had done so much to help him. He wanted to make every effort not to hurt her feelings again tonight, but when she touched his face, he should have pulled away. Such contact was not proper. He was a wolf, but he was still a *man*.

Her caress seemed too tender, too intimate, and she did not know it was a man she touched like that, for all that he was naught but an animal to her. She was so kind. Even a poor wounded animal, infamous for savagery, had her compassion.

Why didn't I meet you before Alisoun? His grief swelled, submerging him, much too great to be contained by the simple functioning of a wolf's humble heart. He wrenched away and averted his eyes, refusing to let Kathryn touch anything more than his shoulder for the rest of their session.

As soon as she had checked his wounds, he hopped down and left the ladies' apartments to seek out his king. *There* he stood on firmer ground. There the wolf understood his place and his duty. *The maiden is too precarious.*

Every moment spent in Kathryn's presence, he slid nearer to a great void, and if he let himself fall in, he would lose the little bit of his humanity that he retained. Despair of that kind was not something from which he could ever recover.

For what could be worse than finding the true lady of your heart and knowing, as you are, that you may never possess her? What could hurt more than finding her, loving her, and knowing in your cursed canine bones she deserves so much more than the beast you have become?

Better to feel nothing at all.

Chapter Five

The garwaf sat by King Thomas at one end of the table, and Kathryn sat by the queen and Llewellyn at the other. Kathryn amused the queen with tall tales while trying valiantly to push the wolf's snub from her mind. Queen Aliénor turned to speak with another courtier, and Kathryn twisted in her seat toward Llewellyn, her restlessness bubbling over. "The queen just reminded me today of the mystery of the lost heir. The king's nephew Gabriel. The Duke of Dorré. His disappearance is an intriguing puzzle, I thought."

Llewellyn quirked an eyebrow and gave her the barest of smiles. His eyelid shivered in a small wink.

She tried not to let the triumph show in her face. She had solved the mystery, then. One piece of the puzzle, at least. She darted a quick glance at the dark-furred duke. The wolf sat in a place of honor by King Thomas, eating the roasted swan set in front of him with becoming refinement.

Scraggly, brown-haired dogs scrounged for table scraps at the feet of everyone's chairs, and she found it amusing that no one, but no one, thought to tell King Thomas that the wolf should join the dogs on the floor. Indeed, she realized with wry amusement, the well-mannered wolf would have been more out of place among the dogs than at the human table.

The king stood and raised his goblet. "The celebration of St. Aaron's Day is upon us at the end of this month, and the custom of this court is to give a great feast. The feast day is also traditionally a time for all my liegemen and the nobles who hold fiefdoms under me to come to the court. Let no man omit this opportunity to serve me as handsomely as he may. The feast is to be a great and solemn occasion." King Thomas raised his goblet, causing everyone in the hall to do likewise. He tossed back his drink, and the rest of his court followed suit.

At the king's announcement, Llewellyn frowned mightily into his lentils, the smile falling from his face.

"My lord magician," Kathryn said, a troubled smile frozen on her own face. "You are ponderous."

Llewellyn glanced up, looking anxious. "The wolf troubles me, my lady."

Kathryn darted an apprehensive glance at the head of the table.

The wolf blinked over and over, licking his jaws convulsively, and he swayed in his chair, his eyes fogged over and distant. Distressed, Kathryn looked to Llewellyn for guidance. He stared at his plate and sighed.

Llewellyn drew his shoulders back and rose. He walked to the head of the table. "My king." Llewellyn bowed and spoke in a quiet undertone, which everyone in the court, whether they showed interest or not, strained to hear—Kathryn included. "I fear your newest courtier is feeling a bit worse for the wear." He gestured to the wolf, who seemed now to be adrift in a mental fog and aware not at all of what transpired around him.

The king looked at once to the wolf, all concern. Llewellyn quickly, but without seeming haste, inspected the wolf. The beast's eyes looked cloudy to Kathryn, and he panted, staring at Llewellyn as though from a great distance. The magician clucked his tongue.

"Use my chambers." A crease had formed on the king's brow.

"The herb garden is closer, my king."

"Of course." King Thomas slapped Llewellyn's shoulder affectionately, though the concerned look still haunted his eyes. "Sir Edric." The king turned to another of his men. "Carry the wolf to Llewellyn's workshop, if you will?"

As the knight picked the panting animal up, the king helped to adjust the weight of the wolf in Sir Edric's arms. Llewellyn trailed behind, his black robes billowing. He cast one look at the high table and locked gazes with Kathryn for the barest of moments before turning away.

His was not a look of reassurance or grief but plainly a call to arms. His meaning seemed clear enough to Kathryn: *come to the workshop.*

She jumped as the queen addressed her in a whisper. "I have a black cloak. Heavy wool. Very discreet. I realize I have forgotten the cloak in your clothing chest. Tomorrow you will return it to me, please." The queen leaned forward, her brow knit anxiously. "Tell me what you can tomorrow? About the wolf?" Aliénor called her tirewoman over and whispered a judicious word in her ear. The woman slipped away, swift but unobtrusive.

Kathryn found resolve enough to meet the queen's gaze. "Thank you." She clasped the queen's bejeweled hand in her own and squeezed gently. "And I will."

After that, Kathryn could hardly contain her impatience. When the king rose from the table to retire, she was barely a beat behind him out of the chamber. She took leave of the queen, who would stay below to listen to the court musicians, and Kathryn hurried back to the women's apartments.

As she entered the bedroom she shared with the other ladies, the barest click betrayed that the door connecting to the ladies' solar had just been closed.

Kathryn dashed to her clothing chest and flipped up the lid. The black cloak lay folded neatly in amongst her other clothing. She snatched the garment up and hastily drew the dark fabric around herself.

While halfway out the door, a rising hesitation stilled her hand. The hour was by no means late enough for the castle's halls to be empty. Any lady caught trying to sneak into the gardens at night in a concealing cloak would be in very great trouble if caught. The harm an indiscretion could do not only to her reputation but also to the reputation of the queen was very great. Another worry was that any men who caught a woman out in the dark would believe her of low virtue and therefore fair game for any and all liberties they should decide to take with her.

Of course, these concerns never seemed to trouble Beatrice—she snuck out most nights—but Kathryn didn't have Beatrice's experience or connections. She suspected she and Beatrice were also sneaking out for *very* different purposes.

What should I do?

The moon shone, pouring silver light over the landscape to illuminate the castle grounds and buildings almost as brightly as day. Kathryn stared down, her gaze arrested at once by a trellis attached to the wall beneath the window. Prickly vines crept up the wall's sides, and the trellis did not seem overly sturdy. Still, if Kathryn managed the first few feet, then she could make her way to the stable roof and climb down from there, following the walls and the shadows to the workshop. *I had far more daring escapades at home, climbing the apple trees to steal the fruit.*

With that encouraging, if somewhat unrealistic, thought, she stepped onto the window ledge. *I hope the queen will not mind a little wear and tear on my borrowed cloak.* Kathryn pushed that and all other thoughts aside and squeezed through her narrow window. Heart racing, she began negotiating the barbed trellis down to her destination. In her haste to get to the workshop, she hardly regarded the various scrapes and scratches the prickly vines inflicted on her.

———————— ◆○◆ ————————

Llewellyn had taken the wolf to his workshop and deftly tied the beast to his worktable before the animal aspect took over completely. The garwaf had been conscious for this and wearily submitted to the indignity. Still, Llewellyn would hardly have blamed the beast if, in his present mental and spiritual fugue, he had forgotten all that.

The magician was currently trying to make sure the wolf's bonds would hold through the night and ensuring the wolf did himself no injury in his madness and glancing every few seconds at the door waiting for Lady Kathryn and, meanwhile, trying to make sure he himself was not scratched, kicked, beaten, or otherwise mauled by the werewolf.

Llewellyn had tried talking to the wolf at first to soothe him, but his voice had only redoubled the paroxysms of rage gripping the beast. The magician had abandoned that remedy. He wiped sweat from his brow before the moisture dripped into his eyes and sighed. "I should have listened to my mother and become a hermit."

The door of his workshop creaked ever so slightly ajar, and a shadow insinuated itself into the room, only to be brought up sharp with a gasp on beholding the wild creature upon the table.

Llewellyn, after nearly an hour and a half of dealing with a crazed, dangerous werewolf, had reached the limit of his usually benevolent patience. "Idiot girl," he snapped out. "Take the damn cloak off so he can *see* you."

The raging wolf lay between Kathryn and himself. Llewellyn wasn't sure sheer fury wouldn't win the wolf his freedom at last if the magician made a move toward wolf or girl now. Llewellyn's bones ached, his head throbbed, and he had to admit he was terrified as he stared at the big animal growling murderous desires to the room at large.

Blood-red curtains of rage clouded his gaze as he growled and thrashed about, not understanding what bound him in this inferno of pain. Images kept flashing through his head. A woman's face. The red chasm of the hunting dog's neck he had ripped out. He salivated, snapping in futility at whatever creature manhandled him. The words the creature spoke were an irritating buzz to his ears. He longed to spring up and create a similar slash of gore on this infuriating creature's neck, if only so it would shut up.

As whatever restraints on the wolf's extremities held, the beast tilted his head back and howled his fury to the moon, the stars, and the chill night air—the only sovereigns he recognized now. The craving to hunt, to kill, swelled strong in him, and only one vision of the myriad display swimming in his head came close to being in focus: the treacherous female with the pale blond hair and the frowning brown eyes. The fragmented pieces of his understanding could not supply a reason for his hatred. He needed the hot rush of her blood spilling down his throat, and soon, or he would wither and die from longing.

A new bouquet mingled with the smell of the herbs and the sweating stench of his oppressor. Judging by her scent, this new one was female. And frightened. She wore a concealing cloak. An image swirled through his afflicted mind of the one he loathed, the one he longed to mangle, wearing just such a cloak.

The female moved only close enough for him to smell her fear and the sweetness of her. Her fragrance alone sent bloodlust pounding in his veins. He reared up, baring his fangs. Let her come near him, let her lay one of those traitorous hands on him, and she would not live the night through with her creamy white hide intact.

Kathryn wavered. She thought of running back into the night, back to a world with nothing more dangerous or mysterious than a tricky piece of embroidery. More than ever, she longed for the dull routine of the queen's chambers. Even the oppression of Beatrice was better than this snarling beast.

The wolf jerked toward her, and corded muscles of iron strained against ropes that suddenly seemed a trifle too flimsy to Kathryn.

She swallowed and, drawing herself up, she stepped away from the door and into the workshop, throwing back the hood of the cloak as she did so. Her disordered coil of hair fell around the shoulders of her blue gown. Stinging scratches from the trellis vines covered her hands and her face.

More than a little ruffled, she caught her reflection in Llewellyn's small looking glass. Her eyes seemed dull, with heavy blue shadows beneath them. The skin around her lips had turned a pasty white, and her battered hands clutched convulsively at the folds of her skirt.

The wolf growled again, feral eyes rolling in a body almost boneless now as he thrashed to free himself.

"He's not—" Kathryn's breath caught on a sob.

"Rabid?" Llewellyn's voice sounded ragged, a throaty gasp of fatigue. "No. This is an affliction of the spirit and the mind, no mere physical malady. I marked him well at dinner. The king's announcement of the Feast of St. Aaron at dinner did this, although the full moon tonight probably isn't helping much." Llewellyn rubbed his forehead.

"Why did you—"

The wolf lunged for her again, and the bonds held him back by only the barest of inches. She stumbled away until her spine banged against the workshop door. She shivered and, swallowing the fear that choked her, looked to Llewellyn. "What can I do?"

He laughed shakily and quite without mirth. "The beast hasn't let me touch him since he slipped into this state with the rise of the moon. He won't let *me* near him except to rip my limbs from my body." The magician's tone was dry, but Kathryn sensed the sobbing, shaking panic that lay behind his cool façade. The same panic she herself kept in check only with a supreme effort of will.

Llewellyn continued, "If he does not quiet for you..." The magician glanced meaningfully at the hatchet hanging on the wall by his head.

Kathryn's stomach dropped. *But I know who he is now.* He had a name, a human identity. Whatever madness gripped him now as a wolf, he *was* human.

The knot of fear in her belly hardened into adamant resolve. "Then he will know me," she declared with more confidence in her voice than she actually possessed. Then she murmured on a sigh, more prayer than pledge, "He has to."

She went to the wolf, as near as she dared, and knelt to put her gaze on a level with his.

Human eyes no longer stared back at her, but the feral and furious eyes of a wolf who, even as she looked at him, was deciding how best to break his bonds and savage her. Yet even as his human soul suffocated, even in this animal rage, there was more than just a wolf there. There was hate.

Hate is human invention. Animals kill because they are afraid. They kill to defend or to eat. The creature looking at her would also kill for his hate. That hatred gleamed in his eyes now, and anything human enough to hate *might* be human enough to bring back.

She hoped.

She prayed.

She moved closer, within an inch of the sharp snap of his jaws. She looked at him, brazenly *looked* at him, daring him to bite the over-inquisitive nose off her too-lovely face. Oh, and how he wanted to. And he would. A few moments more and he would be free, free to have his way and butcher her as he longed to do. Her and then her mate in the corner.

But then...then the female said his name.

He recognized the voice, but it was not the one he had expected to hear, not even one who was supposed to know that name.

Quickly but hesitantly, she stepped toward him. She stood close enough for him to strike. Or close enough for her to get her arms around him.

She did not embrace him. Only the sweetness of her scent stretched out to engulf him, to muddle and drug him with her heady essence, dulling the tearing madness in his heart. She smelled of fertile earth, with a sharp tang of crushed leaves about her, and a caressing feminine fragrance, something that made him think of springtime and sunshine. Like a sweet, fresh fruit ready to be picked. His growling subsided, and he blinked, befuddled senses trying desperately to refocus. She reached out a hand to him. He wanted to snap at her fingers, to scare her back from him, but he could not.

"I will not hurt you," she said quietly and then, almost with wonder in her voice, "and you will not hurt me."

This was not the mate who had betrayed him. This was not Alisoun. He came to himself again, or as near to his human self as he could manage these days. *Oh, I'm exhausted.*

"Go to him, Kathryn," said a disembodied voice over the wolf's shoulder that the beast did not concern himself with. His whole existence was wrapped in the white face shining above him, a safe haven in the dark. Like salvation and redemption and hope.

Kathryn is her name, he thought somewhat coherently as his head lolled back. His wounded shoulder ached and ached, a steady throb timed to his heartbeat. *I'm so tired.*

The wolf whined softly. Kathryn all but fell across his body, tangling her fingers in the soft fur of his neck, her hot tears falling on his face. Llewellyn carefully lifted the silver hatchet from the wall. He waited and watched for a long moment. Then he smiled to himself and, unseen by the others, placed the hatchet back over his hearth. Quietly, he sidled out his back door to give the young people a moment alone.

The wolf licked Kathryn's cheek. She looked into his face and sighed. "So you're back, my lord." She laughed, the sound bordering on hysteria, and wiped her eyes. She traced the line of his scar, then seized the sides of his face to give him a tiny shake. "Dear Sir Wolf," she crooned to him, "don't do that again."

He whimpered and nuzzled her cheek.

She wrapped her arms around him and squeezed. "Do not go where I may not follow you."

Never, never, never, never again. The thought was fierce, vehement. When he contemplated what he had almost done...*if the ropes had snapped*...a shudder passed through him.

"Silly wolf. Whatever you're worrying over, stop." She planted a kiss on his pointed ear. "Don't be a fool. You are a knight of this land, fur or no fur. You are too honorable to break your oaths. Your vows of fealty hold you still and always will, no matter what form you take. No less does the vow you swore to me in the forest hold you.

"You are *my* champion, Sir Garwaf, and whether you will or no, harm will not befall me while you live. You will not let it." She stroked his face again, grinning. "Now let Llewellyn back in and behave yourself while he dresses your shoulder. I'll wait, and then I am for my bed and sleep. As should you be." She turned to seek where the magician had gone. Smiling, Llewellyn approached with fresh ointment and dressings.

Kathryn went to her accustomed bench against the wall. She fully meant to watch the proceedings, but her head kept bowing to her chest over and over again.

By the third time, Llewellyn laughed and said, "Dear girl, I don't require your supervision for this activity. Stretch out and doze if you like until I'm done. Your part in the evening's affair is at an end."

She rubbed her eyes and watched the wolf. He stared solemnly back at her—with the same look he had given the king on first beholding his lord in the forest. She smiled into his eyes and looked reluctantly back to Llewellyn. "What happened? You said something about the king's announcement."

"Since we cannot learn his thoughts, the best I can do is to draw my own conclusions—"

"Yes, yes." Kathryn waved that away. "You're brilliant, Llewellyn, and your suppositions are probably correct. So?" She prompted him with her open palm and an expectant look.

Llewellyn gave her a lopsided grin. "Unless I do the man a grave injustice, I very much believe the new husband of Gabriel's wife to be the one who has betrayed him. Reynard of Troumper. The man courted and married Lady Alisoun immediately, when her other suitors waited out of deference to Gabriel's memory and in fear he might come back to nullify their marriage. The Earl of Troumper had no such compunction."

"Well, why bother when you already know?" Kathryn asked, calling the betraying beast Reynard all sorts of vile names in her head.

"Precisely. I believe our friend"—he patted the wolf's side, and the wolf butted his head against Llewellyn's hand and gave him a look of apology— "was entertaining thoughts that his wife's new husband must be attending the festivities and will be here in the castle, within his grasp. Those less-than-charitable thoughts, when coupled with the new moon tonight, served to bring out the worst of his wolfish nature. His animal impulses robbed the human half of control. The part of him that is still human drowned in these bitter emotions, and reasonable thought could not check the violence inherent to a beast."

"You're saying the wolf triumphed?"

"For a time."

Kathryn rose, awake all at once, and went to her beast. She stroked his head as Llewellyn finished applying the fresh dressing to the shoulder. She continued to card her fingers through the soft fur of the wolf. His eyes fluttered until at last Kathryn had lulled him into a peaceful slumber. She kissed his ears, then looked at Llewellyn. "How do we keep the human half in control?"

Llewellyn scratched the side of his nose and frowned. "The best medication I can recommend is more time spent with his king and with you. The two of you bring out his humanity the best. He is most clearly in control of himself when with you. He knows himself then, who he's supposed to be." Llewellyn smiled gently. "Might say you make him want to be a better man."

Kathryn nodded. "The queen might excuse me for the mornings if I ask. She seldom rises early. The beast dearly loved the training session today, I think. You should have heard him barking for joy. I would hate to take that time from him. I would keep him in my chamber, but he does not think that's proper." She finally glanced at Llewellyn. "Will mornings with me and afternoons and evenings spent in the company of the king and his fellow knights be enough to keep him with us?" She chewed her lower lip, her brows pinched together with concern.

He patted her cheek. "Dear girl, time spent with you is bound to have an improving effect upon anyone."

"And I shall do my part to preserve his oaths and his honor as well," King Thomas said from the doorway.

Even as panic set in, Kathryn dropped a hasty curtsy, her cheeks hot.

She would be cast from the court. Dishonored. Her father would disown her. *Llewellyn.* Llewellyn would be compromised as an advisor to the king. He would lose his position at court. She would never see the wolf again. She—

King Thomas gently clasped her hand. "Have no fear of your king, sweet girl. You are far too high in my esteem for an innocent errand of compassion to lower you in my opinion. Your secret will not leave these walls."

Llewellyn smiled.

King Thomas stared at the face of the sleeping wolf, then looked almost desperately to his advisor. "Is this truly Gabriel?"

"I *believe*"—the magician put gentle emphasis on the word— "this wolf *is* your nephew, my lord."

The king's handsome face convulsed with a spasm of grief and gratitude. Kathryn averted her gaze. When she looked back, King Thomas seemed in control of his emotions once more.

He grabbed her hand. "You gave me a great gift yesterday in the forest, dear child. I will not ever be able to repay you, but from now on I shall devote my life to the effort."

"The act itself was reward enough, my king. You owe me nothing else." She swallowed. "Except...would you give me leave to keep company with the wolf for the rest of the mornings until the feast day? If the queen doesn't mind, that is."

"I shall send him to you in the garden after our morning meal." King Thomas grinned wryly at his nephew the wolf. "I don't think he'll mind." He tucked her hand into his arm. "Now let's get you back. The wolf will be safe with Llewellyn for tonight."

Kathryn traced a hand over the wolf's side, combing her fingers through his soft fur. He stirred vaguely, still asleep. She returned to the king's side and let him lead her from the room. Grinning at Llewellyn, King Thomas said, "Wouldn't the crowning stroke be if he turns out to be someone other than Gabriel?"

Both men laughed, but the wolf stirred on his bench, so they ceased almost at once. One should, after all, let sleeping knights lie.

Chapter Six

Kathryn awoke early the next morning and ducked into the ladies' solar as soon as was seemly. Her queen's presence there startled her, as Aliénor did not usually rise so early. Kathryn had hoped for solitude, but she composed her features, giving a small curtsy.

Llewellyn had sent the cloak back up to her earlier. Kathryn had carefully mended whatever tears she had made in the velvet, but after the patch of bristly vines, the fabric would never be the same. She brushed the cloak off, folded it, and solemnly handed it back to the queen.

Aliénor turned the cloak over in her hands then sighed and handed the garment back. "No, my dear, you will have far more opportunity for clandestine missions than I, unless I very much mistake myself. You keep this. It would not be seemly for a queen to be traipsing about the castle at all hours." She seemed almost wistful as she said it.

Kathryn smiled ruefully and sank onto the stool beside the queen. "It is hardly seemly in *me*, my queen."

"But you have, I think, a creature very dear to you who needed you last night. Such need can excuse many indiscretions."

Kathryn hesitated, wondering what she should tell the queen of the truth, what Aliénor could handle. Not everyone could understand the complicated issues around, well, werewolves. Kathryn decided she would tell the queen everything. Her liege lady had earned that much for her faith. She opened her mouth to say so when the queen held up a hand to silence her.

"I have changed my mind since last evening, Kathryn," the queen said, looking at her lap. "I have only one question I wish you to answer for me."

The queen's flat tone confused Kathryn, but she nodded. "Anything."

Aliénor sucked in a deep breath and looked at Kathryn with wide eyes, shadowed and restless. "Has Lady Beatrice been very unkind to you, Kathryn?"

Kathryn flinched and looked away. "I'm all right, my lady."

"Which isn't what I asked."

Kathryn wet her lips, her pulse jittery inside her. "Lady Beatrice's family is powerful at court, my lady." *And mine is not. I am not.*

Aliénor face twisted, as if she'd heard and understood Kathryn's unvoiced worries. The queen huffed, her fingers clenching in the fabric of her skirts. "Oh, I don't know what my husband was thinking to give that—that *wench* a place of power in my retinue. She's a mean-spirited, ambitious *cow*. And I can't think why my lord would force her presence on me, but everything is in such a muddle." Aliénor's brow tensed. "She managed to bully the other maidens out and put me to bed last night. She told me the most horrible lies about you, Kathryn. That you take part in illicit revels, that you sneak out every night—"

"*Beatrice* sneaks out every night, and the guards turn a blind eye." The hasty words were out just as Kathryn would wish them back in, seeing the stricken look on Aliénor's face. "My queen, I didn't—it's probably—"

"Someone else's husband she beds every night?" A purse of the royal lips, a harsh quirk of her mobile eyebrows, and Kathryn froze. But then the queen thawed. "Ah, child, I'm sorry to take my spleen out on you. You're not the vixen my husband has saddled me with. Anyway, I know it's not true. I know where my husband is every night, and it isn't with you. Or her." A smile of almost feline satisfaction crossed the queen's face before she shook her head. "Except last night."

"He was in Llewellyn's workshop to check on the wolf."

Aliénor nodded, unsurprised. "It's not the first time Beatrice has tried to make me suspicious of Thomas. What can her game be?" She gave a small tug of her hair at the roots, pure exasperation. "Oh, your Lyondi politics. I would have known what was going on at home in the Jerdic court, the internal squabbles, the motivations. Nothing worse than playing a game when you don't even know the rules."

This summed up Kathryn's feelings of her time at court to perfection. She vented a wistful sigh.

Aliénor gave a small headshake and squeezed Kathryn's hand. "Forgive me, my dear. I just wanted to see what you knew and to put you on your guard."

"Thank you, my lady." Kathryn had to quell the urge to find the insolent Beatrice and knock her to the dirt. "Perhaps you should talk to the king? You shouldn't have to navigate court politics by yourself."

"Yes." The queen stared out her narrow window at the rays of sunshine valiantly fighting their way in. "For too long I have let Beatrice poison my heart and pollute my life with her presence, but no more. I swear to that." Aliénor smiled at Kathryn and squeezed her hand. "I should be more like you. Follow my heart and do what it wills me to. And damned be the consequences. I was like that. Once."

"No, my lady, I am no fit model for a queen. I am too much a hoyden to ever make a success of being a great lady like you."

Queen Aliénor laughed.

"Which reminds me: will you give leave to me to dedicate my mornings to the wolf?" The queen's baffled look made Kathryn babble out the rest of her request as she prayed her liege lady would not refuse her. "The wolf needs my companionship, but I can still be here in the afternoons to weave stories for you and help you dress for dinner, if you like."

"Anything you want, Kathryn. Today, though, all my handmaidens shall have the morning off." Queen Aliénor smoothed down the folds of her gown. "Go with my blessing and enjoy yourselves. Please bring my page in to me so I may send to my husband. When he arrives I shall want privacy." The steely glint was back in her eyes, and Kathryn sighed in relief that she did not have to face off against the queen. "I think it is time to discuss Lady Beatrice's position here."

Kathryn felt a small lift of hope in her heart. "I'll pass the message."

As Kathryn headed out the door, the queen called after her, "Oh, Kathryn, make sure the wolf shows you the rose garden today."

King Thomas was not sure what he should be feeling, summoned to his wife's apartments for all the world like a naughty child.

Only the two guards stood at the beginning of the corridor. The rest of the women's apartments echoed with emptiness. He and his queen would be quite alone. A jolt of warm anticipation spread through his gut. Her summons had not seemed particularly warm, but perhaps that was a misdirection. He knocked on the heavy door to her bedroom, and her lovely voice bid him enter.

She sat on her bed, her titian curls soft and loose about her creamy shoulders. She wore a simple, long-sleeved dress of deep blue, cut low across the neck with a voluminous skirt. She looked lovely, and he smiled as he entered.

She did not smile back. No warmth lit her dark eyes at all. "Husband, I asked you here so you could tell me about yourself and Lady Beatrice."

His gut roiled with sudden, clawing fear. He crossed to her bed and sat at its foot, letting his gaze roam all over his beautiful wife. *Is this the day I lose you, my love?* "What do you want to know?"

"What will you tell me?" she countered, voice cool.

Thomas passed a hand over his tired face. He rubbed eyes bleary from lack of sleep and recent stress and shrugged with a sigh. "She was my mistress, but not for several years now. And I've not touched her since I met you."

Aliénor gave a short nod, but she blew a small breath out between her teeth. He thought from relief. She motioned for him to continue.

Thomas ached inside. "There is not much to tell of our affair. Two years ago my nephew Gabriel disappeared, and I thought he'd abandoned me. I was rattled, lonely, frightened, and Beatrice was a pleasing young woman, a lovely if temporary distraction from my pain. I already turned to drink more than I should, and she did not discourage the habit. I could barely function once Gabriel was gone. The boy was like my son. After my first wife died, he was all the family that I had." His jaw clenched, and a spasm of pain shuddered through him before he could settle the hard shield of his self-control back in place.

After a moment he continued in a colorless tone, as if he spoke of someone else's impossible follies. "Beatrice and the boy's wife, Alisoun, fed my rancor toward Gabriel, convinced me that he had left without a word only to hurt me, that he had used our family connection only to better himself and not out of any real love toward me. I think it was easier for me to believe their lies than to go on missing him. How wrong I was, how unpardonably wrong..."

With a mental shake, he returned from his dark reverie. "The bloody harpies got me to declare him dead so Alisoun could remarry. Between them, they convinced me I should strip Gabriel of his lands and gift them to Lord Reynard." He frowned, stomach roiling with rage and despair, and continued with the bleak narrative. "Alisoun's motives are unclear to me still. Beatrice's—well, they became all too apparent. Her brother, the odious Reynard, became the recipient of wife, lands, title, and all. Beatrice's consequence could do nothing but grow as a result. I think she even hoped I would make her my queen."

"What changed? What parted you from her?"

Thomas rubbed his eyes, trying to grind the tired sorrow out of himself. "Llewellyn put his foot down. Saved me. Saved the kingdom probably. He got me sobered up, and I finally realized I couldn't go on as I had been. I ended things with Beatrice. That was about when we received word our southern colonies were in trouble. I should never have left the kingdom, but I still desperately needed distraction from my loss."

"Was that what *I* was for you? A distraction? Is that why—" Aliénor broke off, her brow furrowed, her cheeks pale with emotion.

"No." Thomas dragged her into his lap, banding his arms tight around her. "You were my salvation. You still are. Always will be."

Aliénor burrowed closer to him, pressing her cheek against his shoulder. "As you are mine. Everything I ever wanted."

Thomas brushed his cheek against the silk of her hair, expelling a ragged breath of relief.

But Aliénor pushed back from him, still scowling. "And Beatrice? When you married me, why did you let your old mistress join my retinue?"

Thomas flinched. "Folly and pride. In return for her discretion about my affair with her, she demanded a place in your entourage and a pledge from me that I would help her to a husband. She realized the strength of my feelings for you, you see."

He hurried on with the sequence of events, imagining his skin had peeled off, leaving him raw and exposed. Vulnerable. "She threatened to tell you of all our tawdry escapades together if I didn't help her. The threat acted as the perfect leverage. I am not one to give in to blackmail, but I thought she meant to turn over a new leaf. Out of guilt, perhaps, I meant to let her try. But the shameful wench keeps sniffing about me." He grimaced. "She bribes your guards—which I am, incidentally, changing this very night—to let her out so she can sneak into my apartments. Such behavior is a dishonor to you and, frankly, a headache to me to keep her here longer."

Aliénor remained quiet for a long time, and her husband watched her in trepidation but could think of nothing else to say, not knowing what she wanted to hear.

"I wish you had told me the truth, Thomas."

He shook his head and spoke with difficulty, his voice gruff but soft. "I know. I'm sorrier than I can say, Aliénor. But I did not want to be less in your eyes. I did not want to lose you."

"I am yours, Thomas. By my own choice and Fate's will. My king." She cradled his weathered face in her hands and stared into his eyes, her soul clasping and calming him as surely as her touch did. "I surrendered myself utterly to you, did I not?"

"And I to you, my maiden of the summer-red hair."

"Yes." She pressed both her hands over his heart. "All right, enough of Beatrice and the past. Better we use this moment and enjoy each other. Don't you think?" Her mouth twisted with a mischievous smile full of promise.

"Wise words, my queen." He kissed her deeply on the mouth.

They did not speak again for the rest of that morning, being otherwise and rather pleasantly occupied.

Chapter Seven

Kathryn waited in the castle courtyard at the meeting place she and King Thomas had agreed upon last night. She had barely arrived before she heard soft feet padding to her across the dirt of the courtyard. Turning, she smiled at the wolf's loping approach. His tail wagged, and he barked a cheerful greeting to her.

Her tirewoman was with her again. Propriety demanded Kathryn have such an escort with her whenever she moved about on the castle grounds. By rights, she should also have had a man-at-arms to attend her, but the wolf provided protection enough against any foes she might encounter in the king's rose garden.

Kneeling as the wolf reached her, she caressed the side of his face, smiling into his beautiful eyes. "You didn't do yourself any injury last night then?"

He nuzzled her neck, whining softly.

She grinned. "No, nor me either." She eyed the wound on his shoulder with a practiced eye. The bite had healed well despite everything, even quicker than she would have expected. The edges had closed nicely in a long, healthy-looking scab. "The queen has given me leave to dedicate my mornings to you, Sir Garwaf, from here on out. If you don't object, of course."

He yipped happily and bounced on his front feet. He did not object, apparently.

"Well then, Queen Aliénor has ordered you to show me the gardens."

The wolf paused, cocking his head in a startled motion, but then his mouth parted in a grin.

"Particularly the rose gardens."

Clearly happy to oblige, the wolf set off at a brisk trot through the groves and orchards of the king's stronghold with Kathryn by his side. She, in payment for his services as guide, told him entertaining stories. The tirewoman, acting as the reluctant chaperone, trailed along behind, although the occasional muffled giggle told Kathryn the woman enjoyed Kathryn's far-fetched stories despite herself.

Garwaf, as she had nicknamed the wolf, showed Kathryn all the loveliest ornamental gardens and guided her through the king's lush orchards, waiting patiently while she selected two ripe apples from a tree and happily munched on one, giving the second to her dutiful tirewoman. The wolf led Kathryn past fountains and statues. He seemed particularly proud to show her an ancient marble edifice of a she-wolf sitting regally on the surface of the water, a modest stream trickling from her mouth into the pool at her paws.

Kathryn laughed and tweaked the wolf's ears as he continued his tour. He showed her through the hedge maze without faltering, and as the early morning began to turn toward afternoon, he brought her at last to the rose garden.

The rose garden was a long, charming walk with wooden archways, each bearing a different sort of rose. The flowers were arranged in sections, and the wolf led her on their walk so they encountered first a blinding fall of red followed by a tender caress of peach, then a delicate flush of tiny pink buds against one trellis that blended into the blinding white of a thousand folded dove-whites nesting in the wooden frame of the next arch...and so on. The sight made Kathryn's breath catch. The wolf, probably because he had grown up with the gardens of the castle, seemed bored at first. Yet Kathryn noticed that as her delight increased with each new sight, the wolf's gait became jauntier.

Every type of rose in the world seemed to bloom in the garden, each with its own archway, but just when she thought the footpath would go on forever, the walk ceased abruptly as they rounded a bend. She found herself emerging into an alcove made entirely of roses. The last archway formed a set of twin rose-covered gates that let out into the tiny haven of roses that lay before her.

She looked to the wolf, who nodded, and she stepped into her own little rose-filled Paradise. A naked statue of a young maid posed on a dais, heavily draped in coils of many-colored roses so her modesty remained intact, whether she willed it or no.

At the statue's feet, dozens and dozens of different rose bushes twined together in a great multihued mass. Kathryn walked around the circular platform and discovered a marble bench carved with designs of rose bushes blooming all around the feet. The carvings were so skillfully wrought she was almost scared to sit, lest her hind part receive a nasty surprise in the shape of a very serviceable thorn.

The wolf moved before her and leapt with ease onto the long bench, comfortably settling himself. Kathryn smiled and sat next to him, knitting her hands in her lap, drinking in the wonderful scent in the air of all the roses blossoming just for her.

The poor tirewoman, having done more walking in one afternoon than she was used to doing in a week, collapsed on a humbler wooden bench at the entrance to the alcove and promptly fell into a doze.

Upon realizing they had a bit of privacy, Kathryn grinned at the wolf. "This is probably a popular trysting place for young couples." She had the grace to blush but could not quite keep her mouth from betraying her with a smile.

The wolf huffed and settled his chin on his paws, staring at her with mirth showing in his dark eyes. He did not confirm or deny her guess.

They sat together for a few minutes in companionable silence before Kathryn asked, "Shall I tell you a story, my lord?"

— ◦ —

That evening, when Kathryn returned to the women's chambers after supper, she found a livid Beatrice cramming all her worldly possessions into a large trunk. The other ladies of the queen had clumped together and stared at the furious older girl with barely concealed horror.

Kathryn looked to the younger girls and, shadowed still in the doorway, mouthed, "What happened?"

Beatrice was distracted with a furious tirade at the poor laundress for packing one of her gowns improperly. Lady Avice crept out and closed the door silently after herself, pulling Kathryn farther down the hallway.

Avice's gaze fairly gleamed with mischievous satisfaction. "You missed the commotion on your walk, Kathryn. We came back late as the queen requested, and when we did, the queen asked the three of us—Apolline, Agathe, and me—to wait in our bedchamber while she talked to Beatrice in the solar. We snuck out and listened at the door, of course."

Of course. Kathryn motioned with her hands for the other girl to continue.

"The queen sounded very quiet and composed, so we couldn't hear what she said. But then Beatrice started yelling after a minute or so, 'What do you mean I'm to be banished from court? Does the king know of this?' And then you could tell the queen lost her temper, because we could finally hear her, and she snapped back, 'It was *my husband's* idea.' They got into a bit of a screaming match, and the queen told Beatrice she knew of the midnight excursions out and about. 'I have no use'—this was what the queen said— 'I have no use for a lady-in-waiting who is disloyal to me and courts dishonor at every turn. Your brother has been written to. He will decide what is best to be done and, in the meantime, I want you out of my sight and away from this place. My husband has arranged you should stay with the Abbess Marie.' And then you could just hear Beatrice drawing breath. She near screamed down the rafters." Here the young girl pitched her voice low and whispered breathily as if she were shouting. "'What, you'd send me to the bastard nun?' Kathryn, what does 'bastard' mean?"

"Never you mind." Kathryn ruffled Avice's curling dark hair. "So, dear Beatrice is being shipped off to a convent?"

"That's the way of it." Avice rocked back on her heels happily. "Just as well. There'll be less fighting for the good men with her gone. Her being such a shameless flirt, it was impossible to compete."

The sound of smashing brought their conversation abruptly to a halt. Kathryn rushed back to the room with Avice reluctantly trailing behind.

Beatrice had thrown a hand mirror at their maid's head. Apolline and Agathe clutched each other in one corner of the room while Beatrice vented her fury on them now.

Kathryn thought she would be a more welcome target, and one more able to withstand the barrage, so she said quite cheerfully, "Good e'en, Lady Beatrice. Is aught amiss?"

Beatrice whirled, her eyes fairly popping out of her head from fury. "You. *You filthy strumpet*. You did this."

"Why, Lady Beatrice, did what?" Kathryn blinked innocently, and Avice hid a giggle behind her hand.

"*Ruined* my name in court." Beatrice's face contorted in a paroxysm of rage, turning the usually comely countenance into a wild, animalistic mask. "*Sullied* me before the queen. *Spoiled* all my chances."

"No, Beatrice," Kathryn said softly, her enjoyment of this scene evaporating. "You did that to yourself."

Beatrice leapt for her, but the other ladies had anticipated the attack and latched onto the woman's arms. Even their trembling laundress had her arm around one of Beatrice's flying fists.

Beatrice swung wildly to shake them off, to no avail. When she found her will flouted, she unleashed a stream of ear-burning invective at Kathryn. "I'll get you for this, you whore, you *bitch*." A string of more vile insults poured from her mouth, all of her vitriol directed at Kathryn.

Without missing a beat, Avice skipped from the room and called down the hallway to their guards. "Would you mind helping with Lady Beatrice's luggage? The boxes are a bit heavy for our maid."

Beatrice glared but quieted at once, straightening her hair and the neck of her gown. By the time the guards arrived, she was wreathed in smiles, dabbing at eyes suddenly juicy with tears. "I shall miss you all so very much." She engulfed a petrified Apolline in a bone-crushing embrace. "But when one has a holy vocation, as I have, what can one do but follow the path Fate has decreed?" This as she squeezed Agathe. Kathryn noticed the tiny girl wince with pain and rub her arms afterward.

When Beatrice went to hug Avice, the puckish girl beat her to it, squeezing Beatrice so hard around the midsection the older woman blanched and hurriedly pushed her away. Avice smiled beatifically and refused to let go. "Whatever shall we do without you, dear, *dear* Lady Beatrice? But no, you are to be *Sister* Beatrice now."

"Oh, that will not be for a time yet," Beatrice gritted out through her teeth. "I have still my novitiate to fulfill. One can only hope I will be worthy." For the barest of moments, she looked quite miserable, and Kathryn pitied her.

But then Beatrice stood before Kathryn and pulled her against her generous bosom, growling in Kathryn's ear. "I will get you back for this. Never doubt it."

And then Beatrice was gone, the guards lugging her heavy cases after her. Kathryn couldn't help but heave a sigh of relief as Avice hurried across the room, slammed the door in triumph, then turned and grinned at them all. Kathryn smiled back, and all the remaining ladies of the queen hugged each other, happy in their reprieve from the tyrant Beatrice.

Chapter Eight

F or the rest of the month before the Feast of St. Aaron, Kathryn and the wolf met every day in the gardens. They walked their mornings away in each other's company. Sometimes they "talked," with Kathryn studiously interpreting the wolf's sighs and body language. Sometimes they shared a comfortable silence until they both reluctantly went inside for their midday meal, and the tirewoman, their perpetual chaperone, went in with gratitude to ease her aching feet.

Kathryn and Garwaf each enjoyed their lives apart from their rambling walks as well. The wolf's optimism improved enormously after a very short time living among humans again, among comrades and friends, and not alone in some dank hole in the woods.

The wolf trained with the men and the king in the afternoons. He would stare with longing at the sword and archery practices, which earned him some odd glances from the others. He was always spry and fit for sparring, though, so the men forgot his odd abstraction during weapons training. Mornings were for jousting, and truth be told, the knights did not miss him overmuch now he was always with Kathryn. The wolf's presence used to frighten the horses, and training for the warhorses, at least, went much better without Garwaf.

Meanwhile, in Beatrice's absence, life in the queen's chamber became a joy and a pleasure, as if a storm cloud had blown away to reveal a bright spring day. Not just the queen but also the other handmaidens bloomed in the absence of the stranglehold Beatrice had had over them all. Talk became much more animated and friendly in the queen's quarters.

Kathryn was called on for her stories less and less and invited more and more to talk about the wolf's progress and herself, how she was adjusting to court, how her father was at home, and other such niceties of conversation that had not been addressed to her before.

Kathryn was delighted to discover she had many more friends in court these days. She still loved spending time with the wolf more than anything else, but when he went with the king, she was glad to have some other way to occupy her time.

With one week until the festival, most of the talk in the ladies' solar dealt with the preparation and anticipation of the important day. When talk turned to what finery the ladies would wear and the queen discovered Kathryn's best dress, the blue one, not only needed mending but also was stained and dirty—and Kathryn would wear that one on the feast day—this was deemed insupportable.

All the women, including the queen herself, raided their clothing for Kathryn and quickly equipped her with a beautiful dress and soft leather slippers dyed to match. The queen, in a gift fit for royalty, at least to Kathryn's mind, gave her a matching golden ring and necklace in the shape of a delicately molded rose with soft petals unfolding. The jewelry was so cunningly wrought, and so full and bright was the trinket's bloom, that Kathryn almost expected the rose to wilt as she held the ring. She tried to refuse the gift. "This is too much, my lady."

Aliénor would not have it back, and then, at Kathryn's insistence, she said quietly, "All right, then. Keep one and give the other to your dear one. Unless I mistake the matter, your wolf has no festival finery either."

Not for the first time, Kathryn wondered just how much King Thomas had told his lady about Garwaf. Kathryn and the queen had never discussed the wolf again. Not privately anyway. The queen did not ask, and Kathryn did not tell.

To see the king and queen so happy together pleased Kathryn greatly. Once, in the middle of the month, she and the wolf had been turned from their accustomed place in the rose garden by the unmistakable sounds of the queen's delighted giggling and the king's chuckle, followed by the sound of rustling foliage and a low sigh of contentment.

Discreetly, Kathryn and her beast friend had crept away from the place and back the way they had come. When safely out of hearing, Kathryn gave the wolf a triumphant grin and said, "Told you so. An ideal place for trysting."

Garwaf had, with much dignity, refrained from rising to her bait.

———◦◦———

Garwaf and Kathryn—with the tirewoman enjoying a nap in the shade a little way off—were safely ensconced in that same rosy alcove now, having found the space empty of any other clandestine lovers that day.

"Shall I tell you a story, my lord?" She always asked him this when they sat together in the garden after they had wearied of walking. This time with Kathryn was his favorite time of the day, and he could listen to her talk for hours, for weeks, for all the rest of his days. He loved the sound of her voice, loved the charisma of her personality, loved...

Her.

He worried sometimes she must get bored with only him and her maidservant for company, but when she did lapse into silence and they just walked along with each other, he was always struck by how companionable they were, even in silence. Things were never awkward with Kathryn, silences never strained. She was intelligent, funny, warmhearted. For whatever reason, she seemed quite taken with him as well. She enjoyed running after him, playing tag in the gardens, sitting under an apple tree, dozing. They liked to walk together to look at flowers.

If he could not contribute to the conversation, per se, she did ask him questions often that he could answer with a bark or a nod. They found ways to understand each other.

He perked his ears up and tipped his head to say "yes" when she asked him now if he'd like a story. Kathryn had told him tales many times before. She had a gift for storytelling and quite a vast repertoire of legends. Today, though, he had something else in mind.

"Something of the first crusade? When the king's father founded our colonies down there?"

He shook his head.

"All right. Something from the Tiochene tribe? Do you know of the great lady General Odyssia?"

Garwaf did, of course, but Kathryn would tell the heroine's tale well enough for him to feel the salt spray of the sea on his face and the clash of swords on one another, enjoy the loving embrace of a daughter long missed and the favor of a benevolent Fate. In the garden of the roses, though, he once more declined her suggestion. *No, I do not want tales of heroes and villains, magic and monsters today.*

"Well, then," she said with a touch of impatience, "what story shall I tell you?"

He hesitated, then tiptoed forward on his paws and placed his head on her lap, staring at her soulfully. He nudged her hand with his nose.

She laughed, as he had hoped she would. "You want to hear stories about *me*?"

The wolf blinked. *Yes, that's the way of it.*

She pursed her lips in mock displeasure and sighed dramatically. "Ah well, if you command it, Sir Garwaf, who am I to refuse? Do you command it?"

The wolf barked once. *Yes, I most certainly do. You have saved my life and my soul. I know your mind, your heart, and yet I know far too little about your past. Today is the day to remedy that.*

A corner of her mouth tipped up in a smile she tried to hide. She pushed a few stray hairs from her face and curled around him, resting her head on the soft fur of his side like a pillow. He closed his eyes in contentment, leaning against her thigh.

"Well," began Kathryn. "Every tale of a life must begin *before* that life begins, with the makers of the life. With the parents. That's the way I see it, anyway. I'm sure some scholars would disagree, but they are not here. For my tale we will certainly begin there." And then she fell into her bard voice, as Garwaf called it in his mind. This voice could be any and every character Kathryn chose. Her voice had zest and nuance and could stretch from a florid, gluttonous lord with the deep drum of a thundercloud, rumbling in displeasure, to the high squeak of a mouse doing a good deed for a lion that would probably eat him anyway.

Usually the bard voice had very little of the real Kathryn. Today, though, her voice was *all* Kathryn, warm and melodious, a soothing alto. "I cannot tell you my mother was the sweetest and kindest creature on earth as most mothers seem to be. She had a sharp tongue in her head."

The wolf gave Kathryn a droll look, and she grinned. "Yes, like me. She used her wits instead of burying them at the bottom of her sewing basket. There were not many men would have her, despite her incredible good looks and the fact she was best friend to Queen Rosamund. Now, my father, Sir Stephen, was a lowly knight in faithful service when our beloved king was but newly crowned.

"Together they conquered much of the land that had belonged to our Jerdic enemy. In gratitude, the king created the Barony of Rémeré as a gift to my father, who before was merely the poor second son of a knight. King Thomas's only caveat was that Stephen should find himself a wife, for he would need one when he had his property. Stephen met my mother at the winter court, and he loved Lady Isabella from the first. He wed her within a year of being named Baron of Rémeré. They had me the next year. Not an overly attentive father, Lord Stephen stopped by our apartments to take a look at me every now and again, but mostly my father devoted himself to my mother and left my raising up to her. They were very happy years.

"My father first started showing me around to eligible men when I was ten years old." Now a shadow did fall across her countenance. "Mother died when I was twelve, trying to deliver my father an heir, and he understandably forgot all else, forgot me entirely in his sorrow." Kathryn choked and could not continue, blinking rapidly. Her usual brightness of personality crumbled. She was not always so optimistic and impervious to regret as she led the world to believe. Pain had touched her and still could.

Garwaf tucked his head under her chin, leaning in with the best approximation of a hug he could give with the arrangement of limbs at his disposal. More than anything, he wished for his humanity so he could comfort his lady properly.

A sweet smile lit her face, and she wrapped her arms around him. When she let go at last, he stared at her. Tears swam in the green depths of her eyes, but they did not break the barriers of her lids.

You don't have to continue, he said with his gaze, *if this is painful to you.*

Kathryn caressed the puckered scar along his face. "You would let me end things there, but a good bard does not leave a story half told." She sucked in a calming breath and seemed pleased when the air did not snag on her heartache. "Besides, to tell of the pain helps ease some of it. My Uncle Flavio had lived with us, and he took over my education and rearing after Mother died. He became more of a father to me than Lord Stephen. Uncle never understood why women shouldn't be educated, free to say what they liked and do what they liked, as men do."

She leaned toward him confidingly, and he tilted forward in response, yearning for her warmth, her nearness.

"I had rather an unorthodox upbringing, I'm afraid, and so became the saucy wench I am now."

He playfully nipped at her fingers, and she giggled.

Her dimple peeked out at him. "A sense of what is suitable and not in a young maiden did not hold out long against my reason and my crippling restlessness. Our lands border a great forest and, as I grew, I walked there often, trying to find the Fair Folk our villagers spoke of. I never did."

Garwaf snorted.

"But those adventures gave me a taste for it. I wandered in ever-widening circles from my home after that and taught myself to climb trees. I realize now my luck in managing not to be eaten by wolves at the time." She winked at him. "Or worse."

He shuddered as he thought of some of the things that could be encompassed in that "or worse"—none of them pleasant for an innocent maiden.

"Our gamekeeper caught on to my mischief before any real harm—besides some scraped knees and torn dresses—befell me. Uncle gave me a sound scold when he found out, and a beating. After, he kept a stricter watch on me, and I ended up spending many of my days reading. I had always been a great reader, which is how I learned all my stories, but he added still more books to my library.

"Then, since I had already received far more education than was seemly for any girl, he decided to instruct me in other languages and in the analysis of texts. Teaching me such knowledge was highly improper, but he couldn't see the harm." She fanned her fingers over Garwaf's fur, smoothing it back and forth, snuggling closer to him.

"A few years ago, Flavio fell ill. After three years of pain, he finally passed last year, which meant Father suddenly had to deal with me. Poor Lord Stephen came to discover that all the qualities he loved so in my mother he deplored in me. A respectable intellect is of very little use in a daughter you're trying to marry off, since most men don't like their wives to be too witty.

"Perhaps I'd have been suitable material for a mistress, but having a loud-mouthed shrew like me for a bride? Unthinkable." She laughed brightly, no shadow of ill use showing in a face that Garwaf found comelier by the hour. "None of the neighboring lords in the area thought me worth a glance, especially as I lacked two qualities that would have made me rather more suitable or at least made my shortcomings rather more forgivable. I had no dowry and no beauty."

Garwaf growled a vehement protest.

She grinned and patted his head. "Flatterer. Anyway, after having no luck marrying me off, Stephen wrote to his old friend King Thomas and begged him to take me on. The king had just married Queen Aliénor and brought her home. She would need ladies-in-waiting. My father hoped that court life could put some polish on me and I might find a good husband. So here am I." She hesitated before barreling on. "And grateful, too, to find myself here. With you. That day in the forest, I thought I would die of my loneliness, but then you came. So I thank you, kind sir, for your friendship and your loyalty. Thank you for everything." She bent and delivered a chaste kiss to the top of his head.

He turned and looked at her with longing. *I want to tell you of myself as well,* his heart said. *I want you to know of my father, the benevolent and noble Prince Michael, and his kind and good lady, Phillippa. I want to tell you of my uncle, King Thomas, and how he raised me from a child when they died.*

I want to explain my marriage to Alisoun to you. How I was young and foolish, how I thought a comely and courteous wife all one could want from a woman.

I want to tell you how I became what I am. When my transformations started, how they happened. Why I am trapped now.

I want to tell you all of myself, show you the nicks and dents and scars of my life, and have you love me even though I be grievously flawed. I want to weave a tapestry of my life to show you, so you may see and mend the tears time and betrayal and pain have wrought on my soul.

I have done nothing to earn this regard of yours, but I want to.

I want you to know me. Really know me. Not as I am now. Not in this freakish form I now possess, but as my own true self. I want to prove myself to be the knight I was, that I still am, somewhere underneath all this fur.

I want you to care for me as me, because I am who I am, and not out of pity for what I have become. I want to be a man for you. I already am a better man in this wolf's body than I ever was in a human one. You did that.

He wanted to tell her all this, but he could only stare soulfully into her eyes and sigh.

She leaned against him, and he placed his head in her lap once more. They curled around each other as comfortably as if they were two parts of one whole, connected again at last.

Chapter Nine

T he past month of mornings had been some of the best of her life, and it saddened Kathryn that preparations for the feast would keep her from getting her usual walk in the gardens with the wolf. The day before the feast had dawned, and there was simply too much to do for her to get a moment away for herself. Garwaf had amicably agreed to accompany her on her various errands. He lacked hands, after all, and so was not much good in helping with the preparations of the knights.

Courtiers had begun to arrive the night before and were housed comfortably in the castle now. A brace of dignitaries was also expected to come this morning, and a little snarl of dread formed in Kathryn's stomach. Her father would be one of them.

She wore a dark-gray dress, serviceable and plain, and the rose necklace sat tucked into the pocket of her gown, a talisman against ill luck. The bauble formed a hard knot against her side, and she waited for a quiet moment to make her gift to the wolf, hoping he would like the jewel.

She passed through the courtyard on her way to Llewellyn's workshop, where the wolf had gone to keep the magician company.

A knight on a large brute of a charger rode in through the gates like he owned the castle. A big man, deep chested and tall in the saddle, the knight wore a very rich tunic of striped silk with the red emblem of a curled dog emblazoned across his chest. His breeches and boots were of the finest cut and quality.

Here is a rich and important man if ever I have seen one. Yet his eyes were hard and dark, a sneer disfiguring his too-handsome face as he dismounted. The taut displeasure on the stranger's face unnerved Kathryn, and she shuffled a few steps farther from the man, dropping her gaze.

As the new arrival dismounted, King Thomas, Llewellyn, and the wolf were crossing the courtyard to meet Kathryn. The wolf looked up and saw the newly arrived knight. Garwaf stopped midstride, his eyes widening. Kathryn's stomach dropped with sudden, nameless fear.

"Reynard." Llewellyn grimaced as he saw the big knight. "That bastard."

The attack happened so quickly no one, least of all the man Reynard, knew precisely what had transpired. Garwaf ran toward Reynard, fast as a fiend, and sank his teeth into the man's arm, trying to drag him down to the ground with brutal force.

King Thomas reacted first, and just in time too, before the wolf had a chance to do greater harm to the man. "*Sir Garwaf.* You forget yourself."

The wolf backed off from the fallen man but snarled. Ears back, hackles raised, the wolf tensed for another, probably murderous, spring.

The king had just come back from a brisk morning ride, and so he still had his crop in hand. "Sir Garwaf," he bellowed again, and at last the wolf turned his furious gaze from the fallen knight and looked to his king.

King Thomas raised his riding crop threateningly, but his eyes were tense at the edges, pleading. "You will not harm this guest of my house, wolf, or so help me I shall be forced to beat you from the place."

The wolf looked to the fallen knight. He growled once more before he backed off and sat, glaring, but a threat no longer. Kathryn raced from her hidden vantage point and went to the wolf at once, her heart in her throat. She placed her hand on his head. He glanced up, and the first signs of discomfiture began to show in him. He did not seem sorry for the *act*, but perhaps for the brutality of his attack, perhaps because she had witnessed his wildness?

The man Reynard jumped to his feet indignantly and would have advanced on the wolf had King Thomas not stopped him. "As he has honored my truce, so shall you, Lord Reynard." A threat hung heavy in the king's words.

Kathryn looked to the wolf, but he was watching the king and the wounded knight, whose own blood had stained his fine red-striped tunic.

Reynard fumed. With his nostrils flaring in quivering indignity, he was not at all handsome. "Is it now the custom of the court to keep wild beasts?"

"The practice has only come into fashion of late, my lord," Llewellyn said in evenly measured tones. He bowed his head, his voice so bland as to be absolutely colorless. Kathryn suspected the magician liked this knight no more than she, or perhaps even the wolf, did.

"If you will come to my workshop, I will tend that arm for you," Llewellyn said.

"It would be wise," the king murmured.

Reynard, dignity bruised but unable to cry off, nodded and stalked from the court. The wolf's gaze followed him, and Kathryn would have given much to know what went on behind the gleaming blue depths of her beast's eyes.

When Lord Reynard had passed, King Thomas offered his arm to Kathryn, which she accepted silently while the wolf fell into step with them. King Thomas seemed to be addressing his remarks to Kathryn, but he actually spoke to the wolf. "Was that well done of you, my boy? It most certainly was not wise. All will be made right in time, but patience and prudence are required to accomplish that."

King Thomas walked them out the back and into the garden, where the wolf had just returned from. "I think"—and this the king said to Kathryn— "our friend could use some fresh air. I will speak to my lady wife and see that your duties for the next hour are assigned to some other handmaiden."

After King Thomas left, Kathryn turned a scathing glare on the wolf, and he had the grace to look abashed. He curled his tail between his legs and followed meekly when she led him to their favorite and accustomed spot in the rose garden. She sat on the bench, the wolf opposite her, appearing as ashamed as he could manage with his limited selection of facial expressions.

"The king is right. That was not well done of you."

The wolf hung his head.

She sighed. "But such anger is entirely understandable. Considering the circumstances."

The wolf glanced up. His sharp blue eyes studied her before he slunk toward her, whining softly. Pursing her lips to hold her own emotions back, she held her hand out, palm up in invitation. He rested his chin on her knee, and she smoothed his fur with shaking hands. "I had hoped for a better opportunity than this, but I doubt one will come." She fished in her dress pocket and held her hand in front of the wolf's face. The gold lay glittering in her palm, winking at them in the sunlight.

The wolf sniffed the necklace and looked at her face, curious.

"This is for you if you would like." Heat blossomed across her cheeks. "I have a ring that matches. See?" She held up her hand to show him the golden rose ring encircling her left ring finger. "I thought..." She creased her brows, suddenly shy, awkward.

Before she could grow more flustered, the wolf butted her hand with his nose. She laughed and clasped the necklace around his throat. The necklace looked very distinguished and lent him a regal air not to be found in any common wolf.

She glanced up at the sound of someone approaching, and Llewellyn hovered outside their alcove, wiping his hands with a rag.

"Hello, Master Llewellyn." At Kathryn's greeting, the wise man entered the rose garden.

Llewellyn knelt first before the wolf. "May I check your shoulder, my lord?"

Kathryn, to whom the possibility of injury had not occurred, gasped and hovered over Llewellyn the whole time he inspected the wound, which had *not* reopened and still seemed to be healing nicely.

The examination over, the magician rocked back on his heels and spoke to the wolf. "Our king thinks it best you omit your presence from dinner tonight."

Kathryn gasped with dismay. This announcement hardly surprised her, but it most definitely disappointed her.

Llewellyn's wind-weathered face cracked in a grin. "His Highness does not, however, ban you from attending tomorrow's festivities. He only wants to give you a day to cool down and collect your wits. All right, Garwaf?"

The wolf looked to Llewellyn and inclined his head in the affirmative.

"'Tis well, then, and nothing's to stop you two, now Reynard's cleared out, from taking some refreshment at my hut."

<hr />

The three of them passed a pleasant noon meal together in Llewellyn's workshop. He pulled out a fine batch of apricot brandy and passed the bottle around. Garwaf drank sparingly, not knowing his wolfish threshold for the brew. Kathryn drank rather more than she should have, but that only made her more cheerful. Llewellyn was a deep personality and also a hearty drinker. He imbibed more than both of his guests put together and showed never a sign of intoxication except for a more pronounced glitter behind his pale eyes.

"Oh, do some magic for me, Llewellyn," Kathryn asked after her fourth mug. Everyone called him "magician" and "conjurer," but she had yet to see him display any of these talents he was reputed to have.

Llewellyn clucked his tongue. "I don't do big magic anymore. Not without a good reason."

"Why not?"

A muscle ticked in his jaw, and he gave a small shake of his head. "I...made a grave mistake once undoing another magician's spell. I was foolish, cocky. I nearly killed a great many people. It turned out all right, but it is not an experience I wish to repeat." He smiled brilliantly, throwing off his dour mood. "Anyway, real magic, *true* magic, Kathryn my dear, is subtle and invisible. True enchantment is magic from here." Llewellyn tapped his head. "And here." He placed a palm over his heart. "My magic now is in the earth and the tilling of fields. I help the plants to grow high and tall. I give them resolve to last the winter. I pour laughter and love in when I brew them into wine. I mix in fortitude and hope when they are made into medicines."

Kathryn let all her confusion show in her face, and she heard the wolf muffle a small snort. Probably of amusement.

Llewellyn sighed and relented. "All right, then. Just a little spell." He closed his eyes and breathed deeply. When he opened his eyes, they seemed to Kathryn to glow faintly around the pupils. He pointed a finger at the grate by the fire, and a small shower of sparks fell from his fingers to the logs, causing a chipper flame to leap up in the fireplace. Garwaf barked and jumped away from the hearth with a glare at Llewellyn. Kathryn swore in a rather unladylike manner.

Llewellyn's face flushed, going white around the lips, and he drank deeply of his wine. "Yes, yes, quite impressive, and quite useless in the end. Selfish magic. Silly magic. Why use the supernatural for household chores? Why waste time and energy summoning up an inner flame when some good dry logs and a little friction could do the same?"

Kathryn looked up from the magic fire, which looked like any other fire to her untrained eyes. Llewellyn's skin had paled now and seemed to have hollowed out beneath his cheekbones. She went to him and helped move him to the bench. "Why didn't you tell me magic took this much out of you?" Her voice slurred around the edges.

He laughed. "Truth be told, I was curious myself if I could still do that kind of thing. I haven't done such a spell in a year or more. I'm out of shape."

Kathryn tsked. The wolf growled a short reproach.

Llewellyn grinned his customary irrepressible smile. "I devoted my life to the shallow magics. But now I've discovered a better way—a deeper and ultimately more rewarding way—of putting my talents to use. Instead of using them to build my own fame and glory, I use them to heal and mend, comfort and cure." His tone then became decidedly didactic. "Whatever magic men of my sort do, the power is visited back on them in some way three times as potent. For every shower of tiny sparks I make, I pay the price somewhere else. In my old age the price comes out in physical strength. In my youth, I believe it came out of my brain." He sighed ruefully. "I never did know a more thick-skulled fool than myself as a young man. Now, on the reverse side, every time I use my magic to help a wound knit cleaner, or an old man's bones ache less, or a babe grow straight and healthy, the goodness comes back to me threefold in good deeds and kindness." He smiled beatifically and suddenly looked ten years younger. "Which way would you say is ultimately the stronger?"

Kathryn smiled and clucked her tongue. "Ah, my Lord Magician, you really are just a soft-hearted pup deep down, are you not?"

Llewellyn blushed and made a maudlin face of false modesty. Kathryn laughed. The wolf jumped on him and playfully batted the magician's head with his paws. Llewellyn chuckled as well and unsuccessfully tried to shoo both the youngsters away from him.

The rest of the afternoon they passed together, with Llewellyn lecturing them both a little more on magic. When the magician and the maiden had to depart for dinner, Llewellyn fixed the wolf a meal to tide him over for the night, since he would miss the feasting in the hall. Garwaf settled with seeming placidity in front of the fire to eat his supper.

Kathryn had a nasty feeling, however, the wolf only bided his time. Before she left the healer's hut, she bent down and kissed the wolf's velvet-soft head. "Do not do anything unworthy of who you are."

The wolf gave her a poignant look. Kathryn frowned and left the hut reluctantly but quickly so she would not be late.

———————⊷◦⊶———————

Garwaf sniffed and sighed. *I am a wolf, my lovely maiden. As I* am *there is no ignoble act unworthy of me. I am not a knight anymore. No matter how much I pretend to be. No matter how I wish I still was. No matter how I wish you and I could...* The werewolf growled. *I am what I am now. And Reynard is to blame for it.*

Chapter Ten

K athryn fought with futility against the gloomy mood that settled over her. Garwaf was banished, and now she also found herself seated far away from all of her usual companions at dinner. Llewellyn waved to her from the high table, but she could barely make her fingers crook to wave back. When the magician looked away, she sank her chin into her hand and stared without relish at her food. With so many of the king's highest-ranking courtiers coming to the castle, Kathryn, as the unwed daughter of a minor baron, could not hope to get even a glance of the king or queen tonight.

Another unwelcome surprise came halfway through dinner. Kathryn sat near the doors but with her back to them. Many of the king's vassals were late arriving, stomping through the great hall to take their place at table. So when yet another pair of heavy feet came plodding into the grand room, Kathryn thought nothing of it and did not even look back.

One of the men sitting across from her, a distant neighbor of her father's, suddenly jumped to his feet and waved merrily. "Ho, there, Lord Stephen."

Kathryn slopped wine down the front of her dress as her father's low bass boomed out across the hall. "Had a beast of a time getting here. Roads are nigh impassable this time of year."

Her father, Lord Stephen the Baron of Réméré, had been wiry and spry in his youth, a mass of tight-corded muscle with a hand that could wield a mace like the arm of Doom against his foes. He had done good service for his king and been rewarded for his loyalty. He had married a beautiful woman he loved dearly and had been on such a good road until his beloved wife died.

Now Kathryn's father indulged himself in wine and food. He rarely left his estate—he rarely left his own chambers. The iron sinews of his youth had melted to corpulence in his age.

Kathryn had not expected him tonight. Truly, she had half hoped her father would send his apologies and not come at all this year. A vain, foolish hope. She swallowed with difficulty, her stomach sinking into the heels of her soft-toed slippers. Rising from her bench, she shakily turned to make a curtsy to her father as he approached. "Good evening, Father."

Kathryn spent the rest of the dinner in strained silence. She did not believe she could avoid a prolonged talk with her father. She probably would not even be able to put their conversation off until the next day. So she sat and waited with resignation for her father to bolt his meal down so the dreaded tête-à-tête could begin.

Her father cleaned his plate soon enough with little appreciation for the excellent food the king served to his guests. Softly, Lord Stephen bid her join him in the garden, and Kathryn went without comment. She held her mouth firmly shut until he led her to a wooden bench in the apple groves.

Lord Stephen sat his daughter down and eagerly stood before her, feet spread and arms akimbo, tapping one leg idly with his cane. "Well, girl, how have you done for yourself? If that fancy bauble is any sign, then none too badly." He gestured at the ring, giving her a wink and a broad grin.

Kathryn rubbed her temples, aching with tension. "The queen gave me the ring." She braced herself for his temper.

The anticipated explosion did not disappoint. "The queen? Fool child, I didn't spend a fortune to rig you out for this damned place to have you here making up to a married woman." Lord Stephen calmed himself with a long breath, but this did little to ease the angry flush spreading from the neck of his tunic. "Have you had no offers? No one come to pay court to you? No admirers of any kind?"

What did he expect? Kathryn glared at him, teeth gritting together tight enough to hurt her jaw. "None whatsoever, sir. I am too poor, too plain, and too shrewish to attract the men of the court. Things which you *knew* when you sent me here." The only offers or interest she'd had from men of the court were of the indecent kind, which had abruptly ceased altogether when she became the wolf's companion.

Her father tapped his stick against his boot. "True enough. All of it." His shoulders sagged, and he sniffed with annoyance. "Well, I'm sorry I'm not rich enough to pay a man to take you on. I should have realized my humble barony would fail to tempt these great men here." He narrowed his eyes at Kathryn. "Might as well take you home with me tomorrow then, after the feast. No point in keeping you here any longer."

Her mouth fell open. *But the queen.* The queen and all the ladies were her friends. She would miss them terribly if she left. *And Llewellyn.* Llewellyn said he would be happy to augment her already respectable knowledge of leechcraft with lessons in his herb-lore. *And the wolf...*

"Father," she said in her most carefully measured and reasonable tone of voice, "the queen has taken a liking to me. Let me linger a few weeks more until the court removes to the summer palace. See if I cannot by then firmly cement myself in her good graces." Her stomach churned at having to say these self-serving falsehoods, but her father did not know her well enough to recognize when she lied. "Having the favor and friendship of royalty is no bad thing, after all. She might even agree to keep me here permanently by then. Which would rid you of responsibility for me for good." She paused. "Besides, Queen Aliénor would be very angry with me if I were to leave so abruptly."

Her father thought this over but nodded at last. "You have a point." He scratched his patchy gray beard. "A month more, then, before I send for you? That's when the court will remove to the summer palace." He waggled a fleshy finger in Kathryn's face. "But no new gowns for summer court, girl. You wear what you have or you go about as Nature made you, so tend well what you have."

Her father clasped his cloak tightly around him and bustled inside. Kathryn fell submissively in behind him, all the while her head spinning. She had a month, then. A month to order her life and think of something. A month before her father carried her away from the first home she had enjoyed since her uncle's death.

She *would* think of something. She had to.

———◆———

The day of the Feast of St. Aaron dawned crisply cool. Garwaf sniffed the air, letting the sweet smells fill his body with cheerfulness. A play was planned on the life of the saint, and a market had come to the castle's court, to be followed in the evening by a great banquet.

Garwaf waited with Llewellyn, and Kathryn arrived late for their planned rendezvous. And perhaps that was because she had spent extra time arranging her hair *just so* in a graceful braid falling over her shoulder. Nervously, she smoothed the lines of her new gown. The wine-red dress had a low, square neck, a tightly laced waist, and a graceful train at the back she handled very well, only tripping once as she approached him. The rose ring gleamed in the early sunlight on her hand as she reached down to caress his head.

For his part, he simply stared at her in admiration. *What a lovely creature my little guardian is. She's flushed with the pleasure of the day to come, and her eyes are shining. She can't stop smiling. Ah, if only...*

Llewellyn addressed a remark to him, and the wolf shook himself out of his daze. Garwaf yipped noncommittally and turned his thoughts away from the too-wonderful Kathryn.

The day began merrily enough in the great court with the three of them browsing the market.

Llewellyn made a courtly bow. "We will wander where you will, my lady." He looked to Garwaf for affirmation. Garwaf wagged his fluffy black tail and let his tongue loll out happily. Kathryn grinned in response, all the reward he needed.

Llewellyn halted them and, his face very serious, drew out a small pouch and dropped it into Kathryn's hands. "By order of the king, I present this to you."

She tugged the pouch open and stared down at a cluster of silver coins. "I can't—"

The magician held his hand up. "It is also by order of King Thomas that you are denied the right to refuse this gift." Llewellyn smirked.

Kathryn snorted. "Well, since by royal decree the money is mine, I supposed I should decide how best to spend it."

"A new dress?"

"It won't stretch *that* far. Maybe boots, though. Or a new girdle."

Garwaf noticed her hungrily eyeing a monk's cart laden with books, and he tugged Llewellyn's sleeve. The magician followed Garwaf's gaze. With a pleased smile, Llewellyn winked and guided Kathryn by gentle degrees to the book stall.

"Pick any one you like," he ordered when they arrived. Kathryn dug in heartily, and Llewellyn did likewise. He turned up an interesting volume on the fairies to the north and knelt to look the manuscript over with Garwaf, who scanned the pages with interest.

———◇———

Kathryn narrowed her selections at last down to two volumes. She studied each book carefully, her heart longing for both. Each book was beautifully illustrated by the same supple hand. The drawings made her feel almost as if she could see the sights herself and hear the noises vibrating in her ears, smell the flowers and the chill winter sea. She had selected a slim volume of the lives of many of the more obscure saint-magicians of old and a larger, thicker volume of legends and folktales. The legends were beautiful. Some of them she had never read before, but the volume would cost far too much of the king's gift, and there were still the boots to buy.

Heart heavy, she set the book down and paid the monk what he asked for the saints. Llewellyn took up the book of folktales at once and turned the heavy manuscript in his hands. He smiled and piled the book of legends in with two other volumes on herb lore and a history of the Oracle at Ordinobl.

As they walked away, the books purchased, Kathryn caressed the wolf's ears and smiled at Llewellyn. "Will you let me borrow the book of legends and folktales sometime?"

"Of a certainty," Llewellyn said with his usual grandeur. Then he carelessly handed her the thick tome. "Especially since I bought the book for you."

The wolf barked mischievously.

"But the silver..." She held up the purse, too stunned to finish her thought.

"Was from the king. I like to give more specific presents."

"But—"

"All right, my Lady Stubborn, you may have the book on condition, then." He paused. "And that is that you read to me whenever I ask." The magician winked.

Kathryn chuckled and scooped the book from his outstretched hand. "We have an accord." She stood on tiptoe and kissed Llewellyn's cheek. A pleased flush crept up from his collar to tint his face, and he moved ahead of her to the mercer's stall. The wolf looked at her reproachfully, and Kathryn giggled. "Great silly beast." She delivered a sweet kiss on his nose. She hurried away, and the wolf skipped along behind her.

At the mercer, they met Queen Aliénor and several of the visiting noblewomen. The queen was ordering a new belt with the heraldic imagery of her lord's house, and a buckle in the shape of a wolf.

Kathryn chatted amiably with the other ladies, and the wolf bore the women's simpering regard with patience. Llewellyn, less stolid in the face of feminine attention, darted an appraising glance at the wolf, then made his excuses. He bowed out of the stall, and Kathryn watched the magician walk off toward another.

Very soon the queen had completed giving the specifications for her belt. She stepped aside so Kathryn could be measured for her new boots.

The mercer was quick and efficient. He was also very shrewd and had apparently noticed on what easy terms the young lady purchasing the boots was with Queen Aliénor. In consequence, Kathryn got a better deal on her footwear than she would have had she come to the mercer's stall when Aliénor was not by. The mercer, for his part, also admired the wolf, or more particularly, the wolf's pelt.

As the mercer and Kathryn concluded their business, he said quickly, "I'll give you the boots for free, throw in a pair of gloves and a new belt if you'll trade me for that animal."

The wolf snorted, his lip curling back, and Kathryn hid her smile behind her hand. She managed to compose herself quickly. "I'm sorry, sir, but the wolf is not mine to barter away so easily. He is the king's man."

The mercer deflated. "King's pet then, is it?"

"Why no, sir." She widened her eyes. "*He* is the most devoted of the king's personal retinue of knights." Kathryn swept from the stall with the wolf on her heels. She looked down at Garwaf. "And don't you forget that either."

The beast broke into a grin and playfully nipped her fingers.

"Behave yourself, or when I get my boots tomorrow, I really will trade you to the mercer. I could use a new belt."

They looked for the magician after that, but Llewellyn had lost himself somewhere in the tangle of stalls, apparently. "I don't think it's worth looking for him in this mob, do you?" Kathryn asked.

The wolf growled a cheerful negative. The stalls were a mess in the middle of the court, but the fair was not overly large as these things went. They were bound to run into Llewellyn sometime. Neither Kathryn nor the wolf fretted about the magician's absence. They were enjoying themselves too much.

As it happened, Llewellyn was trying to find them, but a visiting noble had hindered his attempts. The magician had been corralled into conversation and could not get free. Llewellyn disliked the man and was bored to tears by his endless tales of hunting, but the noble was an earl of the highest consequence—even if he was a muttonhead. It would not do for Llewellyn to offend him.

The wolf is not *the Duke of Dorré*. Reynard had to believe that, because if the wolf *was* the duke, then Reynard was about to find himself inhabiting a world full of woe.

Reynard's wife had been the strategist in their marriage from the first, but she remained at home. His sister, Beatrice, would have been helpful as well, but the fool girl had gotten herself sent to a convent in disgrace and was of no use to him now. So Reynard had decided—and not just because he liked his flesh intact—to avoid the wolf and to leave as soon as possible after the king's convocation of his liegemen.

The convocation would take place on the morrow. Reynard intended to make all ready to leave this bloody castle and ride as far away from the wolf as he could as soon as he could. Word of the wolf's attack had already spread, and the knights from the castle, who knew the wolf, were beginning to whisper to the ones who did not. Reynard fancied he could hear them now, chattering away behind his back as he passed.

"Yes, attacked him."

"Right in front of the gates, I heard."

"I saw the fight. The wolf knocked him into the dust."

"Would have torn him to pieces if the king hadn't called him to heel."

"Yes, but my dear, the wolf has never shown a bit of violence to anyone else before this."

"Makes me wonder what old Reynard did to the poor wolf to make him attack. Seems to me, the beast must have had a pretty good reason."

"I wouldn't put anything past Reynard."

"The lecher..."

Reynard's hands were beginning to cramp from being clenched into fists all morning. He wished he could just retire to bed for the day with a good bottle of wine and a kitchen maid, but his wife always hammered home to him the importance of appearances. Not the cleverest of weasels, Reynard still recognized that the antagonism against him would increase tenfold if he suddenly went missing for the day.

So, like a marionette with his strings being plucked, he wandered idly through the market stalls. He picked up a pair of scented, embroidered gloves for his wife, smiling grimly to himself as he tucked them into his pouch and paid the booth keeper.

His wife. Reynard could not think of Lady Alisoun these days without a twist of distaste coiling in his gut. *My wife. And what a fine wife she is.*

The press of bodies in the fair had begun to overwhelm Garwaf. Three people had tripped over him so far, and even Kathryn's soothing presence could not calm his raw nerves.

She reached down to caress his back. "Perhaps, Sir Garwaf, you would accompany me to the play? They've set up a pageant wagon in the gardens."

Garwaf gratefully led her into the castle. Sitting next to Kathryn in the shade, safe from the crush and stench of so many bodies, seemed a very palatable idea.

Together they stepped outside into the gardens, where the pageant wagon had been set up. It was a tall cart, nearly twice the height of a full-grown man, gaudily painted, and the massive structure rolled along on six huge wheels. Chairs and stands had been set up in the shade of the apple orchard for people to watch the performance.

The play had not started, but seats filled up fast. Two golden, high-backed chairs on a special curtained dais were marked out and waiting for the king and queen whenever they should make their appearance.

Kathryn grinned as Garwaf chased his tail for her amusement while they walked toward the wagon. But the smile abruptly fell from her face, and she stopped short before leaning in to tug him away. "I've changed my mind. Let's steal a quiet moment in the rose garden, eh? Away from all this bustle?"

Wolf or no wolf, he was not a fool, and he had already scented the foul odor she meant to distract him from. *Reynard.*

A clear path lay between Garwaf and his nemesis. *One pounce, that's all.* He tensed his muscles to spring, but suddenly arms closed about him. Tiny arms. Arms that had not the strength to stop him if he followed through on his attack. He barked angrily in Kathryn's face.

A hurt look twisted her features, and guilt stabbed through his gut, clear to his backbone, making him nauseated. He whipped his head away from her. *This is revenge. Women have no truck with vengeance. They do not understand.*

He writhed against her, trying to break free without hurting her, but she held him fast. Reynard stood so close, half turned away, oblivious to Garwaf's presence. The wolf wheeled on Kathryn, putting a fierce demand in his gaze. *I am just a pet to you, little better than a dumb animal. And* this, *this grudge is about honor.* He braced his muscles to break free of her hold. *I can never have Kathryn anyway. Honor is all that is left to me.* He growled low in his throat, a warning to her.

Reynard wheeled about and fell back at sight of the wolf. Garwaf twisted and thrashed in Kathryn's arms, scratching at her and snapping his jaws, snarling red-hot fury at Reynard.

Kathryn's build was slight, but the years of tailing after the servants in her manor and being put to tasks when she got in the way had given her a fair bit of wiry strength. To have such strength was very unmaidenly in her, of course, but her muscles were the only way she managed to hold a struggling wolf trying to free himself.

Reynard swore freely, though he was among ladies, and drew his sword on the wolf. "Fate's tits, what madness has gripped the king that he keeps such a beast about?"

"The beast amuses me," King Thomas said from behind them. "If he does not please you, Reynard, you are welcome to take your leave. I can well understand a wolf companion may not be to *your* liking. But you will sheathe your weapon first. I ordered peace ties, did I not? I do not allow naked steel in my home."

Reynard sheathed his wicked-looking blade and glared. He began to stalk out of the garden, but the king laid a restraining hand on his shoulder and grinned. "Tie the sword first, and then you may go."

The nobleman flushed angrily, found a thong of leather, and tied his blade to its scabbard so he could not draw his steel so easily again. Reynard made the most perfunctory of obeisance to the king before storming off.

King Thomas knelt, and the wolf stilled his struggles at once, but his ears were flattened back. Anger still rumbled low in the beast's throat as his gaze followed Reynard.

King Thomas laid a gentle hand on the wolf's shoulder. "There is a time and place, good sir, and that time is not here and now. Compose yourself." And then so quietly that Kathryn, who still restrained the wolf, barely even heard him, he exhaled in a tiny whisper, "Please, Gabriel."

The wolf looked at him, and his shoulders sagged, so that he turned biddable, almost boneless, in Kathryn's arms. The king helped her to her feet and winced in dismay. The wolf's claws were sharp, and he had not been gentle in trying to free himself. Because of the beast's struggles, Kathryn's gown had been torn to ribbons. She also had several nasty scratches on her thighs and arms. She was dirty and suddenly very tired. She desperately wanted to disappear before her father got wind of the whole incident and appeared on the scene.

Queen Aliénor stepped forward and slid her arm through Kathryn's, leading her toward the castle. She summoned one of the servants. "Lady Kathryn needs a fresh gown and a bit of a wash. Bring water to her apartments and lay out my dark green gown for her."

The servant withdrew, and the queen gave Kathryn a rueful smile. "I wish I could go with you, but I must stay by my lord."

Kathryn agreed mutely, lending only half an ear to the queen.

Garwaf had almost *attacked* her. A moment more and he would have. King Thomas and not she had saved the wolf's humanity this time. Garwaf was already sorry, of course, and he would probably not attack Reynard again after this. But other things in the world could provoke the werewolf in a like manner.

How much longer could she deal with this? Would he attack a human? Would he attack *her*? Kathryn could not control him forever if he could not exert some control over his own impulses. But had that really been an animal impulse? Or a human one?

Maybe she cared too much. Maybe the wolf would be better left to Llewellyn to manage. Maybe she *wasn't* helping the wolf. Maybe all Kathryn did was remind him what he did not have. Maybe she should—

"The wolf did not mean it." Aliénor squeezed Kathryn's hand. "Men lose themselves sometimes in trying to do the honorable thing. But they come back to themselves in the end. And back to us." She patted Kathryn's cheek and left her to find her own way to the women's chambers.

Kathryn really hated the idea of the queen giving her one of her own gowns to wear, but she was just too weary to refuse the mercy at this moment. As soon as she recovered some strength, Kathryn would make sure the dress was properly laundered and returned to the queen.

That would be the first thing Kathryn saw to before she left the castle.

Chapter Eleven

L lewellyn was found, looking very much the worse for wear after his encounter with an interminable bore of a lord. The magician was also very much the worse for the furious dressing down King Thomas gave him after the play of the saint for leaving the wolf unattended. Garwaf felt heartily guilty about the whole affair.

Head hanging in shame, Garwaf meekly went along with Llewellyn's escort as the magician kept him subtly to the side at dinner, which did not help the curious stares of the court, though the maneuver did give them a new direction.

Kathryn emerged just in time for dinner, clean and in the queen's lovely dark green dress. She did not sit with Llewellyn, nor the king, nor the wolf, nor even her father, though that worthy did try throughout the meal to catch her eye.

Kathryn remained stubbornly oblivious to the advances of all her usual associates and said not a word to anyone during the meal. Eventually, she removed to an isolated corner of the room and hid herself half in the shadows so she could not be easily seen. She hardly attended to her food.

She looked pale and sad, and her eyes were red rimmed and deep shadowed. Garwaf hung his head and did not touch the food placed before him either. *Even if I had ripped Reynard's throat out, it would not have been worth this. Nothing is worth this.*

"You, my lad, are in rather a bit of a mess," Llewellyn said out of the side of his mouth. "Throwing you and Kathryn together the way we did was unfair. But how the king and I were supposed to know the effect the girl's charms would have on you is beyond me. Gabriel had such terrible taste in women. How could we know you would see the worthiness of Lady Kathryn?"

Llewellyn plucked a thick roll from his plate and proceeded to break it gently into pieces, stuffing small bits into his mouth as he spoke. "I must admit *I* never saw the appeal of Alisoun of Canille." He rubbed the side of his nose thoughtfully. "This way will be better for Kathryn." He fell silent and Garwaf looked up at him. Llewellyn continued, "Far better Kathryn have a clean break now with the *wolf*—before the *man* has a chance to snub her."

Garwaf growled at the magician. *If you are implying my intentions toward Kathryn were ever anything other than honorable, that I ever entertained thoughts of—well. Reynard won't be the only one with a scratched face, and he won't be the worse off, either, if you don't shut your mouth.*

The magician seemed to read at least some of Garwaf's less-than-charitable thoughts toward himself, and a twinkle crept into his eyes. "Of course, if *I* were still married to Lady Alisoun, I wouldn't help anyone to turn me back to a human in a hurry either. Especially since, as a man, Gabriel does still have rights to his wife if he should return."

The wolf jerked and knocked over Llewellyn's goblet. The magician, unperturbed, righted the mug, poured himself more wine, and began drawing small runes in the spilled liquid.

I'm not married to Alisoun any longer. I cannot be. I—but... Oh. Fate spare me. I am still married to that harpy. The wolf huffed. *And everyone believes Reynard acted on his own. No one else knows what a lying, two-faced spawn of the devil she is. And if I let myself stay like this, no one ever will.*

When the beast came out of his reverie and looked at the magician, eyes pleading, Llewellyn grinned. "No one will mark our absence tonight. Let us retire to my workshop. I have certain relics about the place that might be useful. Perhaps some of them will enable you to tell me what I need to know."

The wolf hopped down from his chair, leading Llewellyn out to the garden.

—◦—

Reynard had rallied his allies around him at table and gathered the scraps of his dignity close. Everyone still whispered that he had injured the wolf in some way. Thankfully, no one had come close to the truth yet. Although that blasted pet magician of the king's kept an infuriating eye on him all through dinner.

Reynard shifted in his seat, thinking not for the first time how bloody grateful he would be to escape to his own manor. If all went well with the plan he had set into motion, by the next convocation of lords, the damned beast would not be here. Or even alive.

Seated at Reynard's left hand during dinner was the flighty daughter of some baron. Apolline, her name was, and an old friend of his sister's. She flirted with him and, when he found she was one of the queen's ladies, good friends with the wolf's companion too, he turned his considerable charm on her and pumped her for information. He might have pumped far more into her after the meal, but unfortunately, duty called. He had plots to carry out and no time for sport. Piecing together what Lady Apolline let fall with things his sister Beatrice had ranted about in her letters, Reynard began to see an opportunity.

Lady Apolline excused herself from the table, casting an inviting look over her shoulder at Reynard. He left his seat almost at once, but with much regret, he did not follow little Apolline. Instead he wandered from table to table before he "discovered" an empty seat next to Kathryn in the shadowy corner where she had secluded herself.

She did not notice Reynard until he said, "Lady Kathryn, is it not? We met last time I was at court." He slid into the empty seat and eagerly leaned toward her. "And now you are the caretaker of the king's prized wolf?"

Kathryn looked up in surprise and recoiled.

When she made to get up, he laid a restraining hand on hers. "Ah, now, let me remind you how improper it would be for you to make a scene here." He flashed her a grin. "My lady."

She frowned but sat back on the bench.

He released her fingers and smiled into her pale green eyes while she glared back at him. "An intelligent woman," he sneered. "What a rare find in these times. So, you are the wolf's...?"

"Friend," she said, denying any impropriety with the bluntness of her tone and the direct regard of her gaze.

"Ah, yes, of course." Reynard selected a large piece of pheasant from the platters. He proceeded to rend the leg, and just as much of the meat ended up in his mouth as did in his beard and clothing. "You know," he said around the meat before swallowing, "the beast is naught but a simple wolf."

She smiled innocently back at him. "Did I ever say otherwise, my lord?"

He grinned at her, and she looked away from him in obvious revulsion. Unperturbed, he continued, "But if the wolf were other than he seemed...say, a certain knight. A missing heir." He paused and picked some dirt out from one of his fingernails with his dinner knife before he spoke again. "If he were that knight, say, who has been missing these two years from our king's court, well, then it is only natural he should try to kill me."

The wench widened her eyes at him, trying to play innocent. "But *why*, good sir, unless you betrayed him in some way?" She tilted her eyebrow up with just the right combination of cool haughtiness and defiant challenge to deter a thousand forward knights. The queen would have done well to match her hauteur.

What an amusing wench. This game grows better by the minute. "You poor, dear girl." He caressed her wrist. "He still loves *her*, of course."

The girl froze, her cheeks going a little pale. "Her?"

"Why, the Lady Alisoun, of course. I married the sweet lady when her husband so callously abandoned her." Reynard smiled. "A most remarkable woman, I can tell you. Sweet. Humble. Lovely beyond man's dreaming. The knight would have to get me out of the way if he were to have any hope of reclaiming his former bride." As Kathryn's hand clenched on the table, Reynard smirked.

He traced his fingertips over her knuckles and leaned in to her. "If Gabriel ever returned, he would not have a moment to spare for the destitute daughter of a shabby genteel baron." He inhaled against her hair, and his voice turned husky, a sharp rasp as his lips brushed her ear. "I, on the other hand, could find many uses for you." He lifted a section of her hair and rubbed the lock between thumb and forefinger. "Many uses indeed." He tilted in to wrap his arms about her, bending toward her mouth.

He was stopped short, however, by the small but quite sharp dinner knife Kathryn clutched in her free hand.

<hr />

Kathryn fought to keep her voice steady and her hand firm on the knife's handle. She placed the blade against Reynard's inner thigh, very high up. The offensive knight stopped as if turned to stone.

She wet her lips. "No doubt you received most of your intelligence about me from the charming Lady Beatrice. She has, I am sure, informed you that my family brought me up like a heathen. So, in case you wondered, *yes*, I will use this knife to gut you if I so choose." She shifted the knife infinitesimally, and Reynard flinched.

Kathryn narrowed her eyes. "Now, you're probably wondering if you can get the knife away from me. But, I remind you, the time to test my prowess with a blade is *not* when it, and I, are a hairsbreadth away from removing all hope of your ever having an heir."

"*You little bi—*"

"Nor is this a time to be forgetting your manners," Kathryn reminded him with a quick prod of the blade. "Now..." At this she stood and, still brandishing the small blade, backed away from him. "I think I have been more than tolerant in allowing you to say your piece, let alone to paw at me as you have done. So, in deference to the becoming patience I have displayed..." She moved out of reach of his long arms, scooting around the edge of the table. If he made a grab for her now, the action would attract considerable attention. She tucked the knife up her sleeve. "You will stay away from me and, more importantly, you will stay away from the wolf." Her heart racing with fear, she whirled around and rushed from the dining room.

⊰◦⊱

Reynard watched the swish of her skirts as she left and smiled to himself. Well, she had not been as biddable as he would have liked. A fine filly, and it would have been very satisfying to mount her. Still, all in all he had done a good bit of work for the evening. He examined the food platter and, having selected a prime cut of meat, sank his teeth into the flesh with enjoyment.

⊰◦⊱

Kathryn sat by the window in her room. None of the other girls were back from the feasting yet. She sighed and watched the grooms at their work in the stables without really seeing them.

She supposed she had finally figured out what about the wolf's repeated attempts to harm Reynard so upset her. The wolf had allies. The king himself knew his true identity at last and, with so many people acting on Garwaf's behalf, plans would be set in motion before long to restore the wolf to his true form. They only needed Garwaf to cooperate with them, which he had not yet been willing to do.

Maybe he was only waiting until he had dispatched Reynard. Maybe that was why the wolf wouldn't let Llewellyn examine him, because the missing duke needed Reynard gone and the path to his beautiful wife clear.

Reynard *had* probably cursed the duke to stay a wolf in order to steal his wife. The wolf would soon be human again, and all that stood between him and the old life he had lost was Reynard. If Reynard died, then the duke would be free to return to his wife without messy entanglements and scandal.

Garwaf had attacked Reynard to save his wife and to set the stage for himself to win her back when he was human again. With thoughts like these swirling through her head, Kathryn marveled she did not start sobbing into her lap. She didn't know what she had hoped for. She didn't even know what she had thought would happen when the wolf was human again. She *was* certain she had all too conveniently forgotten the duke's wife.

That was the most troubling thing of all. What *had* Kathryn hoped for? She had not thought that when the Duke of Dorré was himself again, restored to his proper station and honors, he would marry *her*.

Or had she?

No. And yet... *No, not the Duke of Dorré.* Kathryn laughed ruefully. *The honorable Duke of Dorré is not whom I have cared for, nursed, and...liked very much.*

She never had been able to connect the image of the king's noble nephew with the wolf and his soulful eyes. Garwaf was not the Duke of Dorré to her. She did not know that man. Kathryn knew only Garwaf. And Garwaf with his flashing eyes, impish moods, and quiet dignity was the one Kathryn wanted. *Not* the great duke.

Strange as the idea sounded even to her, Kathryn *had* always thought of the wolf as a person. She saw in him the trapped mind of a man, capable of deep thought and complex emotion. She had just never been able to take the extra step and connect the rational creature trapped as a wolf with the name of the Duke of Dorré, which rightfully belonged to him.

Garwaf was her friend and companion. Her dear heart.

Gabriel the grand Duke of Dorré was a stranger.

But if they did manage to break whatever spell held him as a wolf, then Gabriel, and *not* her Garwaf, would be here. And the beautiful Lady Alisoun was whom he would go to. Not drab little Kathryn.

Kathryn might as well leave with her father. Garwaf needed her only while he remained a wolf, and the way events were falling out, he would not be a wolf for long. To be here when he was not a wolf would be much, much too painful.

Kathryn did not relish the thought of witnessing the happy reunion with his charming and lovely wife.

Well, if he wanted his wife, then she wished him all the best, but she should get on with her own life, her own troubles. She wished him all the best, but she just didn't have a part in this drama anymore. As events had turned out, she never really had had a part anyway. But really, she did...she, well, she wished him all the best.

One stray tear breached her defenses and fought its watery way down her cheek. Just so the others didn't get any ideas, she viciously dashed the droplet away with the back of her hand. "Silly girl."

As soon as her eyes had dried sufficiently, Kathryn rose from the window's bench and went to find her father. The sooner she left the castle, the better.

Chapter Twelve

G arwaf waited patiently in Llewellyn's workshop while the magician left to get the final ingredient for the arcane ritual he planned. Whatever the magician did, whatever information he wanted, Garwaf would surrender.

Enough is enough. Time to return to being a man. Most of the time. I'll always be a werewolf, but that's only three days out of every month. Kathryn won't mind three days. Kathryn will— Oh, hurry up, *Llewellyn.*

When all Llewellyn returned with was a large black glass bowl full of water, Garwaf cocked his head in surprise. The magician set the bowl on a small tripod made of laurel boughs and poured just a single drop of black ink into the water. He waited a moment for the water to still, then stepped back, beckoning to Garwaf. "Look into the bowl for me, if you will."

Tense, Garwaf crept up to the bowl and peered into the water's black depths. Shapes swirled until a face formed on the surface. Garwaf yipped in shock and fell backward off the bench. His ears flattened to his skull, and he gazed in wonder at the magician.

Llewellyn muttered a few words and passed his hand over the bowl. He filled his lungs and closed his eyes as he let the air out in a slow sigh. When he opened his eyes again, he stared at the face in the bowl.

The face belonged to a young man in his late twenties with smooth terra cotta brown skin. His thick hair had the dark, luxurious finish of a raven's wing. A long beard shadowed his well-chiseled cheekbones and strong, square jaw. His features were generally reminiscent of the king's leonine countenance, except broader and stronger. His aquiline nose had a crooked bridge from at least one bad break. A puckered white scar cut through his eyebrow and scooted just to the side of his right eye before going all the way down to the top of his cheekbone.

The man's eyes were truly beautiful: deep set and almond shaped, with dark lashes and irises of cobalt blue. The top of the young man's broad, well-muscled shoulders showed, and Llewellyn could just make out signs of small, half-healed bite marks there. The man also wore a gold rose pendant around his neck on a delicate chain.

Llewellyn had not seen this face in a very long time but, nevertheless, he recognized the man on the instant. He touched the wolf's shoulder. "I'm sorry to have startled you, my lord." He bowed his head and grinned at the wolf. "But that's one mystery solved for certain, at least. You *are* Lord Gabriel."

The wolf huffed and rolled his eyes.

Llewellyn chuckled. "Well, yes, but I had to be sure." He slapped his thigh in satisfaction and stood. "Now on to the next mystery."

Llewellyn shuffled back to the tripod and picked the bowl up. With great care, he set the container in front of the wolf's paws. The magician hurried to his worktable and selected a small, wickedly sharp knife. He bowed his head again in respect before the wolf. "My lord, this next form of scrying requires a bit more. I could use spittle, but that doesn't work as well. I am as likely to see what you had for dinner in the bowl as I am anything of significance. Have I your leave?" He brandished the knife.

Garwaf lifted his paw readily enough, and his muscles tensed as he braced himself. Llewellyn held the wolf's limb over his scrying bowl. "Think of all you wish for me to know." With precision, Llewellyn made a small slash on the wolf's forearm and let three drops of blood plop lazily into the bowl of water.

Llewellyn released the paw and swirled the contents of the bowl with his knife's blade. He quickly set the bowl back on the wooden tripod and let the surface of the water still. After a moment, he leaned forward to watch the play of events flit in crystal-clear images across the surface of the water.

He saw the duke at once, and the Lady Alisoun swam into focus a moment later. The lady appeared very upset, hanging on to her lord's arm, her face pinched and white.

The bowl could do many things. Producing sound was, unfortunately, not one of them. Llewellyn, being intuitive and quick witted, had a gift for interpreting the images he saw when he scryed.

At first, the duke seemed reluctant, apprehensive even. He kept shaking his head and turning away from her. She grabbed his arm and pulled him back, tears streaming from her eyes. At last he gave in and pulled her into his arms. In a whispered conference, he conveyed to her whatever secret she had been trying to pull from him.

Llewellyn watched the Lady Alisoun closely and saw the look of horror and revulsion cross her countenance. He also saw, barely a moment later, the look of cunning as it fell like an executioner's axe across her face. She schooled her beautiful features into a look of love and concern as her lord looked at her once more.

Garwaf had by this time climbed up to watch the play of events in the bowl. How well he remembered this conversation.

Alisoun addressed a question to him. Her tone had been so mild, full of such simple curiosity. "My lord, do—do you undress for your transformation into a wolf, or..."

He had laughed. *Laughed*. The idiot. "Wife, I go stark naked." He had wiggled his eyebrows and leaned in for a kiss.

She turned away. "My love, where are your clothes, then, while you're changed?"

He shook his head, retaining that much common sense, at least. "I cannot tell you, nor anyone. If I am ever discovered, if my clothes are taken, I will be trapped as a wolf until they are returned to me." He'd tucked a strand of her flaxen hair behind her ear. "That's why I don't want to reveal their hiding place. Can you understand?"

Tears trembled on the edges of her eyelashes, and her lips turned down into an adorable pout. "I have given you all of myself. I love you more than all the world. I am your *wife*. You must not keep secrets from me. Do you fear your wife?"

Yes. Dammit. And rightly so.

"Quiet, please, so I may think," Llewellyn murmured.

Garwaf realized he had growled as the water mirror turned to that bit of the scene. Duly chastened, he looked back at the shining surface that was water and yet more besides.

Ah yes, another bout of pleading and begging and raging and storming. Alisoun had certainly known how to throw her tantrums. *Quite impressive ones, really.*

"You don't *trust* me." She threw a jar of perfume, and he jumped back as it shattered against the wall. "You hide your deepest self from me, and then when you finally *do* tell me, I find there are still more lies to unravel, more secrets you keep. You claim to love me, but this doesn't seem like love." Her lower lip trembled, and a small catch formed in her voice. "What dire sin have I committed to make you doubt me?"

His guilt got the better of his common sense. In those days he had believed himself to love her. Before he'd learned the truth of things, of course. *Before Kathryn.*

"Dear heart." He perched on the edge of the bed while Alisoun sat next to him and watched him with eager, hungry eyes, drinking in his every word. "Near the woods where I abide as a wolf, there is an old shrine that has often done me good service. Beneath one of the bushes of this same holy place is a hollow rock. I hide my clothes there until I am ready to return home." He told the truth to his wife and opened his soul to her, exposing the deepest shadow that hung over his heart. Fool that he was, he had told her everything.

Garwaf could take the memories no longer and looked away again.

But Llewellyn kept watching. That was the point of this whole exercise, after all.

The interview apparently over, Gabriel reached for Alisoun, but she waved him off and, having soothed him with a tender kiss, crossed to a small table filled with correspondence. She sat at once and scribbled a hasty note on a small sheaf of parchment. Gabriel, meanwhile, sighed heavily and went to fetch a servant to clean up the mess she had created in her pique.

On his way out, he glanced down at the letter to which she was just applying a wax wafer and the seal of her husband's house. As the scene dimmed, Llewellyn squinted fiercely and just managed to make out the name written on the letter: Lord Reynard, Earl of Troumper.

"Ah," was all Llewellyn said as the water flowed in the bowl into a different scene. Gabriel stood in the forefront of the scene, in the middle of his castle's inner bailey, checking the cinches on his great black palfrey's saddle.

Llewellyn looked at the wolf. "What was that horse's name again? Old temple name, wasn't it?"

Garwaf returned him rather a dry, droll look. The magician quirked an eyebrow and grinned. "Goliath." He shook his head and turned to the bowl. "Good horse."

Gabriel checked the gear strapped to the grand brute Goliath. The duke paused before mounting and cast about for something, his dark eyes probing every corner of his keep. He glanced upward, and the Lady Alisoun rushed headlong down the castle steps to her lord. She threw herself into his arms and kissed him with abandon. While poor Gabriel had his eyes firmly closed—all the better to enjoy the sweet attentions of his beloved wife—Lady Alisoun had her brown eyes open—all the better to watch the werewolf whose kisses she suffered through one last time to allay suspicion. She pulled away, and Gabriel mounted and rode off. He turned at the castle gate to wave, but Alisoun had already hurried inside.

Gabriel seemed disheartened, his broad shoulders slumping and his brows drawing together. He looked worried. He shook his head, and a strained smile crossed his face as he rode off into the gathering gloom of the night.

Llewellyn sighed. "Idiot."

Garwaf growled and rolled his gaze toward the ceiling, sighing, as if to say, *I know.*

A cozy little hermitage and shrine off the main road appeared in the bowl. Gabriel tied his horse there and went in to leave an oblation at the temple. He prayed on his knees before the tiny altar to the ancestors and, when he rose, walked straight out of the building and down the road.

He stepped behind a bush to strip off all of his fine clothes and every piece of jewelry he wore, right down to the golden signet ring of his house. He made a small bundle and wrapped it around with sacking, then turned over a hollow rock and snugly tucked the package inside the stone before tipping it back down. This accomplished, he looked skyward. Night had fallen, and clouds screened the sky. The moon rose.

Llewellyn had never seen a werewolf transformation. He had been trying to do some research on the subject, but whenever people tried to observe a werewolf secretly, they inevitably ended up observing from the werewolf's innards. Scholarship on the subject remained somewhat limited.

Llewellyn wouldn't say he was disappointed on witnessing the event—just surprised at the subtlety of the transformation. Moonbeams fell across the land. Gabriel watched them with apparent equanimity and waited silently behind his bush. As the moonbeams fell across his body, the parts they touched just...turned wolfish. Where the light strayed across his leg, dark fur was suddenly revealed to the light, or was made by the light or...something. Llewellyn couldn't tell which.

Gradually, the moonbeams had lovingly caressed every inch of Gabriel's body with the sensuous silver light. Where the fine and noble figure of Gabriel had been, there now stood the same black wolf that even now sat placidly at Llewellyn's feet.

The wolf, his transformation completed, threw his head back with delight and howled his freedom. He bounded happily into the night to create whatever mischief wolves do when left to their own devices. The bowl didn't show Llewellyn these nightly revels. He was sure they would be fascinating, but they were hardly the meat of the matter.

"Customarily three nights, yes?" Llewellyn turned to the wolf, who nodded solemnly. "But sometimes you didn't turn back during the day. Such a bother, after all."

The wolf looked a trifle abashed, and he shifted his paws in seeming unease.

Llewellyn clucked and smiled. "Ah, my boy, I understand. Being a wolf has certain enjoyments when it's only three days out of every month. But two years of nothing but being an animal? The experience wears thin, I'm sure. You didn't this last time, correct? Turn back human and change into your clothes, I mean. That's why you didn't notice they had gone missing until the time to change back for good?"

Garwaf nodded. Excitement bubbled in Llewellyn, making his hands twitchy for something to *do*. Garwaf blinked, and the pictures in the water spun again.

The wolf returned in the predawn light of what Llewellyn guessed was the final day of his transformation. The wolf sniffed at the rock, turning it over with a paw. Empty. Just a hollow rock.

The wolf sniffed the area. Again and again. Round and round in circles. Down the road, up, back into the woods. All over. Dawn came and went, and still the wolf continued his fruitless search.

Llewellyn cast him a look of sympathy. "Even then?"

Yes, even then. The wolf sighed. *I didn't believe it.*

In the next scene, he would go home to look, ashamed to let Alisoun see what he had become, yet he needed her help if he was ever to be a man again. He went home, and he had found Reynard there before him.

Next came the scene in the garden where Alisoun had said—where she and Reynard had first—

Well, Garwaf had seen the moment enough in his mind's eye. He didn't need to watch Alisoun's betrayal again outside his own head. He went away from the table and waited for the last scene of his silent testimony to play out.

When the magic had finished, Llewellyn leaned back, rubbing his eyes wearily. "Very illuminating." He patted the wolf's shoulder as he had when Gabriel had been a lad. Llewellyn gave him a lopsided grin and set about making a small bed for him on the floor, since the castle was far too cramped with visiting nobles to accommodate either of them that night. "And now, some much-needed rest."

Garwaf was suddenly reminded of hunting with his uncle and the magician in his youth, before his marriage. Grinning inwardly, Garwaf stretched out next to his friend.

Llewellyn crossed his arms under his head and stared at his ceiling. "Now that I have seen what you had to tell me, I have an idea what is best to be done. You and I need to speak to the king tomorrow. See if he fancies a bit of...hunting." Llewellyn's breath slowed with sleep.

Garwaf yawned and placed his chin on his paws to sleep as best he might with all the worries and woes pressing on him. He studied the sleeping wise man, hope stirring in his wolfish heart that, despite his fears, something could be done to save him.

There had to be a way to unravel the tangle that he and the lady he loved now found themselves caught up in.

Chapter Thirteen

T he next morning brought the convocation of the king's lords and the
ceremony in which the king's liegemen would renew their oaths of fealty.

By general accord between the king and the wolf, with a solemn promise on
Garwaf's part, they agreed he would attend the meeting, closely chaperoned by
Llewellyn at all times.

The king had observed firsthand some of his liegemen in their carousing of the
night before. In consideration of their aching heads, the meeting was never called
before noon. The event took place in the great hall. Only men were allowed inside.

The king spent the morning settling land disputes, hearing the grievances of
one lord against another, and taking tallies of what taxes and how many fighting
men could be called up should the need arise.

The slog through the morning's work finished rather more quickly than usual
with Garwaf sitting by the king's side. The hearings and adjudications being over,
the time had come for the oath to King Thomas. As one, every man in the hall
knelt to speak the oath, which renewed his fealty to the king for another year of
honorable and righteous service.

Garwaf swallowed as he looked about him at all the bowed heads. He looked
to the king. His king. His lord. The man who, for as long as he could remember,

had acted as a father to him. Garwaf's heart stirred, swelled sweetly inside him, a fierce desire kindling to swear again all the oaths of knighthood.

He bowed over his forepaws. His chin touched the cobbles of the court, and he closed his eyes.

The men of the king's retinue all knew the customary words of the oath well, and as one man, they spoke. For Garwaf, the promises of fealty and righteousness etched themselves into his heart, the words acting as an incantation, drawing their shining light from his worthless hide to lift him higher than his stifling, corporeal form. In his heart, the words of the oath sang out in all sincerity and love for his king.

"I will to my lord, the high king, be ever true and loyal. I swear by my oath I shall love all which my king loves. I shall shun all which he shuns, according to the will of Fate, the order of this world, and the laws of our land. I swear by no word or deed of mine shall I ever do anything to displease or anger my lord. I will be without fear, upright, and good as he dictates, and always I shall defend his realm and his person with my very life. This I swear on my honor as a knight and servant of this land."

To which King Thomas replied, per tradition, "In return for this service you render unto me, I swear to hold stalwart to you all as you deserve. I will perform every act I have promised and so I am bound to you as you are bound to my will and my service." King Thomas raised a hand in acknowledgment of his vassals, then slowly lowered it, officially ending the convocation until next year.

Garwaf trembled from the fervor with which he had expressed his vows. He had not yet moved nor risen from his bowed position on the floor.

Two years. Two years and now I'm back again. He wasn't sure how he kept breathing after such joy. Almost nothing would be able to tarnish this moment. *Almost* nothing.

Lord Stephen muscled his way through the crowd to the king's high seat. The baron fell respectfully and with some difficulty to one knee and bowed his gray head. The king motioned, and the Baron of Réméré stood once more with a little huffing and puffing.

Kathryn's father. Garwaf rose and padded softly to the king's chair. He settled his limbs on the floor, gave a jaw-popping yawn, and pillowed his long snout on his paws. He attempted then, very overtly, to give every evidence that, despite his display of moving fealty a bare moment before, he really *was* little more than a dumb lapdog.

Lord Stephen eyed Garwaf with misgiving, but the king waved encouragement that the baron should speak. The Baron of Réméré, looking rather put upon, drew himself up and began an obviously prepared speech. "My lord." He bowed again, sighing all the while. "My daughter, Lady Kathryn, came to me last night. She's unhappy—"

"Lady Kathryn? Unhappy?"

Garwaf fought but could not keep himself from pricking his ears up.

King Thomas tipped his head to the side. "I've seen no indication of her discontent. At least not lately. For the past month, at least, I would stake my life she was happy as can be."

Visibly flustered, the baron floundered on, "Well, you see, I think, um, something happened yesterday to alarm her." He leaned in to the king and said in a confiding whisper, "I believe she and the queen had a bit of a spat over a gown she borrowed that, um, well, the wolf, he ruined the dress and—"

King Thomas waved that away. "Easily mended. I'm sure your daughter apologized, and I'll certainly be happy to buy my wife a new gown to replace the ruined one. Is that all that makes Lady Kathryn dissatisfied with her situation here?"

The baron ran a hand through his hair and wiped some sweat away. "She had other reasons, I believe, ones she did not want me to convey to you, sire." He darted a meaningful look at Garwaf, who peered at the man through his lashes.

Garwaf's insides writhed with guilt. *This is about yesterday.*

Lord Stephen flicked a look at him, then hurriedly glanced away, his hands clenching and unclenching with unease. "Long has Lady Kathryn contemplated a spiritual life, sire, and she begs me to take her with me today so I can escort her to the convent at Bourlonge."

Garwaf's eyes sprang open, and he stared at the baron, his heart suddenly racing. *Kathryn's leaving?*

Still glancing anxiously in Garwaf's direction, Lord Stephen smoothed his hands down the front of his tunic, leaving damp stains from his sweating palms behind. "She will have, by now, conveyed her deepest regrets to your estimable lady, and so it is only left to me to express to you her sentiments. She will always remember her time at your court with fondness, and she regrets that she could not linger here longer." The baron let his breath out in an obviously relieved sigh.

Garwaf leapt to his feet, staring at the man in unconcealed horror.

"Now I must convey my sincere compliments to your lordship and take my leave so we can make an early start. The road to Bourlonge is a long one."

Garwaf staggered down the steps. *She is leaving now? But I haven't seen her since the feast. She hasn't even said good-bye to me. I behaved badly yesterday, but surely my actions don't warrant this.* What could have changed her feelings so quickly? As he glanced around in dazed horror, he found himself staring into the smug face of Reynard where the man stood behind the flustered baron.

Without thinking, without pausing to draw breath, Garwaf pounced and landed on Reynard's chest, bringing the large knight crashing hard to the cobbles of the court.

The effect on the assemblage of lords was instantaneous. Some knights leapt to Reynard's defense. Others drew their weapons to protect the wolf. Lord Stephen only scrambled to get out of the way. Llewellyn shoved through bodies and fought his way to the standoff in the center of the hall. Garwaf perched on a defenseless Reynard, snarling into the terrified knight's face, sharp fangs bared in menace. *You did this. You drove her from me.*

———◆———

Llewellyn elbowed his way through the throng of onlookers. Salvation of the situation lay in the fact the wolf had only knocked Reynard down. He had not yet seriously injured the knight.

The king moved to intervene, but the crowd was too thick, jostling, and dense. There was no time to waste. Time for Llewellyn to try his hand at taming the wolf. He just hoped he didn't lose an appendage in the process. Llewellyn did so very much like his hands.

Reynard had gone white as a sheet and had not so much as batted an eyelid while he lay pinned beneath the wolf. He had hurt the back of his head, and it now oozed blood. His eyes were slightly glazed. Still the knight was enough in possession of his senses not to give the homicidal wolf sitting on top of him any reason to strike. That wouldn't last forever.

Llewellyn crept up to the wolf on his hands and knees. "Gabriel," he whispered, "whatever this man has done, however he has driven a wedge between you and Kathryn, this won't help. You are *not* a wolf. Use your mind. Come back to yourself. *Gabriel.*" He leaned down to force the wolf to look into his eyes and to move between the wolf and Reynard. Garwaf would have to hurt Llewellyn to get at Reynard. "*Remember*, my lord. Do not forget the oath you have but lately spoken. You are more than what you have become. Prove it now and let this pig offal go."

The wolf looked down. Humanity flickered in his eyes, and Gabriel stared back at Llewellyn from the wolf's face.

But suddenly Garwaf's face contorted in a fierce snarl, and the wolf lunged. Reynard flinched and cried out.

The wolf let the man shriek himself hoarse for exactly one heartbeat, then pulled back from his feint. Garwaf then wagged his tail, climbed off the prone knight, and sat back in obvious satisfaction. The hall erupted into relieved laughter at once. At Reynard's expense. Llewellyn pressed a palm over his mouth but could not contain his relieved laughter.

Reynard bolted upright, rubbing the bump on his head and nursing his wounded pride.

Llewellyn sat on the floor, hands draped on his knees, laughing too hard to get up. He fought valiantly around his mirth, then finally managed to stumble to his feet between chuckles. "Would you like me to look at your head, my lord?"

Reynard glared at Llewellyn, drew his fancy cloak tight about himself, sneered at the wolf, then stomped from the hall.

———◆———

Garwaf yipped happily, scanning the crowd for the king. After a moment, he realized Reynard's was not the only scent absent from the hall. Lord Stephen's smell of fresh-turned earth and beef stew had gone as well.

Kathryn. Garwaf charged from the hall, pounding through the doors and onto the cobbles of the court just in time to see Reynard galloping into the distance only a few horse lengths behind Kathryn and her father.

Llewellyn, not one to shirk his duty, had followed Garwaf from the hall. The magician and the king stood side by side, panting for breath as one man. "My lord, Reynard may harm the Lady Kathryn if left to his own devices on the road with her." He clutched his chest and rasped for more breath. "Her father is not as young as he was."

The king nodded. "Nor as heavily armed as Reynard."

Kathryn and that hideous beast? No. She may not want me with her anymore, and small blame to her after how I have behaved these past few days. But I care too much to risk her all alone on the road with that slimy filth. Without pausing, the wolf bounded out of the court to follow the dust trail of the horses that had but lately left the king's castle.

Chapter Fourteen

Kathryn made sure she was ready to depart and had taken her leave of the queen quite early. Lately, the queen had been ill, and all the other ladies were too squeamish to wait on her. A small amount of guilt tickled at Kathryn to be leaving Aliénor now, but she hoped the queen's sickness would pass before too long.

Kathryn's father had brought only one horse and, when she explained to the queen that she and her father would probably take turns in walking and riding to the convent, Aliénor offered up her own mare. Kathryn protested, but the queen only clucked her tongue. "Not for you to keep, you tiresome creature. Just to borrow. Besides, if you have my pretty girl with you, I shall have a good excuse to visit you sooner than later." Aliénor smiled but with sadness in her eyes. She hugged Kathryn and kissed her cheek.

The queen escorted Kathryn to the courtyard and ordered her own dainty horse, Gaenor, saddled and loaded with Kathryn's meager luggage. "Shall I wait for your father with you?"

"And deprive the court of their beautiful queen?" She laughed and shook her head. "Go back to the garden and your ladies, my lady. I'll be fine."

Aliénor left with obvious reluctance.

Kathryn would miss the queen and the court and the ladies and the knights and the king and Llewellyn...and the wolf. She would miss it all, but still she knew this was the best possible decision. She would only be in the way when the duke returned. If she was near, there would be awkward and painful scenes to play out. By leaving, she acted in the best interests of everyone.

I'm being a coward.

"Oh, quiet, you," she snapped at herself.

Fortunately for Kathryn's inner solidarity, her father came rushing out just as the sun rounded the horizon toward late afternoon. Winded and flushed, her father's face blazed as red as a tomato. Lord Stephen wiped sweat from his broad brow, then grasped her by the arm to drag her to their horses. "Come on, fool girl. Best to go while the going is good."

Baffled rather than bolstered forward, Kathryn dug her heels in and would have asked questions but for the look of sheer terror her father turned on her. Silence seeming the best course, she mounted the queen's mare and set off at a brisk gallop beside her father through the castle gates.

They rode for some time. Not until the sun began a headlong rush toward its bed for the night did Kathryn notice the sound of a third pair of hoofbeats behind them. When she turned and recognized Reynard, a manic glint in his eye, she was immediately too scared to notice anything else.

Eventually, she perceived the small dot behind Reynard farther down the road. Too small to be another horse, yet her other pursuer ran on all fours. Her throat closed with fear. She prayed this second following shadow was not who she was almost certain that it was.

———— ◦◦◦ ————

Unsure precisely what he planned for the wench, Reynard wanted only to hurt the bastard who had humiliated him so completely in front of all the court. Kathryn was the best and most readily available means of doing this. Her father was a trifling matter not to waste one's time on. What defense could an overweight graybeard mount against Reynard, who was cunning and in the prime of his vigor?

Reynard kicked the flanks of his horse hard to get an extra burst of speed. They neared the forest, and dusk would be the perfect time. Once into that line of trees with the concealing cloak of night to abet him, who was to know what had happened to the poor girl? Or who had done such thoroughly appalling violence to her?

Oh yes, Reynard intended to be *very* thorough.

Kathryn. Oh Kind Fate, please, please, do not let me be too late. Don't let him so much as touch a hair on her head. Please. Oh please...

Garwaf's lungs were on fire, and his legs ached as if four monsters stabbed every nerve ending in his limbs. He had never run so fast or so hard in his life. Not even the day the hunting dogs were after him, the day he'd met Kathryn. Then he'd been running for *his* life. Now he ran for *hers*, praying the whole way that he would be fast enough to reach her in time.

Lord Stephen still galloped his horse hard for the forest as if a demon bit at his ankles. Kathryn was more reticent to enter that enclosing darkness with Reynard so close at their heels and night riding along at his shoulder.

Any number of accidents could logically befall one in there, and any number of excuses would be ready to Reynard's hand should they befall Kathryn in a hive of such reputed villainy. She reined in her horse. "Please, Father, the day is too far advanced. Let's return to the castle and get a fresh start in the morning."

Her father halted just shy of the tree line. He wheeled his horse around violently. "No, girl, best to be away before that damned creature gets any ideas and comes after us."

He's running from the wolf? *Oh dear.* Had something else happened at the assembly to make her father fear the beast so?

"Father—" she started, then broke off with a small gasp.

Her father turned his horse too sharply. The beast bucked and threw Stephen before running into the forest.

"*Father.*" She jumped down and ran to where her father lay dazed in the dust. Just as she began really to worry, Stephen came to himself.

"Filthy nag." His voice sounded thick, his words slurring.

"*Now* will you go back to the castle?"

The sound of hooves made her whirl around as Reynard at last caught up with them. With a creak of leather, Reynard dismounted. "Can I be of assistance?" He tried but could not conceal from Kathryn the smirk playing about his cruel lips.

Her father rose at once and swayed, holding his head, which bled a little on the side from a blow with a rock. The baron collected himself and made an obeisance to the higher-ranking noble. "If your lordship would lend his assistance, I should be most gratified." He tried to bow without falling over but just managed to stand with Kathryn's steadying hand on his arm.

"You're destined for Abbess Marie's convent at Bourlonge?" Reynard asked, a speculative gleam in his eye.

"Aye." The baron blinked bleary, unfocused eyes. Kathryn almost toppled from supporting his weight.

"Well, then our way lies together." Reynard smiled. "For I am on my way to collect my dear sister from that same convent. Your horse has run off, sir?"

"Yes," her father slurred, becoming more muddled by the moment. He sagged again, nearly knocking Kathryn down too. "In there." He pointed to the forest and blinked as if trying to get his eyes to focus.

"We shall go in together and search, then. Before the sky gets much darker." Reynard clasped Kathryn by the arm, his grip like steel bands around her flesh, and jerked her away from her father.

Lord Stephen fell over in a faint at once without Kathryn's supporting shoulder.

Reynard yanked Kathryn toward the forest. "You, my little peach, will now be taught to mind *your* manners."

She struggled, and he pulled her to him impatiently, bending her arm behind her back. She let out a cry of pain and tried to kick him, but her skirts blunted her blows.

Reynard's smile was predatory as he looked at her, a thin sneer pulling back over his bright teeth. "You will come to wish you had not refused my kindly attentions before. I shall have to make sure your wolf gets a good look at my handiwork when I've finished. That way he will never forget what I did to you."

Summoning her courage, Kathryn spat in Reynard's face. "Garwaf may be a wolf, but you are the animal." Her other hand still free, she swung her fist back and clipped Reynard full force across the jaw.

He cursed and rubbed his mouth. His face contorting, he hauled his arm up and backhanded her. This was no laughing matter, as he wore a heavy leather gauntlet and had a fist like an anvil.

Her head snapped back, and she sagged in his grip, though she remained conscious. Barely. She stumbled but still tried to break free, tugging and shifting her weight away from him.

He easily pulled her forward. Hauling her close, he slapped her again with casual brutality, then once more for good measure.

The pain of the first blow fused into the second as her face erupted with stinging heat, her cheek throbbing. Her cheek stung, and her lip had split open against her teeth so that she tasted thick, coppery blood.

Her head grew fuzzy. She should have been struggling, but her arms did not obey the signals of her addled brain. She was limp limbed and half unconscious as Reynard drew her to him, grunting in pleasure. He pushed her roughly to the ground. While he pinned her legs with one of his, she wriggled beneath him. Reynard slapped her again, and her head lolled back, her cheek scratching against the road. The dirt of the ground felt coarse and cool beneath her cheek, and her nostrils filled with the scent of Reynard's sweating body as he loomed.

Grinning in savage satisfaction, Reynard bent toward her. She closed her eyes, trembling, but her eyes popped open the next moment at the sound of paws skittering in the dirt.

———◇———

The wolf leapt forward and sank his teeth in. He dragged Reynard to the ground and proceeded to maul the fiend, striking, yanking, thrashing to get him off Kathryn.

She managed to wobble to her feet for precisely one moment. Her eyes closed, and she tumbled bonelessly to the ground and lay there as still as death.

No. Garwaf whined. *Please, no.* He was about to go to her, but Reynard tackled him from the side and punched him about the head and ribs.

Growling himself, Reynard hefted a large branch and swung hard at Garwaf. The branch hit with rib-cracking accuracy but disintegrated in a shower of rotten wood chips. Reynard shook the dust off his hands and grimaced. "Oh shit."

Garwaf landed on him, all flashing teeth and sharp claws savaging Reynard in the failing light. Reynard shoved him off and scrambled away. Garwaf moved to stand between him and Kathryn, hackles raised, teeth bared.

"Nice doggy," Reynard crooned.

Garwaf snarled and moved forward a step.

Reynard backed off, stumbling to his horse.

Garwaf darted a glance to Kathryn. She was still not moving. *No* was the only coherent thought spinning through Garwaf's mind. He crouched in the dirt beside his lady and keened softly, butting her bruised cheek with his snout. She still did not move.

Shaking with grief, he collapsed into the dirt beside her body, his cold nose pressing against her wrist, his lupine head on her arm. He closed his eyes. *Let Reynard come. Let me die, then, if she will not move.*

Kathryn stirred. "Your nose is cold." Her voice was thick, but she spoke. She *lived.*

Garwaf leapt to his feet and nudged her with a paw. *Up, my beauty. Up. We're not back to the castle yet. Up.*

Kathryn shakily propped herself on her elbows and gazed at him in the near dark, her eyes vague, dazed. She rubbed her head with her other hand and winced as she brushed her bruise. "*Reynard,*" she said and turned.

Garwaf had much keener eyesight than she did, especially so near nightfall. He clearly saw the crossbow Reynard leveled at him. He growled defiance at the knight, preparing to spring. Garwaf might get an arrow bolt through his gut, but Reynard would end up with a broken neck. Garwaf's probable death would be worth it to hear *that* satisfying crack.

———◇———

Kathryn moved before the wolf could. Half conscious and head aching, she still knew him better than he could lay claim to knowing himself. And damned if she'd saved him from the king's hunt just for him to get shot by Reynard the Lecher, a stone's throw away from sanctuary.

What she did was not graceful or particularly well executed. The maneuver was not so much heroic as it was an awkward, frantic, sideways topple.

But it did the trick.

And it saved the wolf.

And it got Kathryn an arrow through the shoulder for her trouble.

———◇———

The low sound of rage that rumbled out of the wolf was enough to make Reynard piss himself in fear. The beast tensed, leapt, then some unseen force propelled the wolf backward so he landed in the dust twenty feet from Reynard. King Thomas deliberately put himself between the wolf and Reynard so the wolf could not pounce again.

Reynard's eyes grew wide, and rolled his gaze toward the king's pet magician. Llewellyn muttered a few words and sketched a hasty symbol in the air, which left a faint sign of luminescence where his hand had passed. Then Llewellyn ran to Kathryn.

Reynard threw his prized crossbow to the ground. His face grew warm, and his eyes were open wide in horror. "I didn't—she just fell right into it," he choked out and swallowed. Then he leveled an accusing finger at the wolf. "*The beast did this*. Damned wolf was going to attack me again, and I only defended myself. I didn't mean to..." He trailed off quietly. Reynard had injured women before, certainly, and he killed men as a matter of course. He had never actually *killed* a woman, though. He found he hated the feeling, actually. Much as he had disliked the wench Kathryn, he had not wanted her *dead*.

"Llewellyn," the king yelled and jerked his chin toward the wolf, who growled and paced on the edge of his invisible barrier.

"The spell will hold," the magician said, without looking up from Kathryn's injuries.

Sure enough, the wolf lunged forward only to be repelled again by some force. He skidded through the dust a few feet from whatever imperceptible barrier Llewellyn had erected.

"Then go, Reynard," the king said, lip curling. "Go home and let me not hear a word from you. About any of this."

Almost smiling in relief, Reynard ran to his mount and flung himself into the saddle. Riding fast, he beat his horse to within an inch of its life to get him home as swiftly as possible. He needed to return to his wife and make a complete report to her. She possessed all the intellectual cunning in their relationship and would know how to mend things with the king.

"I had to let him go," King Thomas said quietly to no one in particular. "It would be his word against a wolf's, and unfortunately some people would believe Reynard."

Once Reynard was gone from sight, the king knelt next to Llewellyn. The magician looked up for a bare moment from the hasty field dressing he had applied to Kathryn's shoulder. Lines of care and fatigue had etched deeper into his face than the king had ever seen them. Llewellyn waved his hand once, muttering a soft syllable King Thomas didn't catch.

The wolf, magical barrier removed, ran to Kathryn.

"Well?" King Thomas gulped. The wolf, his quarry obviously forgotten in the face of Kathryn's distress, nestled under the king's arm, seeking comfort like a child.

"She lives." Llewellyn's voice broke. "We need to get her to Bourlonge. The convent is nearer than the castle, and we may be able to save ourselves scandal if Marie will help us."

"The abbess will do all she can," King Thomas said, still petting the head of the stricken wolf.

Llewellyn pushed himself up with a hand on one knee, staggering only slightly before he gained his footing.

"What can I do?" the king rasped out, gazing in horror at Kathryn. She looked like a broken doll lying in the dirt of the road.

"My lord, press firmly on either side of the arrow." Llewellyn ran to fetch their horses. "We must keep the edges of this wound together until I can get the damned arrow out."

A groan from Kathryn's father made them all jump.

The baron sat up and held his aching head. He shrieked when he saw the wolf. Then he saw his daughter, and the look on his face made them all want to weep. "Wh—what happened?"

"Bandits," King Thomas prevaricated smoothly. The wolf shot him a sharp, betrayed look, but the king shook his head and, smoothing the wolf's fur, said, "My boy, be patient. Do you think Reynard will not pay? He will. Just you wait." The king nodded grimly. "And oh, but how he will pay."

Apparently satisfied, the wolf looked to Kathryn, then to Llewellyn.

"We must get her back to the convent—it's closer," Llewellyn repeated. "I have to"—he sucked in a frayed breath— "get the arrow out, and the procedure would be too dangerous to do here. I have no bandages, no gauze, no herbs, nothing to clean the wound. I'll have to cauterize the opening as well—"

King Thomas silenced him with a sharp gesture, his hand slicing through the air. "All right, Llewellyn, I'll carry her on my horse." He lifted Kathryn in his arms, trying to be careful of the arrow and the hasty padding of bits of clothing and such that Llewellyn had scrounged to bandage the open wound without pressing on it. The king mounted his horse, kicking the beast forward at once without waiting to see if the others followed.

———◦———

Their party rode quickly, thinking haste more important than jarring the arrow. The longer Kathryn was left to bleed, the less chance she would ever awaken. Llewellyn eventually took the wolf up before him on his horse. The confused Lord Stephen nursed his aching head and brought up the rear on Kathryn's borrowed mare, his own horse lost in the forest for now. The king's horse first reached the sturdy wooden gates surrounding the convent. King Thomas tugged furiously at the little bell of the wicket gate, and very quickly the portress, looking bleary-eyed and ruffled, came to open the gate for them.

"Are you and your lady benighted, my good lord, or—" Then she saw Kathryn. "*Oh*."

The king brushed past the portress. Knowing the convent well, he barked orders to the sister as he hurried across the court to the closest cell, there to deposit his sad burden. "Summon your abbess at once, and anyone with herb lore or leechcraft."

The elderly nun hesitated, and the king whirled on her, becoming all at once a blood-soaked barbarian barking in her face. "Go, idiot woman, or this girl's blood will be on your head."

By this time, Llewellyn and the wolf were within the enclave as the convent's healer and her abbess ran forward.

"Marie." The king intercepted the dignified abbess, taking her by the hands while her healer went forward to assist Llewellyn.

"Brother?" the abbess said, wiping sleep from her eyes. "What's happened?"

Marie was the king's half-sister, a by-blow of their father's, but one King Thomas had loved his whole life long as though she were his full-blooded relation. She had a lovely face, narrow and leonine like his, with the long, sharp nose of their father, which showed so strongly through the line. Her eyes were large and the same gray-blue as his. Her hair shone a dark, rich brown, though she had hacked it off on becoming a nun, and now her lovely locks were forever hidden from sight under her wimple.

Unable to ever make a good marriage because of her illegitimacy, Marie had accepted the temple as her vocation and made a fine job of the pursuit too. She was abbess at Bourlonge, and a more respected and renowned abbess could not be found in all the land.

Hurriedly and very quietly, the king gave his sister an abbreviated version of events without omitting even Reynard's part.

Marie nodded. "All will be attended to. But first we must ensure the girl is safely on the mend."

King Thomas clasped her hand. "Yes."

The baron, once he arrived at the convent, demanded to stay by his daughter's side.

In the sickroom with Llewellyn and the convent's healer, Lord Stephen was startled and scandalized when the magician placed a hand on Kathryn's forehead and uttered strange incantations under his breath. A glowing aura formed around the magician's palm before sinking into Kathryn's body. For a moment, Kathryn seemed illumed from within by healing light. That passed quickly, but afterward she seemed less pale, her breath less labored.

Lord Stephen did not hold with magic, but he would not protest anything that might give his daughter back to him.

The attendant nun pursed her lips but likewise said nothing. The Sisters of Fate had a strained relationship with the magicians of the land. Their two belief systems were oftentimes at odds.

The baron, though usually rather squeamish in all things having to do with healing and the gore entailed therein, nonetheless volunteered to be the one to assist Llewellyn in removing the arrow. The arrowhead had, thankfully, passed all the way through the shoulder already, and so the arrow only needed to be carefully broken off and pulled out. Lord Stephen almost forgot himself when Llewellyn cauterized the wound, but the baron recovered his wits in time to leave the room before being asked to help stuff the wound with moss and apply the dressings.

Outside the sickroom door, the wolf paced back and forth. Their party had taken over one of the front rooms of the convent, as Llewellyn had no wish to waste a moment and let Kathryn bleed any longer than was necessary. The holy man had unceremoniously kicked out the nuns who had been sleeping in the room.

King Thomas sat quietly by a fire in one of the convent's receiving rooms, waiting for news. Lord Stephen joined him and, shortly thereafter, the wolf came to the baron, bowing his head respectfully as if in an act of contrition.

Lord Stephen looked at the wolf and frowned. A feeling of wonder stole through him as he realized what he was witnessing. Lord Stephen hesitated for a moment. Then, at the king's encouraging nod, the baron placed his hand on the wolf's head. "I'm sure this misfortune was not your fault, my boy."

The wolf nodded, then left the king and the baron. He curled up to the side of the sickroom door.

Lord Stephen eyed the beast, then looked to his king. "He...*loves* her. Doesn't he?"

King Thomas looked at the wolf with a strange light of affection in his eyes. "Yes, he's truly learned the nature of real love now with your girl. I hope..." The king trailed off, pursing his lips as his eyes shone with moisture.

Lord Stephen swallowed and let the subject drop, sensing his liege's grief and too overcome with his own in that moment to speak.

Hours later, Llewellyn emerged, the convent healer only a beat behind him to close the door of the sickroom. Garwaf jumped on Llewellyn at once and placed his paws on the magician's shoulders, staring Llewellyn solemnly in the eye as he delivered his news.

Llewellyn sighed, a frail smile trembling on his lips. "She's alive, and I think she'll survive. But this coming night will make the difference. If she takes a turn—" Llewellyn's voice broke, and he looked away.

Garwaf eased himself off Llewellyn's shoulders at once and started into the sickroom before remembering himself and looking back to Llewellyn sheepishly for permission.

Llewellyn scoffed. "As if I could stop you. Go on."

Garwaf padded into the sickroom.

Kathryn was very pale. *Too pale.* A light sheen of sweat beaded her brow. Red and puffy all over, her face was covered with bruises. One eye was swollen shut entirely. A florid bruise spread across her cheekbone around a small nick there. Where her split lip had scabbed over, Llewellyn had wiped the blood away. From the small hint about her nostrils, her nose had bled as well.

A knot of hatred formed in the pit of Garwaf's gut. *I'll get him for what he did to you, Kathryn. Whether you want me to or not. I will* hurt *him for this.*

Tucked tight with many blankets, Kathryn had been propped up against the bed's headboard with her feet elevated. Thick layers of dressings had been applied to her shoulder.

Her caretakers had let him see her before they had even taken the time to clean up all the bloody cloths or pick up the discarded arrow. The stench of Reynard was all over the arrow's shaft, and a heady reek of Kathryn's blood that made Garwaf dizzy. He kicked the arrow away under the bed so he would not have to look at its bloody point and think. Instead, he went to Kathryn.

Llewellyn had said she would probably be fine. Llewellyn was hardly ever wrong, and he would never lie. She was still unconscious, which was probably a good thing to judge by her bruised face, the large bandage, and all the blood-soaked rags about. Kathryn would be in a lot of pain when she did wake up. If *she wakes up...*

Don't even think that.

He nuzzled her limp hand on the sheets. *I am so sorry.* He closed his eyes. If he had human eyes, real human eyes, he would weep. But he was not human, so he keened softly and whimpered into her palm.

If I could have explained things to you, I would have. I wish I could explain everything to you. I wish I could have told you once in more than just actions. In words. In exact and precise words what you mean to me, Kathryn. I want to be able to tell you all that is in this twisted, damaged heart of mine. I want to be able to tell you that I love you. Out loud. Out loud and as often as I can form my lips around the words.

I was lost. More than halfway to being an animal all the rest of my days. I had forgotten what being human felt like.

Ah, my beauty, I need you to live. Even if you never speak to me or look at me again, I need you to live. I need you to be in the world. Having you in the world makes it an easier place to survive.

So breathe in, breathe out. Mend and heal. Do what you have to, but stay in this world.

Just stay, Kathryn.

Stay.

As her hand stirred, he jumped in surprise. Her fingers moved closer to him, and he leaned toward her. Her delicate hand shook as she cupped his dark muzzle in a caress. Hope flared within him as he gazed into her face. Her good eye opened a crack, and she smiled at him, careful of her lip. He gingerly leapt onto the bed so as not to jar her shoulder and settled his chin in her lap.

She smiled again dreamily and stroked his head. "Ah, Garwaf." Her voice was the barest whisper of breath, hoarse with pain. "Events like this should tell you that the time to be a man again has come." Her hand stilled on his fur.

He looked up in alarm and fear only to be reassured that no, now she slept true sleep and not the unconscious stupor of injury. This was healing sleep and would do her good.

He stared at Kathryn a long while, frowning over the darkening bruises on her. The marks would leave no lasting scars, but for the moment, her face remained hideously marred by Reynard's handiwork.

Garwaf found he no longer craved to rip Reynard's throat out with his teeth. The thought of the man's blood in his mouth revolted every part of him. He wanted none of that poisonous stuff anywhere near his innards.

No, the werewolf craved instead a contest of arms. To challenge the vile beast Reynard to trial by combat, then hack him into little tiny bits with a sword, a dagger, whatever weapons he had to hand, but to make a thorough job of his revenge, regardless.

To challenge Reynard, though, he needed to be a knight. To be a knight, he would need his clothes back. To get those, he would need help.

Kathryn shifted, and he stilled. *All in good time*. He could wait a while longer. He needed to be with Kathryn now. *When* she lived through the night, well, then would be the time to seek restitution and, maybe, redemption.

Chapter Fifteen

Kathryn lived through the night.

In the morning, when Llewellyn came to check on her, Garwaf lay curled at her feet. He perked his head up, then hopped down so Llewellyn could examine her.

The magician let out a profound sigh of relief as he examined Kathryn. Garwaf wagged his tail and was persuaded to leave the sickbed to get some food. A young novice came to sit with the invalid in their absence.

Lord Stephen went to rest in a guest room now that he knew his daughter would live. Garwaf broke his fast with Llewellyn in the little receiving room, where a cheerful fire crackled. The king and the abbess entered shortly thereafter, and all four of them sat to council. The abbess gazed at Garwaf, and when he grinned at her, she bent to stroke his ears.

"We'll keep her here until she's well enough to travel," Marie said.

"Agreed." King Thomas poked at the fire. "And you will help us to keep this from blossoming into a scandal. Even if we put about the bandits story, people will believe Kathryn's virtue compromised, especially if Kathryn is seen like this. If even a whisper reaches the court of her condition, her reputation could be forever tainted. I don't want that for her."

"We'll keep her here while she mends and, if it is her wish, we'll send her back into the world again when she is whole and no blemish remains of the incident to cause suspicion. She was coming here anyway. If her father keeps silent about the whole affair—"

"Which I'm sure I can persuade him to do," King Thomas said.

"Then we need not worry," the abbess replied. "She's supposed to be here. She *is* here. If any come seeking her, I can say she wants solitude for reflection before beginning her novitiate."

"Ah, Marie." Llewellyn patted her hand. "How we've missed your level head at the castle these years."

Marie smiled back. "I'm sure you've managed."

King Thomas settled into his chair, gazing about expectantly. "Now what do we do?"

Marie snorted. "My people are well able to care for her."

Garwaf yipped and glared at his aunt.

"I think what the king is trying to say," Llewellyn said with careful diplomacy, "is that all of us are reluctant to leave Kathryn's side while she is like this."

"She's *fine*," Marie said. "People will comment if you all stay away longer. You'll have a hard time explaining why you left so suddenly and stayed away for the night as it is."

King Thomas waved that away. "The wolf ran off because he sensed his friend Kathryn leaving. Llewellyn and I went to reclaim the beast. Chased him all the way here to Bourlonge, and by the time we arrived, the hour was too late to leave. So, the kind abbess"—a gesture to his sister— "graciously offered us bed and board for the night. Much as I hate to admit you're right, we can't stay here any longer without courting scandal."

Garwaf whined stubbornly, but eventually the king convinced him of the wisdom in leaving. The last thing the wolf wanted was to harm Kathryn's reputation by some act of his own. So, after repeated assurances on Llewellyn's part that Kathryn would be fine, Garwaf agreed to leave.

Kathryn's father, on the other hand, refused to depart from the convent until Kathryn became well enough to *order* him away. Since they had secured his promise to stay quiet and let the king deal with the "bandits" who had injured his daughter, Stephen was given countenance to stay. King Thomas and Llewellyn didn't need Lord Stephen back at the castle to make their story plausible anyway.

⸺◈⸺

Garwaf peeked inside Kathryn's room, his ears perked forward. She beckoned him in and smiled when he bounded happily to her side. He gingerly jumped on the bed and rested his head in her lap.

Kathryn tweaked his ears. She didn't remember much from the previous day as yet, but she still understood what she must do. Fragile in her heart and body, she still had strength enough, bravery enough now, to start the discussion she had been dreading since the feast. Her haphazard flight had been an attempt to avoid this moment, but with the wolf at her bedside she *had* to speak. "Garwaf."

He looked up at once and crept closer, slipping against her side so she didn't have to speak too loudly. His scent filtered up to Kathryn, and she smiled. He always smelled strangely nice. Of leather and manly works, also meadows and roses, sharp and strong but tender and sweet as well.

She bestirred herself. She would never get to her point if she let her thoughts continue in that vein. "I don't want you to have any sense of obligation toward me." She scratched his ears and touched the wound on his shoulder, which had started to scar over. "I think you've more than discharged any debt you might believe you owe me. Go with King Thomas, return to your real life, and forget the wolf's bookish little friend."

Her words tumbled out in a rush. Like tearing the dressing from a wound, she hoped to get her ordeal over with quickly. "You still love your wife and—" Her throat threatened to close up with the knot that was forming, but she *would* get this out. "When you return to her—"

The wolf growled.

Kathryn startled at the noise. She blinked, confused by the disgusted look on his face. "*Do* you want to return to your wife?"

A belligerent and violent head shake. *No.*

"But Reynard said—" Realizing how stupid the rest of the sentence forming in her head really was, Kathryn cursed her own folly fluently in two languages. Reynard, scoundrel that he was, had still seen through her and plucked just the right chords inside her soul to send her dancing to his tune. "Well, thank Kind Fate, no serious harm has been done."

The wolf snorted and nudged her side.

She gave a small, pained laugh. "Right." Being of a very pragmatic nature, Kathryn had conveniently forgotten the arrow in her shoulder. "Well, then. That's good. That we have an understanding." Her heart clenched with hope. She gazed into Garwaf's eyes and saw the human heart shining out of them. He gazed back adoringly.

Kathryn, the more practical of the two, was the first to shake out of her reverie. "Well, you great ass, the sooner you make off with the king and Llewellyn, the sooner we can be about the business of life." She made an impatient shooing motion. "Out, you great silly beast. Get thee gone. The sooner you leave, the sooner you can come back, yes?"

The wolf started to go, then whirled back, jumped up, and licked her face before galloping out of the sickroom in search of his king. She laughed and wiped her wet cheek.

A shadow fell over her heart after he'd left. The soulful eyes gazing out of a wolf's head were one thing, but she found herself wondering what she would do if she ever saw those same eyes shining out of a human face.

Chapter Sixteen

A lisoun had always been cunning and careful. Originally naught but a poor steward's daughter, through guile, good looks, and rather a bit of luck, she had managed to snag one of the best catches in the kingdom. Gabriel, the king's nephew and heir, the Duke of Dorré, had chosen *her*.

Then, when her first husband, after nearly a year of marriage, had shown himself to have rather an inconvenient problem, she managed affairs to dispose of him accordingly. After, she'd replaced Gabriel with a much more malleable tool in Reynard, and one willing to use the power she secured for him.

Closeted away in her chambers, she reclined on her bed while her lady's maid read a romance verse aloud to her. Hooves clattered on the cobbles of the court below. Someone was arriving at Dorré.

The maid dropped her book with a resounding thud, her soft slippers shushing across the floor toward the window. "Lord Reynard has returned." The serving girl stammered as she said his name.

Alisoun laughed to herself. If Reynard had not already bedded her maidservant, then his failure wasn't for lack of trying. Alisoun had never met a hornier old goat than Reynard of Troumper in all her life.

"I suppose my husband will come to pay his respects as soon as he may." Alisoun motioned for the maid to resume her reading but no longer attended to the ballad herself. Rumors had reached her of the king's new pet. An uncanny black wolf, unnaturally large and well trained for a beast so lately plucked from the wild. Alisoun was curious indeed to hear Reynard's impressions of this wolf.

Not that the wolf's sudden appearance meant anything. Pure coincidence merely. It had to be.

When Reynard arrived at her chambers with unaccustomed promptness, a sense of foreboding pricked at the clever Lady Alisoun. When her husband peremptorily dismissed her maid from the room, he gained Alisoun's full attention.

"I bought you some scented gloves, my love." Reynard sneered the endearment, mocking her as he tossed the parcel onto her bed to hit her legs. Alisoun made no move to pick up her present.

"How was the feast?" she asked him.

Reynard scratched at his beard, a sharp rasp of skin on stubble in the quiet of her chambers. "Alisoun, we have a problem." He then proceeded to pour out to her all the disastrous occurrences of the past week, up to the preceding night's happenings with the injured girl.

When Reynard had finished, Alisoun smoothed her skirts, hissed in a deep breath, and proceeded to give him the tongue-lashing of his life. "The wolf attacked you, and you let it live? You bloody *fool*. What better excuse did you need for killing the beast? And if the wolf is *him*, all the better. That loose end has long haunted me. It would be a comfort to know he's been dealt with."

"Quite the loving wife, aren't you, my darling?"

Alisoun snatched at the package he had given her and threw the parcel at his head.

"You missed, my lamb."

Alisoun curled her lip in distaste. Her husband had old scars from Alisoun's other fits of pique. She had a habit of throwing breakables and smashing furniture when someone flouted her will. A pity that her aim had deteriorated of late.

Reynard held his tongue for now. He never fought her back anymore. He was probably scared of killing her accidentally. At least over the tedious, dark time of their marriage he had learned to value her cleverness. Her husband was a great fool, but he still knew he needed her cleverness to see him through this crisis.

Once the wolf was gone, things might change, but Alisoun would plan carefully for that as well.

What a shame it was that Beatrice had been away from court for the feast. A singularly stupid girl, Reynard's sister yet had her uses in keeping her brother from costly blunders. *Ah well, the damage is done. Now, how to repair matters?* "I will unravel this knot you have tied," Alisoun snapped. "Never fear, dear heart. Now leave."

Reynard left with haste, boot heels ringing, and slammed her door on his way out.

She gave a small laugh. *My dear husband is not overly fond of my society these days.* Well, the feeling was mutual.

———— ◆ ————

King Thomas arrived in his castle in time to sit with his knights for the noonday meal and catch them up with a fictionalized account of the past night's adventures. Garwaf came in for some lighthearted scolding and passed the deception off well enough.

Queen Aliénor, since Kathryn was her dear friend, would be put in possession of the truth. The king didn't relish the task but went at once after his meal to break the news to his lady. King Thomas made plans to meet Llewellyn in his workshop as soon as possible afterward to discuss their next steps.

Garwaf, listless and unequal to enduring the rowdy knights, went to the alcove of roses. He sat there for some time, turning things over in his mind. Surrounded by the scent of roses, awash in memories of his happy days with Kathryn, he reached a decision. Sliding off the rose bench, he ran in search of King Thomas.

Garwaf found the king closeted in Llewellyn's workshop, a plan of a siege tower spread out between them. He gazed at the plans with mild interest before puffing out an unimpressed snort.

The king laughed. "Yes, we found them highly impractical as well." He patted the wolf's shoulder and proceeded to roll up the plans. He turned away, and Garwaf looked at Llewellyn.

The magician frowned and touched the king's shoulder. They both looked to Garwaf.

The wolf scratched with his paw in the dirt outside Llewellyn's hut. Gabriel had learned his letters as a boy and, though not a great reader, he had been able to pen a letter or two if the need presented itself. No one had yet, however, seen him display any such talents in wolf form. Indeed, he labored hard at his task, blinking, his tongue lolling out. At last, his effort completed, he stepped back from his great work so the other two could read his message.

HELP ME was all Garwaf had spelled out, but the two words had the desired effect.

King Thomas and Llewellyn traded looks and nodded. The king stepped forward, kneeling to bring himself eye to eye with Garwaf. "I thought we both might enjoy a little hunting." He grinned. "Near Dorré."

The king set out from his castle the next morning with the wolf, Llewellyn, and a significant number of men-at-arms. He said he fancied a spot of hunting after all the trials of the feast. If some of his courtiers wondered what he was about going with so many soldiers, well, as king he could be excused his odd little indulgences.

Word of the king's movements came to Lady Alisoun a few days after her husband's return from court. These tidings were as unwelcome as they were surprising. Alisoun's estimable wits had been thrown into a complete disorder. She was flustered. *She*, the triumphant Duchess of Dorré and Countess of Troumper, was *panicking*. She could not think of a suitable strategy. Her cool intellect and her steady calmness had abandoned her.

Finally, she realized there was nothing to do but go to Sûr, where the king quartered himself, and meet the king's wolf. To so expose herself was a terrible gamble, but she didn't trust Reynard to go alone. He would undoubtedly bungle everything. *Again.*

Her maid laid out all Alisoun's very best finery. She had to be flawless to-morrow to allay any and all suspicions. She had to look perfect. The ideal of womanhood.

Perhaps she did not take such a very great risk. She would go for only a short while, just to take the measure of this wolf everyone spoke of. Perhaps, that being done, she might settle on an appropriate course of action. And then she would be able to calm some of the dread that consumed her every moment.

———— ◦ ————

Robert of Sûr was a simple creature, a good landlord, and a kind man. On the king's arrival to stay as his guest, Robert cast doubtful looks at the wolf. Still, the creature traveled with King Thomas and, as such, under Lord Robert's fundamental code of conduct, the beast was to be welcomed as a guest and treated with all courtesy.

When the beast demonstrated he could be quite the prettiest-behaved vassal in the lot, Robert was impressed and gave the wolf the good bedchamber adjoined to the king's.

Garwaf glanced in concern at the slighted Llewellyn. The magician grinned. "Ah, lad, I don't mind being bumped down to lesser apartments." He laughed. "I'm used to it, after all. From the old days, remember? I always got the worst chambers when I traveled with you two."

Garwaf whined, unconvinced.

Llewellyn tweaked his ears, not hard enough to hurt, and smiled broadly. "Believe me when I say that I dearly missed being a second-class houseguest these past two years."

Garwaf snorted and let the subject drop but returned to his own plush apartments free of guilt.

By the second morning of their stay with Sûr, word had predictably spread throughout the surrounding areas that King Thomas had come to call. All his vassals, who had by now returned home from the feast, hastily made their reverences to their lord. Again.

The king sat at the opposite end of the great hall of Sûr on a raised dais in the finest chair the Baron of Sûr could offer him. Garwaf, like some mythical beast of old, sat at the king's side like a figure carved of black marble, noble and aloof. Barons, castellans, and knights all made homage to King Thomas while Garwaf remained as removed from the proceedings as if the courtiers were ants scurrying for his scraps.

There was only one face he wished to see, only one person in all the throng massed about the hall that he wanted to step forward and make her obeisance. His fur stood all on end as he smelled her at last. Never could he forget that spicy floral scent.

The smell was tinged now with some other scent, an odd pungency almost sickly in nature. The scent reminded him somehow of the goats he used to hunt for meals around the forest. He shook that thought off. She *was* here, and he would bide his time until she revealed herself. Then...well, then matters rested in Fate's hands, for Garwaf couldn't guess what he would do when he saw Alisoun.

One lowly knight scooted to the side, and she was revealed. The Lady Alisoun, Duchess of Dorré through her marriage to the duke, Gabriel. Countess of Troumper now she was Reynard's wife. A lithe, glowing vision, she stood before them, the early-morning radiance pouring in through the Baron of Sûr's leaded windows creating a coronet of sunlight on her head.

Clad all in white, Alisoun wore a graceful gown of silk fixed with delicate seed pearls at the hems and the cuffs of her long sleeves. She wore elegant gloves, embroidered with silver leaves and delicate buds of flowers over her hands.

The sight of a tight wimple modestly covering her golden hair startled Garwaf. Before she had displayed her hair with lamentable vanity whenever an opportunity had presented itself to do so.

Her second husband walked with her, and she delicately rested her hand on his wrist as they shuffled forward in the receiving line. She limped now. She had forever been riding like a madwoman across their lands, and Garwaf would not have been surprised if, at last, Alisoun had suffered an injury for her recklessness. A long, plain white veil covered Alisoun's face. Her resemblance to an innocent maiden made rage boil over in his gut.

The sight of her was too much. Nothing could have strangled the wolf in him in that moment. There he was, humbled beyond all measure, imprisoned in a body not his own, tortured, conflicted, and in peril of his soul, and this betraying witch had the gall to play at being the devoted wife. All modesty, chastity, and humble duty to her lord. *How dare she?*

The wolf took over, and he pounced from his place by the king and knocked her to the ground. The wolf in him might have ripped her limb from limb, but Llewellyn leapt into the fray to drag him back. The magician whispered a few of his rusty magic spells to calm and hold Garwaf in his place.

Men closed in on the wolf from all around and tore him from Llewellyn's protective embrace. Someone knocked Garwaf a resounding blow to the head, and he crumpled unconscious to the great hall's floor.

———— ◦ ————

The nobles might have torn the beast apart right there and then. For what honest man would stand back and let a defenseless woman be savaged right in front of him and not move to act?

Llewellyn staggered to his feet, throwing himself over the wolf. "Listen to me. My lords, you *will* listen to me." His voice rose in the highest tones of command, echoing with supernatural force throughout the hall. His command froze them where they stood. "Many of you know this beast. There is not a one of you who has not watched him, marked his noble bearing and gentleness. Never before this has he shown violence to any human creature save this woman." He pointed to Alisoun, who had not moved one inch from where she lay on the floor. "And her husband." He leveled a finger at Reynard, who sheepishly stepped back from the wolf he'd been about to kick in the ribs.

Reynard immediately assumed a none-too-convincing air of outraged innocence.

Clenching his hands, Llewellyn raised them high, his voice tight with the fervor of his words. "By my troth, I swear our wolf has some cause to hold such a bitter grudge against Lady Alisoun *and* her husband, Lord Reynard."

Reynard steadily edged his way out of the hall.

"You all knew the other Duke of Dorré, our dear Gabriel." Llewellyn placed his palm over his heart, dropping his gaze to look at the wolf. "Can any man among you tell me the truth of what became of him?"

The crowd eyed the unconscious wolf in wonder and confusion.

Llewellyn had hit his stride by then—he had the crowd in his thrall. "I say we question Lady Alisoun to see what she knows about this wolf. *And* her first husband's disappearance. Let us discover the truth of why the wolf hates her so. *Make* her tell what she knows of his curse."

At this time, Reynard made a rather pronounced bid for freedom, knocking people down as he ran for the doors. Very quickly, the crowd apprehended the knight, and some of the king's men-at-arms dragged him back.

King Thomas went to Lady Alisoun. She still breathed, but she had not stirred on the ground. He touched her shoulder. "What have you to say, my lady?"

The duchess turned over, and a collective gasp of horror went around the crowd. Her veil had fallen away, and blood poured from her nose, staining her gown in gore.

Worse, though, was the wreck of her face. Lesions and old, scaly sores covered her once-lovely face. Her nose had caved in on itself long ago and was all but gone, save for two ghastly slits where her nostrils had been. A chalky pallor hung over her face, and puckered white lines from old sores, long healed, marred the once-perfect creaminess of her skin.

Worse than all this, however, was the look of pure hatred in her bloodshot, unseeing eyes. "I say, I hope the beast *rots*."

Chapter Seventeen

T he king detained Reynard in a sturdy cell in their host's underground stores with several of the king's best knights posted as guards.

The wolf rested in his bedchamber, and the Lady Alisoun had been moved to a private room in the servant's wing. Meanwhile, Llewellyn and the king conferred.

King Thomas grimaced. "Her face. Was it—?" He shook himself and looked at Llewellyn. "What was it?"

Llewellyn chafed at his arms. "Without a closer inspection I can only guess, but I believe she's leprous, my lord. A well-advanced case. She's blind already, and her face—" He cleared his throat and scratched at the pale blond stubble on his chin. "I wouldn't say she was much longer for this world." He shook his head in disbelief. "The disease is not usually so quick moving. Leprosy should have taken *decades* to inflict such wreckage on her, but I would say she's been infected only these past few years. I saw her whole and well not more than two years ago, and I would swear on my life she wasn't leprous then."

"She became leprous only *after* she betrayed Gabriel?"

"It would seem so, my lord." Llewellyn spread his hands in a small, noncommittal gesture. "Fate's justice can manifest itself in strange ways."

"She was always such a ruthless little—" The king broke off, huffing out a breath. "Well, she always enjoyed the pleasures of court, so I had wondered why she suddenly ceased to attend. I believed then that the cause was grief over Gabriel's disappearance."

"When I interviewed him below, Reynard said Alisoun instigated everything." Llewellyn scrubbed a hand through his hair, shaking his head. "Reynard would never have discovered Gabriel's condition if Alisoun hadn't sought him out."

King Thomas clenched his fists. "No wonder Gabriel attacked her as he did. I'm surprised he didn't kill her."

"The nobles gave Garwaf quite a crack on the head for his pains. But he should've come round by now."

A look of concern crossed the king's face, but Llewellyn waved his fears away. "Not to worry. He'll be fine. Best he's out of this now, anyway. The rest of the work is up to us. Come, let's go see the woman, sire."

Alisoun had been made comfortable in a small, bare cell, and her silk dress had been changed for coarse blue robes scrounged from the rag pile. Without her cleverly concealing garments, her disease made itself plain. She was not recognizable now as the once-beautiful woman who had captivated the court and held a dozen young men in the hollow of her hand.

Her hair had mostly fallen out. Where strands lingered the sight was all the more grotesque, for the hair was goldenly luxurious even while mingling with the old sores and bald patches now covering her head. Her right hand remained firm and supple, but the bones of her left had all but disappeared, forcing her appendage into a crooked claw composed of festering sores and rotting skin. Not just her nose but also her upper lip had rotted away, revealing yellowing and broken teeth, and her lower lip drooped with unnatural heaviness.

Her eyes, once so bright and sharp, were now clouded and milky, bitter. She had gone blind from her disease and could no longer blink, as her lower lids were paralyzed. The sight unnerved the king, but Llewellyn had had truck with lepers in his many travels and was not put off. He had only pity for the poor woman.

She turned her ravaged head toward the sound of their footfalls. "This is a judgment on me for what I did to the beast," she rasped out in a voice barely recognizable as the bright, clear tones both men remembered from her earlier, unblighted years. "I banished my first husband to inhuman exile, and Fate condemned me to live like this. To live and die a leper and an outcast, so I may know threefold what I have inflicted upon the filthy werewolf. But never, *never* will I help him back to his human form. If I must die accursed and contemptible, then I will not go alone into the fire." Her good hand clenched around her covers while her other arm lay limp and nerveless on the sheets.

King Thomas and Llewellyn retired to a far corner of the room and held quiet conference. "Usually the mind remains whole and untouched until the end," Llewellyn explained. "One of leprosy's more bitter aspects is that the infected remain in full possession of their wits as they watch their flesh literally rot off their bodies. But I think, in her case, the loss of her former beauty has touched her mind. She is a trifle unstable."

"Do you *think*, oh wise man?"

"Don't get testy." Llewellyn rubbed his cheek with one thumb.

"Reynard, then?"

"That might be the best course, and also—" Llewellyn frowned, darting a cautious look at the king.

King Thomas folded his arms. "And *what*?"

Llewellyn scratched his nose and gave a small shrug. "Might be a good idea to bring Garwaf round to talk to her as well."

Naught for nothing was Thomas a king. One does not get to be ruler without considerable amounts of discretion and self-control, even if you *are* born to the position. It required all of that particular virtue the king possessed to keep quiet until he and Llewellyn had discreetly removed themselves back to Thomas's own quarters.

Once there, however, and safely behind closed doors, the king's voice boomed out across the Baron of Sûr's estate. "Did you *see* what she looked like? She's a *wreck. A horror*. The sight of her face is going to haunt me for *years*. If you think

I am going to subject him to *that*, then you're a bigger fool than I always thought you were. She was his *wife*—"

And on and on. Llewellyn bore the harangue with composure and said not a word in retort.

The king's tirade went on for some time and might have been enough to wake the dead. His yelling was certainly more than adequate to wake a sleeping werewolf.

———◦———

Garwaf jumped up and turned the door handle with his paws. Groggily, he trotted into the king's bedchamber adjacent to his own and encountered his liege lord still yelling at a resigned Llewellyn.

The wolf sent Llewellyn a questioning look. The magician winked and waited for King Thomas to draw breath for his next barrage. When the king paused, the magician jerked his chin. "Behind you."

The king glared, turned to look, met Garwaf's gaze, and deflated.

"Perhaps," Llewellyn said in a bone-dry voice, "you should ask Garwaf what *he* wants."

Garwaf looked to his uncle expectantly.

King Thomas frowned. "My lad, do you remember what happened in the great hall just now? Did you see Alisoun?"

A shudder passed through Garwaf. He had seen.

"She refuses to tell us where your clothes are," Llewellyn put in.

"I want to bring the conspirators together, demonstrate to them the fruitlessness of holding out—"

"*I* don't believe that ploy will work," Llewellyn said. "I think you, my lord"—this he directed toward Garwaf— "must earn your own humanity back from them." The king glowered. Llewellyn groaned and threw his hands up. "But we will, of course, yield to your wishes, my king."

The king stalked to the window, his shoulders tense as he looked out.

Llewellyn came to Garwaf and clasped an arm around him. "If that fails, what will you do, my lord?"

Garwaf looked away. *I will go to her. I think I need to. Somehow.*

As if reading his thoughts, weary Llewellyn creaked to his feet and crossed to King Thomas. "Shall we?"

The king squared his shoulders. "Fetch Reynard to his wife's chamber." A beat passed and the king sighed deeply. "Bring Garwaf as well." He held up an admonishing finger. "I don't want him to see her like this if he doesn't absolutely have to."

"Only if there is no other way." Llewellyn nodded.

Garwaf growled. He understood what the king was doing, of course, and it infuriated him. *I am not a child, Uncle.* Garwaf also understood this was *his* task to do and no one else's. How to convey this to the king and his magician was a different matter.

Times like these truly made him miss his power of speech.

<hr />

King, magician, and werewolf padded through the castle to where they had left Alisoun in her solitary sickroom. King Thomas had sent ahead, and Reynard, under heavy guard, awaited them. When they reached the door, the king tried to keep Garwaf out of the cell.

The wolf glanced at him with defiance in his dark blue eyes. *I have more of a right to confront these two than anyone.*

Sighing in resignation, the king opened the door to let Garwaf precede him into the sickroom—now makeshift interrogation chamber.

<hr />

Upon beholding the wolf, Reynard flinched and retreated. Alisoun stirred beneath her covers, but she didn't speak. She certainly knew King Thomas and

Llewellyn had returned, but had she also recognized the light padding footfall of the wolf?

Reynard thought not. He stood silent and fuming by his wife's sick bed, unable to keep the contempt and disgust from showing on his face when he looked at the ruin his wife had become. "The betrayal was all her idea," Reynard growled when they questioned him. "Long had I admired Lady Alisoun. Often did I offer her my *services*. Always before she refused my attentions and sent me on my way. I was never more shocked in my life than when I received the letter from her. She named a time and place. Faithfully did I keep the tryst with her. There she told me of the werewolf and how to trap him so she should be free of him."

King Thomas cast a black look at Alisoun. "If you desired your freedom, you could have come to me." He glared at her, though Reynard knew her sightless eyes could not see the expression. "Gladly would I have parted you from my nephew." The king's voice held a note of disgust.

Reynard laughed. "And give up being the Duchess of Dorré? My king, we all know Alisoun better than that. And you were so angry, so hurt, so *drunk* once Gabriel disappeared, getting you to sign over all his lands to me was an easy task. I'm not sure you even realized how malleable you were. But Alisoun did."

The lady in question said nothing all the while. She remained blank faced throughout, betraying her interest in the discussion only by the restless stirring of her good hand on the sheets.

Reynard continued his account of his part in events. His sudden burst of chattiness had actually come about after a few not-so-subtle hints from Llewellyn regarding sharp objects and certain soft parts of Reynard's anatomy. After his colloquy with the king's magician, Reynard had wisely decided a full confession would be best. After all, persecuting a werewolf, even if in the daylight hours he was the king's nephew, would hardly be regarded as a crime by the general populace. Reynard had no desire to be tortured into divulging his part in the werewolf's betrayal. Not when, on closer inspection, it seemed his willing confession could hurt him not a bit.

King Thomas and his two pets here in the room could actually do very little to Reynard. He had fallen out of favor, he might lose his lands, and banishment was an option. There were, however, other lands and other kings more susceptible to manipulation and flattery. One way or another, Reynard would find his way to power again. And then the wolf and his little girlie would be in a world of pain. Reynard would see to that. *Somehow. Someday.* He smiled.

"So," Reynard continued smoothly, betraying nothing of his thoughts, "Alisoun told me where the werewolf went and by what road. I stole the clothes from the rock and, having faithfully discharged my errand, returned to her to receive my reward." He wiggled his eyebrows in a smug manner at the wolf. The beast curled his lip to show sharp teeth but did not growl. Reynard ceased his gloat and went on, "I gave the clothes to Alisoun and forgot them. I haven't seen them since."

"You have no idea what she did with them?" Llewellyn asked.

Reynard grinned. "None whatsoever."

"Send him back to his cell." King Thomas dismissed Reynard with a casual flick of his wrist.

The guards jostled him toward the door but, before Reynard left, he stopped and leaned down to glare into the wolf's face. "I got everything I wanted. Your lands, your title, *your wife*, and I left you worse than dead. Dishonored. Broken. An animal living in the woods. What a delicious day that was when your wife propositioned me." Reynard snorted. "But you've had your revenge full measure now, haven't you? I and not you have ended up cursed. Cursed with a leper to wife. Oh yes, what a grand deal clever Reynard made that day. You've already had your revenge, my lord, on the pair of us, and now you know it."

The wolf curled back his lip.

Reynard leaned in and said, so only the wolf could hear, "Even if I did have your clothes, I wouldn't help you back to them."

———◆———

The wolf snapped in Reynard's face. Before events could further devolve, Llewellyn directed the guards, and they carried Reynard out between them.

Llewellyn, for the past few minutes, had closely watched Alisoun, and he observed a new animation seeping into the rotting husk of her body. *Ah, so she did not know her first husband was here. Not until this moment, when Reynard addressed himself to the wolf.* Still she said nothing, though.

"Well?" King Thomas snarled at the lady. "Ungrateful wretch that you are, you might still redeem yourself, gain a modicum of forgiveness in this world and the next, if you will tell us where those clothes are."

She laughed. "You do not scare me, my king. What threat could you possibly hold over a leper?" Her voice rasped, faltering to form the words with her disfigured face.

The king glowered.

Llewellyn laid a hand on his shoulder. "By your leave, my lord?"

King Thomas, face tense, went to lean against the door.

Llewellyn knelt by the bed and clasped her good hand in his. From the corner of his eye, he noticed the king recoil, but Llewellyn knew this disease and had no fear of contagion. "Lady Alisoun, when did you find out your husband was a werewolf?"

She frowned, the lines of pain on her face deepening. "He always left me at the end of every month with no explanation." Her enfeebled body stirred to life again under this blazing indignation. "I was his lady wife. I had a right to know where he went." Her maimed hand convulsively patted the sheets at her side while her still-functioning appendage plucked at her gown. "If he was being unfaithful, I wanted the truth."

"Did you love Gabriel?"

The question seemed to surprise her. Then, oddly, the ravaged lines of her face softened. She was not lovely, but she became less painful to look at. "I thought him everything a knight should be. Everything honorable and good. He was so kind, so gentle. And the way he looked at me. So proud. As if I was the greatest prize in the land, and he had won. I thought I had the best husband Nature could make."

———◆◇◆———

Garwaf sighed. She *had* been a prize to him, an honor, an ornament, the final trophy with which to decorate his fine castle. The fact she had seen herself as such did not excuse his misconduct. He had regarded her as chattel and treated her accordingly. He had enjoyed admiring her, contemplating his great triumph in winning Alisoun for a bride. He had never actually talked to her. Not at their courtship, which, he remembered, had been all too brief.

I think the night she confronted me about my absences was the first time I saw she had thoughts and feelings of her own. And I wanted then, so much, to share all of myself with her. To let just one person in this world really know me. His thirst for acceptance had outweighed his discretion. *I saw Alisoun only as my wife. I was naïve. I trusted without understanding her.*

"I badgered him," Alisoun continued in a lower voice, sinking into her bed now the first blaze of her anger had burned itself out. "I would let him have no peace, and finally he told me." The stricken lines of her face hardened. "He told me and turned my life into a *nightmare*. My husband was a monster, I was a fool, and all the power that I had worked so hard to achieve hung on a knife's point. If he should ever have been discovered, I would have lost everything. The shame was not to be thought of, not to be endured. And the thought that I had let this creature touch me. That I had been longing to bear his brats." She shuddered. "He had to pay for so defiling me. For so *humiliating* me."

I should have told her from the first. Garwaf hung his head.

"So I cuckolded him with Reynard, and I stole his vile clothes so the world would forever be able to see what he *really* was."

"Lady, why did you not confront your lord with this when he told you his secret?" Llewellyn asked.

Alisoun scoffed. "Unfold my mind to an *animal*? Bad enough I had lain with the creature, been deceived for so long. To what purpose should I have continued the charade and indulged the beast in believing he was human?"

"He is not a beast!" The king's face blanched with fury, a vein on his temple throbbing. "Even in the form you have trapped him in, he retains a dignity and understanding you could never aspire to have. He has a compassionate soul, which your curse has done nothing to tarnish. It is *your* wickedness that is to be condemned. *Your* betrayal. *Your* lies. Mayhap he should have told you from the first of his affliction, but *you*"—his lips curled back in repugnance— "you judged and condemned him at once, and in that same moment when he had most trusted you. You, *my lady*, took a man's life away from him with never a thought of the blight you inflicted on his soul. With never a thought to spare for his humanity—humanity, which, I assure you, remains intact, no matter what his shape."

Alisoun looked sullen. "What can a werewolf know of humanity?"

The room fell into a silence positively thrumming with tension. The king spoke again. "What do *you* know of it, Alisoun?"

Llewellyn rubbed his forehead, his brows knotted in a frown.

"If I have done wrong, see how I am repaid." Alisoun lifted her maimed hand and turned the ruin of her face toward the king and Garwaf.

A tremble passed through them both.

Obviously sensing their revulsion, Alisoun laughed in triumph, a mad light in her dull eyes. "Almost at once my iniquity was rewarded with the contagion that reduced me to this. Within a week of stealing the clothes, I stabbed myself with a needle. The point went clean through my finger, and I didn't notice until the blood stained the cloth.

"By the end of the first year I had sores all over my body. I saw the flesh liquefy from my bones, my bones dissolve and fall like dead leaves." She twitched the covers aside to reveal a disfigured foot, bereft of all but the two largest toes. "My foot first, then my hand, my face, my hair—all putrefied. My eyes went last, so I was privileged to behold every deformity and relish the sight of my beauty laid to waste." A delighted rictus of a smile crossed her face. "I bedded Reynard for months after I first noticed my symptoms. He threw up for a whole day when he finally realized the truth."

Sick at heart, Garwaf trotted over to the king. He gazed into his lord's eyes and gave a small keening whine, willing the king to understand him.

King Thomas sighed. "Llewellyn," he called softly. The magician looked up. "Let us leave them alone for a moment."

Alisoun sat up. "What? You'll leave me to the wolf?"

"No wolf, madam," King Thomas gritted out. "Only your husband." And then the king and the wise man left.

Garwaf sat there for a full minute, willing himself to move but unable to get his limbs to obey. Alisoun leaned back and stared fearfully around with her sightless eyes. After a moment, he padded as slowly and as loudly forward as he could so as not to startle her. He watched her eyes the whole time, ignoring the ruin her face had become. Her eyes were sightless now, but some of the lovely brown tint remained. He focused on that, on the familiarity in her eyes.

His anger toward her had abated. He had lived a horrible life these past two years, cut off from family, friends, and all the world he had known. He had been cold, hungry, miserable, but he would recover. Mend. Alisoun never would, which made him sorrier than he could say.

He leapt up onto the bed. She recoiled, drawing back and lifting her hands to shield her face. "Don't. Don't."

He whined and crept toward her, at last resting his chin on her good hand.

She remained stiff for a long moment, but then her expression softened. He rubbed his chin on her hand, wondering if she could even feel his fur. She hesitated, then blindly reached toward him. He tilted his head into her palm, and she caressed his ears. "Oh, Gabriel, it *is* you in there."

I did not do right by you, Alisoun. I should have told you. I should have told you from the first, I should have given you a choice. I am sorry.

She sighed and leaned back, letting her hand fall. "What have I done to you, Gabriel? What have I—" For a long moment, she did not speak, and Garwaf let his presence comfort her. He could say nothing to ease her guilt, but he could show her she was forgiven.

She reached out to him again, and he met her questing hand, ducking his head into her fingers. She touched his jaw, and her sightless eyes somehow found his and gazed into them, unseeing. "What Reynard stole from you, what *I* stole from you, you will find it amongst my things at Dorré. In my clothing chest, the one you had carved for me at our wedding. Your things are underneath my old bride clothes."

Garwaf nodded.

"I tried to burn them once," she spoke dreamily, almost conversationally, her thoughts wandering. "They wouldn't burn. And I meant to drop them in the river or bury them but, whenever I went to rid myself of them, I would pause, and I could not finish the deed."

No, Garwaf thought, *you would not have been able to. No one could destroy them for good but me.*

The light in Alisoun's eyes faded. Garwaf sat on the bed for a long while with the body before he went to the door where King Thomas and Llewellyn waited.

Llewellyn went to Alisoun first and checked her. The magician shook his head. "Reynard is a widower now."

"And you." The king addressed this to Garwaf.

Garwaf shook his head. *No, our marriage ended the day she sent for Reynard. Alisoun and I might have lain and lived together, but we never had a true union. We said the words in temple, we went through all the motions of love, but our union was never what a marriage should have been. What love is supposed to be, what it is ordained to be.*

I will do better next time. I must do better. My beauty deserves that. If she'll have me. The werewolf looked up at the king.

"She told you where we may find your clothes?"

Dorré was but a half day's ride. Garwaf blinked in wonder.

Llewellyn hazarded a guess and directed himself to the wolf. "Somewhere at your home, my lord?"

Garwaf nodded.

King Thomas slapped his thigh, stomping with deliberation from the room. "Then to Dorré we ride."

Chapter Eighteen

The ride to the Dorré estates was not a long one but still seemed to last an eternity to Garwaf. He could not ride alone, obviously, and it was uncomfortable to go on horse, so the king and Llewellyn rode with him in a carriage.

As the day darkened, they clattered up to the Dorré estates—there to tear the house down about their ears if such an action would help them find the lost clothes. Clothes that, through some magical property unbeknownst to even the king's wise magician, would somehow restore to Garwaf his human form.

Garwaf was apprehensive and restive, shifting perpetually in his seat, absently whining. The past few days, from the feast onward, had passed in a dizzying whirl. Everything had moved so fast, and *now*, if all went well, he could be a man again by the end of the night.

A shudder passed through him. He thought his heart might explode for the happiness swelling inside his chest.

They had brought Reynard with them, thoroughly tied and gagged. King Thomas was challenged at the gates of Dorré but, once he identified himself, their party passed through unmolested, led off to the inner bailey of the castle with due deference.

When they arrived in the castle's inner sanctum, Garwaf longed to bound up to Alisoun's room at once. Still, he was wise enough to realize that a strange wolf galloping unescorted through the castle would be a wolf with a very short life expectancy. He stifled his anxiety and waited for the king to sort matters out with the castle steward. Eventually, King Thomas was given free rein of the castle and leave to search the grounds to the smallest jar of seasoning for what they sought.

King Thomas waved this generous offer away. "That will not be necessary. I believe we have a fair idea where to seek what we desire." He patted Garwaf's side. "Don't we, lad?"

Garwaf shuffled forward and whined. He wanted to *go*.

"All right, all right." King Thomas smiled indulgently, but the expression wavered on his face, and he trembled. "Let us go."

Garwaf charged into the castle keep, navigating with ease through the many corridors and rooms. Scents came back to him—the musty smell of smoke, the cool chill of the stones, the dust of the tapestries. *Home.*

On the threshold to Alisoun's bedchamber, Llewellyn and the rest of their party hesitated. Garwaf, a lifetime ago, of course, had been there many times before. He didn't hesitate to enter. Not much of the décor had altered, and Alisoun had not moved the wedding chest from the wall that had ever been its accustomed place. Regret filled Garwaf for the ruin Alisoun had become, and he paused for a moment to grieve.

With a sigh, he scratched his dead wife's trunk. Llewellyn picked up on his hints and lifted the intricately carved lid. The magician shuffled back the fine gowns to find a package of dirty wool wrapped and carefully folded, tucked securely at the very bottom of the chest. He pulled the parcel out, presenting it to Garwaf for his inspection.

Garwaf's nostrils flared as his gut churned. He barked and jumped. He could barely breathe from the anticipation.

"My king." Llewellyn grinned from ear to ear. "I believe we have the items." Llewellyn laid the clothes in front of Garwaf and waited expectantly for him to make some move toward them.

Garwaf only sat there, giving them all an impatient look, growling low. Llewellyn understood first. He pulled King Thomas aside and dropped a discreet word in his ear.

The king, likewise, looked abashed at his own stupidity. "Of course." He shook his head and winked at Garwaf. "So sorry, lad. We weren't thinking."

Llewellyn chivvied the other nobles, guiding them off to another part of the castle. The king acted as Garwaf's servant and carried the package of clothes to the old room Gabriel had used when the castle of Dorré had been his. Reynard, miraculously, had not taken the suite over when he became master of the fortress, and the room had been left almost untouched since the rightful duke was last in residence. King Thomas laid the clothes on the end of the bed, patted Garwaf's shaggy, fur-covered head, and left to give him his privacy.

———— ◆ ————

Garwaf stared at the parcel for an hour without moving. The thoughts in his head were eddies of turmoil, barely coherent. He just kept thinking, remembering, pondering, wondering, worrying, and the thoughts in his head would not still long enough or make themselves rational enough to allow action.

After an hour of perching in silent indecision and fretful inaction, he finally bestirred himself. With difficulty and regret, he pawed at his neck until the golden rose necklace slipped off. Then he padded to the bed and tore away the wrappings of his bundle.

To someone who did not know their secret, the clothes were innocuous enough: a pair of dark leather breeches with worn patches at the knees, a stout linen shirt, a green woolen cloak with a heavy hood, and hardy riding boots. A leather pouch lay among the clothes too. Garwaf grabbed the bag in his teeth and tilted out its contents: an ornate cross etched in gold on a delicate chain, a length of three braided ribbons, and...nothing else.

The wolf growled. The smell of Reynard was all over the pouch.

———— ◆ ————

When Garwaf burst forth from the chamber still—well—a *wolf*, the king looked surprised and understandably dismayed. Garwaf ignored him and all others as he galloped through the castle—all thoughts of caution thrown to the wind. He bounded out of the keep and into the courtyard. Reynard leaned against the gate with his guards.

Reynard let out a muffled cry and threw up his hands to ward the wolf off. The guards, no fools, threw themselves out of the path of the furious animal. Reynard was not worth dying for.

Garwaf knocked Reynard to the ground, bouncing Reynard's head on the cobbles, so the knight lay momentarily stunned.

The king's retinue recoiled in horror, and the archers on the walls drew their bows. Llewellyn and the king ran into the courtyard together, winded and pale.

"*Hold,*" King Thomas bellowed to the archers, his voice cracking from fear. "*Hold.*"

Garwaf continued to ignore them and sniffed furiously all about Reynard's hands and torso. Letting out a snarl of rage and triumph, the wolf struck at Reynard's neck. The watching crowd gasped.

Garwaf sensed their fear, but he had no intention of ripping Reynard's throat out. Instead, the wolf delicately drew a leather cord between his teeth from the man's neck and bit the string in two. Carrying the leather thong and the gold ring dangling from it in his jaws, Garwaf cheerfully trotted away from the prone Reynard and back into the castle.

———◦———

Shut up in solitude in his old bedroom, Garwaf laid his ring out on the bedclothes. The heavy signet was bright gold with a flat lapis lazuli set into it, a wolf passant chiseled into the stone. He had not seen the ring in more than two years. The signet had been his father's, crafted in the far southern city of Ordinobl and brought back to wear in all honor as the Duke of Dorré. The ring had passed to Gabriel at his father's death.

The delicate cross had been his mother's, brought home from the distant southern colonies by her father from the then newly conquered city of Anutitum. The Lady Phillippa had gifted the bauble to her son on his naming day. There was a heavy cross in the middle, with four smaller crosses bordering it to symbolize the four paths down which the will of Fate guides man.

The grimy braided ribbon had been a gift bestowed on Gabriel by Alisoun. She had braided it in her hair, then given the ribbon to Gabriel as a sign of her favor afterward. The ribbon had frayed at the ends, dirty and discolored now. The colors of the three strands had once been red-orange, dark purple, and yellow, though the third ribbon, which had been bright yellow, had faded now to a dingy mustard hue.

Garwaf gazed at the cross, the ring, and the braided ribbons. They had been the most precious of all his belongings. These treasures, and not his clothes, defined his humanity. Without these three items, he would have been stuck forever as a wolf.

He jumped onto his bed, and with some frustration about his lack of thumbs, he managed to get the signet onto the toe of one paw and twist the chain of the cross around his leg. He went to get the ribbons and found he was loath to touch them. Before they had been a reminder and a comfort to him. *Now* they served only to remind him of his incredible folly—first in marrying and then in trusting poor Alisoun.

He nudged the ribbons off the bed with his nose, letting them fall to the floor. Better to continue a wolf forever than to remain indentured to the memory of Alisoun and their disastrous marriage.

A glint of gold caught his eye. The rose necklace lay in a glittering pile. He had taken the necklace off to create the clean slate required to transform, but he realized he needed that bauble more than all the rest, after all.

He smiled to himself. Not the past but the present, his *future*, his hopes, were what he needed now. Even if he had been able to bring himself to take up the ribbons, he doubted very much whether they would have worked for him any longer. That life was over and his new one just beginning.

Breath shallow, muscles tense, he shrugged his head into the gold chain with surprising ease and waited...

...and then the world changed.

———❧———

Two hours later, the king could bear the tension no longer. Garwaf had been alone quite long enough. If anything was going to happen, it would have happened. The king went to the room and knocked. When no answer came, he pushed the door open a crack to peek inside.

His nephew sprawled on the bed, bathed in the fond caressing beams of moonlight, sleeping soundly, snoring loudly, with an odd assortment of items draped over various limbs and the old clothes tangled all about him.

He was still a wolf.

King Thomas clenched his jaw and shut the door with precision to stop himself from slamming it. Then, to avoid having to contemplate the repercussions of this failed experiment, the king staggered off to get quietly and thoroughly drunk.

———❧———

Dawn arrived next morn as vibrant and brightly pink as a maiden flushing with delight at a pleasant surprise.

Llewellyn managed to rouse King Thomas with difficulty by noon. The magician had spent most of the morning already looking for the silly bugger. When Llewellyn *did* find his king, Thomas sat hunched in a corner of the great hall with a bottle snuggled under his arm like a lover. Llewellyn's gut turned over with remembered pain. He had never wanted to find King Thomas in such a state again after the lost years when Gabriel had been missing. Fighting against his frustration, Llewellyn was not *very* gentle in rousing his liege lord.

A few industrious dunks in the ice-cold water of the horse trough did the trick.

King Thomas, sober now but not entirely awake, aimed a blow at the magician's head, which he ducked. Llewellyn grabbed the king by his shoulders and
gave him a hard shake. "My lord. We must check on Gabriel. See how he does."

The king's face fell. "I have." He collapsed into Llewellyn's arms, nearly knocking Llewellyn down, and sobbed as only the extremely hungover can do. "The
clothes didn't work, my friend. He remains a wolf. We've lost Gabriel forever. I'll
never see the damned boy again. He's doomed to spend the rest of his days as a
house pet. And *Kathryn*. Poor sweet girl." King Thomas moaned and held his
head, sniffling.

Llewellyn shook the king again, gripping the other man's shoulders. "Did you
check on Gabriel this morning?"

King Thomas blinked, eyes red from sorrow and drink. "No. Last night."

Llewellyn rolled his eyes. "Am I the *only* one who noticed the full moon last
night?"

Befuddlement, comprehension, then a piercing hope flitted over the king's
face. Llewellyn barely had time to absorb any of these emotions before King
Thomas broke from him and bounded away up the stairs to Gabriel's room.

In his delight, the king was not entirely considerate, and he threw open the
bedroom door so hard the heavy wood collided with a bang against the wall.

A long lad lay stretched out on the bed. Sometime during the hours of darkness, the clothes, which had lain discarded, had been put on. The young man lay
coiled among the thick blankets with one hand curled under his tanned cheek like
a child. The glint of the signet ring on his finger caught dawn's early rays.

King Thomas stood in the doorway and simply stared.

The man in the bed stirred, long lashes fluttering against tawny cheeks, and
looked up. Dark blue eyes opened at last and stared at the king. The sleeper
frowned and raised one strong, well-muscled arm to run his fingers through un-
kempt black hair. He passed a hand over his handsome *human* face and scratched
with his knuckles at the long white scar along his cheek, black-shadowed now
with a dark beard. The apparition grinned impishly, and said in a voice a trifle

raspy from lack of use, "Good morning, Uncle." He nodded brightly to the king's magician too. "Llewellyn."

That King Thomas did not break the lad's ribs was a wonder as he ran forward and embraced his nephew. The king kissed Gabriel's forehead and hugged him, sobbing with elation and *not* the inebriated melancholy of the night before. "My boy, my son. Oh, Gabriel, my dear, *dear* lad."

Gabriel cradled his uncle's face in his hands and laughed and laughed, tears shining in his eyes. He hugged him close when they both finally began to weep in earnest.

Llewellyn hung back, quietly shutting the door. He smiled drunkenly to himself, besotted by the joy of this morning. "Welcome home, my Lord Gabriel."

Chapter Nineteen

L lewellyn allowed uncle and nephew as much time as he could to bask in the glow of reunion before he discreetly ducked his head back in and coughed.

"My good friend." Gabriel strode forward to clasp Llewellyn by the arms.

Llewellyn made a formal bow. "My lord." He smiled and playfully batted Gabriel's bearded cheek. "Good to see your face again, m'lad."

Gabriel laughed. "I must agree with you."

King Thomas said nothing, just stared at his nephew, his gladness written plainly in his glowing expression, his eyes still shining with happy tears.

Llewellyn hated to be the one to break the mood, but... "Perhaps it's time we strategize."

The king let himself take one last look at Gabriel, as if he were memorizing the lad's features. Then, with a visible wrench, he looked at Llewellyn. "Strategize?"

"How we're going to reintroduce Gabriel." Llewellyn scratched his nose. "Account for his absence."

King Thomas required a moment longer than usual to comprehend Llewellyn's meaning. When he did, his look of joy was shuttered at once. An immense frown creased his brow instead. He paced and chewed his thumbnail. "You're right. We must find someone trustworthy to groom Gabriel, find him suitable clothes, bustle Reynard out, bustle a double for the black wolf in..."

Llewellyn nodded at these plans and made mental notes of his own, already delegating tasks, planning how best to dig up a large black canine on such short notice.

"No, no, no, and no." Gabriel stepped between the two men, stopping his uncle pacing. "*Not* like that. Never again. Besides, most of the court has already figured my secret out. The ones who would be fooled by such a charade are not the ones worth fooling."

"But—"

Gabriel shook his head and clasped the king's shoulder. "Uncle, I lived half a lifetime like that. Now I have a second chance, a second life. I will *not* begin my second chance with a lie. Let them know me for what I am and judge me as they see fit. I will stand trial as a werewolf if I have to, but whatever happens, I won't be banished to the dark again to hide my head in shame." He drew himself up proudly, a son of kings. "I am what I am. And I can live with it now."

The king opened his mouth as if to protest then snapped it shut. He darted a glance at Llewellyn, who only shrugged. Who was he to meddle in the affairs of kings?

Well, the king's advisor, yes... But really, that was definitely beside the point.

"Lot of help you are, my old sage." King Thomas snorted. He sighed and looked back to his nephew. "All right, then."

Gabriel clapped his uncle on the shoulder and headed for the door.

The king caught him gently by the arm, hauling him into the room and kicking the door closed. "Gabriel, lad, at least let us clean you up a bit first, eh?"

—◦—

Most of the king's vassals who had come to pay homage at Sûr had by now followed their liege lord to Dorré. Strange happenings had transpired.

And obviously these old fools mean not to miss the finale. Reynard studied them with disgust.

The crowd had gathered in the courtyard of the duke's hereditary seat, wiping sweat from their brows. The bravest among them would dart glances at Reynard where he stood chained and gagged between two of the king's knights. He bared his teeth at one of them.

No one seemed surprised to see Reynard in chains, and he wasn't terribly shocked himself. Most of the nobles about likely wondered which of his many infamies had finally gotten him caught.

Reynard glared at the puffed-up idiots and waited with resigned curiosity. He had spent the night in his own oubliette and been pulled out early that morning to sit on chill stones in his own courtyard. He too was ready for this farce to be over.

A commotion at the gate set the crowd humming, and the castle's lanky steward strode out with his usual bustling gait, issuing orders to every servant within his sight.

The spokesman of the assembled lords went to the steward and stopped him, speaking loud enough for all to hear. "Pray, steward, what transpires?"

The steward bowed respectfully to him and said in a tone of deep condescension, which only the highest-ranked of servants can master, "King Thomas bid me summon every servant of this house down to the lowliest drudge and bring them to this courtyard, my lord."

"Why?"

"I am not in the king's confidence, my lord," the steward said with a crushing blandness before sweeping away to discharge the rest of his orders.

Very quickly, the courtyard of the castle became a sad crush. All the nobles and servants crowded around, pressed tightly together, kitchen drudges rubbing elbows with earls. His guards pulled Reynard roughly to his feet to avoid him being trampled by the crowd. Reynard frowned, standing on tiptoe to see what was happening. His skin prickled with a deep unease. *Surely they won't—*

King Thomas appeared with Llewellyn at his back and addressed the now very restive audience. The king held up his hands and received quiet at once. "My lords and the inhabitants of this castle, the Lord of Dorré wishes to address himself to you. I pray you hear him out in all courtesy and compassion." With that concise introduction, King Thomas stepped aside, only the anxious flickering of his gaze betraying his nervousness.

Some heads turned toward Reynard, who blandly returned their stares, but others looked toward the castle's entrance where the king had appeared. Obviously, they remembered Reynard had not always been the Lord of Dorré. No doubt they remembered the king's pet wolf as well.

Reynard swallowed, a heavy lump of dread roiling in his gut now.

Gabriel came to stand framed in the doorway, and the clouds crowding in around the castle parted briefly and the sun bathed him in an approving beam before moving on to shine elsewhere. Gabriel's hair had been cut and brushed back, the wild tangle tamed into waves that framed his face. He knew after looking in the mirror this morning—for the first time in *two years*—that his countenance was more lined now, but his fellow nobles apparently recognized him instantly nonetheless.

A whisper passed through the crowd, swifter than the birds of the court could have flown to carry it.

"The duke!"

"Lord Gabriel—Why, that's really Gabriel.*"*

"The man himself."

And so on.

Gabriel let them chatter amongst themselves for a moment, then lifted his hands high to silence them all.

Except Reynard, who let out an indignant scream through his gag. The displaced Reynard was soon better muffled by his guards, and his indignant cries went unheard.

Gabriel planted his feet and squared his shoulders, projecting a confidence he was far from feeling. "A long time has passed since my face was last seen in this land. I have been remiss in my duties to my people and my title. For too long I have been absent. I acknowledge that, and I am sorry for this neglect.

"Some of you have met the wolf that King Thomas has kept with him of late. Some of you encountered him for the first time here when the king rode in yesterday. I tell you now, wondrous as it may be, that I..." He frowned, swallowing and nerving himself up. *Oh, Kind Fate, please guide me to do the right thing.* "I was that wolf."

Cries of shock, horror, and confusion erupted from his servants. His peers did not disappoint either. The resulting clamor from all assembled rose to deafening heights.

He held his hands up, and the crowd quieted again—their curiosity overcoming their shock. "Many of you have known me since I was a young lad. And I've been informed by my steward that many of the old servants who answered to me are still here. I tried ever to be a fair master and a good one. I hope serving me was not an onerous duty."

He nervously combed a hand through his hair. "But I *am* a werewolf. There are those who will swear this makes me unfit to walk the earth. I can only say in my defense that I do retain my mind if not my shape. I am the same creature as a wolf that I am as a man. I swear it." *I'm just shorter. And furry.*

Gabriel drew a steadying breath. "Many of you fear the garwaf and have heard dreadful tales of him from your mothers and grandmothers, on back to the beginning of time. I do not want any who serve me to fear their lord or to fear retribution should they decide to leave my service. Search your hearts and your minds. Decide what you can live with and then leave or stay as you see fit.

"And to my loyal friends." He embraced the circled lords with a toothy grin. "My *dear* friends will be pleased to learn King Thomas has gifted back to me all my old lands." He grinned at Reynard. "And many of Reynard's lands as well to keep in trust. So you need not concern yourselves over Dorré's welfare any longer. I will see to my duchy's safety and keeping as well as I ever have done before. Believe me that pain and woe shall fall on the head of any man who tries to take my lands from me again." He flashed them another predatory smile before continuing his speech.

"I've hidden my secret as long as I can remember, even from my kind uncle. No one knew but my wife, and she betrayed me. Left me accursed. I never thought to be human again. Now that I am, I don't wish to return to you cloaked in lies. If my people serve me, if my friends stand by me, let it be because they know the worst and still judge me as fit and able. Good and honorable. That's why I've told all here assembled of my secret. I leave you now to make your choices. No blame shall follow anyone should you choose to seek service elsewhere. If you believe I did you wrong as a wolf, go to the courts and seek justice there. I will answer for myself and take responsibility for what harm, if any, I have done.

"But, if it pleases you to let my prolonged banishment serve as punishment enough, I am happy to resume my duties and take up my old life again. If the world will let me." He nodded once, satisfied, then ducked into his castle. He stood just inside the doorway, back pressed to the wall, and let a long, slow breath out through his teeth. All he could do now was hope that he would not be torn apart by the crowd.

———◆———

Llewellyn stood quietly, wreathed in the shadows, listening to every nuance of the crowd's reaction to Gabriel's speech. King Thomas had set a contingency plan in place should Gabriel's gamble fail: at the first sign of trouble, Llewellyn was to give the signal and the guards would whisk Gabriel out of the castle to safety. And exile.

Please, let the lad's foolishness work. Please, don't let it come to flight. Llewellyn drew closer to a knot of people, eavesdropping as they whispered together.

The nobles fell into a buzz of conversation at Gabriel's exit, discussing what the most politic way would be to duck out of Dorré now they had been seen. *No harm there.*

Llewellyn moved on to the humbler folk of the crowd.

"Well, I'm not sure," said the grizzled old groundskeeper. "I've heard some strange tell of werewolves."

The cook, a solid, roundly built woman, folded fleshy arms across her bosom and huffed. "Well, I'll say this for ol' Gabriel: I'd rather be locking up my chickens than my daughters, and that's a fact. Say this for the werewolf—he never was one to tumble the maids as was unwilling."

"No," piped up the head groom, "never did catch him with any willin' ones either, 'ceptin' his late lady, of course." They bowed their heads. Word of the duchess's death had reached them before even the king had.

The cook spoke again. "Well, I must say I think, werewolf or not, he ain't any better nor worse than the rest of the nobles when you come right down to it. In fact, we could do *much* worse for a master."

"We already did," some brave soul muttered.

Everyone darted a look at the glowering Reynard and edged a few steps farther away from him.

"I s'pose I'll stay on," the cook declared, "despite all this to-do. I don't reckon Lord Gabriel will make a habit of these grand dustups when the dear lad never did before." With that charitable pronouncement, she wiped her hands on her spotty apron and wandered into the castle to continue terrorizing the kitchen drudges.

The rest of the servants came to pretty much the same decision and shrugged amongst themselves as they went back to the work they had been summoned from.

"Well," the head groom muttered as he walked off arm in arm with a friend. "What was all that fuss for anyway? Lad should have known we'd welcome him back with open arms. 'Specially after living with *Reynard*."

Llewellyn grinned as he strolled into the castle to find Gabriel and the king.

——◄O►——

"All right, Gabriel's safe. Now what, may I ask, are we going to do with Reynard?" Llewellyn popped a grape into his mouth and glanced expectantly at King Thomas.

"Banishment," the king said.

Llewellyn looked to Gabriel, who said nothing. A crease appeared between the duke's brows, though he did not look up from his steward's inventory report. "Well, my lord Duke?"

Gabriel sat back in his chair. "Reynard is not walking out of this land alive if I have anything to say on the matter." His voice was hard, flat.

"Gabriel—"

"No, Uncle. You stopped me from ripping his throat out as a wolf, but you shall not keep me from challenging him to fair combat as a knight. He beat Kathryn. He *shot* Kathryn. I'll take the payment he owes for that out of his hide."

"Gabriel, this is not—" The king broke off as Llewellyn gave him a look and shook his head.

Llewellyn stood, crossing to Gabriel and gently touching his shoulder. "Lad, why would Reynard consent to fight you? He's already been stripped of his lands. He's not so desolate that I think he would let you kill him, so *why* would he fight you? What does he have to gain?"

Gabriel's mouth tilted up in a grin. "I shall strike a deal with the former Earl of Troumper." He stalked from the room, boots resounding on the stone floor. King Thomas anxiously hurried after him.

Llewellyn rubbed a hand over his tired eyes. "Fate preserve me. We finally get the boy back his body, and nothing will suit him better than to get himself killed." He followed the others, hiking his robes up above his knees, his pale legs flashing as he ran to catch his liege lords.

Gabriel beat king and magician both to the courtyard. The pack of nobles still milled about in indecision, discussing the morning's marvels and revelations. They eyed Gabriel warily as he bypassed them, walking up to Reynard.

Reynard's back rested against the wall with his knees propped up and his eyes closed. Chained wrists rested on his filthy knees and, but for the manacles, he might have been taking a refreshing nap in the early-morning sun.

"Remove his gag," Gabriel ordered.

Mouth free, Reynard worked his face in an obvious bid to return feeling to his lips and tongue. That done, he curled his lips into a smile and gave a mocking nod. "Sir Mutt."

Gabriel smirked. "Well said by one who well knows my bite."

Reynard cocked an eyebrow and laughed. "What do you wish of me, my lord Duke?"

Llewellyn and King Thomas had caught up by this time. Gabriel spared them a glance, hastily thrown over his shoulder, before turning to Reynard. He leaned in to the other knight, lowering his voice. "I wish to have an opportunity to pay you back in full for what you did to Lady Kathryn."

Reynard narrowed his eyes. "You wish to fight me."

"I do."

Reynard sniffed. He tipped down to rest on his elbow and arranged himself languidly as he could on the castle's hard stones. "Why would I do something so stupid?" He picked dirt from beneath his nails with his teeth and seemed content to lounge on the dirty cobbles of the court for the rest of his life.

Gabriel hesitated. He looked over his shoulder at his two mentors again and then, squaring his shoulders, he risked all on one throw. "If you agree to fight me fairly in single combat, and if you win, I will cede all my lands, all my titles, *everything*, irrevocably back to you."

"*No*." This was a horrified gasp torn from the king's throat.

Llewellyn merely sagged to the nearest wall and sank his head down to his chest in despair. Gabriel could easily guess his mentor's thoughts: Reynard was older, more experienced, *stronger*, and he hadn't been out of practice with the play of weapons—not to mention the practice of managing human limbs—for more than two years. No doubt the magician thought this duel suicidal.

But it has to be done, and damned if I'll let anyone else do it. Gabriel watched Reynard's face, waiting for his answer.

A smile of triumph twisted the haughty lips of Reynard of Troumper. He jumped to his feet and clasped Gabriel's hands. "We have an accord. Witnessed by king, court, and all. Let it be so." Reynard twisted Gabriel's hand in a bone-crushing grip, but Gabriel, by dint of will, kept himself from flinching. "Now to the battlefield," Reynard cried.

"No," King Thomas said, his voice harsh. He pushed between the two men, leaving one hand firmly pressed against Reynard's chest to hold him back. "If we are to do this, then we do it fairly. You will eat and rest, and so shall the duke. We'll wait until late afternoon. Then you and Lord Gabriel can hack each other to bits for all I care."

Gabriel winced. *Uncle really is quite furious with me if he's calling me "the duke" and "Lord Gabriel." But this duel has to happen. Reynard's bloody and bruised carcass is not worth one drop of Kathryn's blood.* He looked at Reynard's smug face. *But it's a start.*

Gabriel ate his midday meal in stony silence with Llewellyn as his only companion. Eating cooked food with utensils again was odd but extremely gratifying nonetheless. He had so missed having *thumbs.*

King Thomas had gone off to make preparations for the duel. He returned when Gabriel was finishing the last of his roast boar. The king walked straight to the room's largest window and stood there, staring out without saying one word to either of them.

At last, Gabriel could take the silence no more. "Uncle."

Llewellyn laid a restraining hand on Gabriel's arm, but he shrugged the older man off and went to the king.

"Uncle," he said again, more gently. "It has to be done. If I don't defeat him, he will follow me forever. And Kathryn. Fighting him will end it."

"What will this bloodbath end? What satisfaction do you hope for?"

"I want to know the filthy brute won't be coming after me, won't be sniffing around Kathryn. That Reynard the Lecher won't be haunting me all the rest of my life." Gabriel clenched his fists in frustration. He had to make his uncle understand. "Disgrace Reynard. Banish him. Beat him from the land with stones, and he will still return. Reynard has to *die*—not just for what he's done to Kathryn but for what harm he can do in the future if we let him escape. His evil ends now, and I'm the one to end it."

A muscle ticked in his uncle's jaw. "You're a young fool. I only pray you'll be a *live* fool at the end of this." He stomped from the room, slamming the door behind him.

Gabriel turned to Llewellyn, who had lingered. "And what do you have to say, Master Magician?"

Llewellyn gazed at the ceiling and let his breath out through his teeth. "My lad, I don't know whether to strangle you or weep in despair." He scrubbed his fingers through his white-blond hair and at last met Gabriel's gaze. "I haven't yet decided on which one appeals more at the moment. I might do both."

"I'm right to do this. You *know* that."

"Perhaps." Llewellyn swept out of the room too.

Gabriel was left to prepare himself as best he might for the coming ordeal. Alone. "Merciful Fate." He let his breath out on a gusty sigh. "Things were easier as a wolf."

Chapter Twenty

The expectant blush of the morning flared to a bright yellow at noon but, by the time of the combat, it had waxed to the fatigued red of someone florid from overexertion.

The two combatants faced each other across the open fields before the great castle of Dorré. Men-at-arms ringed them round with their shields. Gabriel and Reynard each wore leather jerkins over their light linen tunics and breeches. The jerkins were sturdy enough to deflect a half-hearted stroke or a dagger graze, but certainly not enough to ward off a killing blow. Each fighter carried a sword, serviceable and as light as could be managed. The knights might be at this all afternoon, so any extra weight that could be left off the weapons and their bodies had been. Each man also bore a matching dagger tucked into his belt.

King Thomas clenched his hands at his sides. *There has to be a way to stop this.* How could he let his dear nephew, a boy as good as a son to him, square up against the beast Reynard? *I've only just gotten Gabriel back, and to lose him now? How can I stop this?*

His mind raged, but he was taking too long. King Thomas needed to move, or one of the fighters would strike without his leave. Once started, neither combatant would pause for their ruler's displeasure either. If the king did not start the contest soon, the looks on both of the fighters' faces promised they would.

With an almost physical wrench and a choked-out oath, King Thomas gestured for the duel to begin. He jerked his gaze away. He did not condone this duel, he could not stop it, but he would not watch.

—◦—

As the fight officially began, Gabriel hefted his sword and waited with patience to see what his opponent intended.

Reynard advanced several paces. "You've scratched your last flea, Sir Mutt." The larger knight swiped at Gabriel with his sword.

Gabriel easily parried the blow and thrust for Reynard's midsection.

He turned Gabriel's sword aside with a deft twist. "I'm surprised you remember how to hold a sword." He stepped in and seized the wrist of Gabriel's sword hand. Taking advantage of Gabriel's position, Reynard held Gabriel's wrist tightly, trapping their blades together in a crossed arrangement. As they strained, pushing against each other, Reynard laughed in Gabriel's face. "Hard to get used to having thumbs again, m'boy?"

Gabriel shifted his stance and drove his knee into Reynard's midsection. Reynard doubled over. Slicing savagely with his blade, Gabriel broke the cross of their swords and left a sizeable gash across Reynard's back.

A few of the men-at-arms cried out in jubilation as Gabriel drew first blood. From the corner of his eye, Gabriel caught sight of Llewellyn pumping his fist in the air, calling out to Reynard, "I hope that will serve to remind you, Troumper, not to waste your breath so idly on foul words."

"I'll see you skewered on a pike, you pasty bastard," Reynard snarled at the magician.

Gabriel kept his gaze focused on his opponent, waiting, unwilling to rise to Reynard's petty taunts. Gabriel had no breath to spare either.

Reynard straightened, working his back muscles with a grimace. In a sudden burst, he raised his sword and ran at Gabriel. Gabriel met him, and they traded blows. Overheated and hampered by his light jerkin and flimsy shirt, Gabriel struggled for control. His boots made him unsteady. He would have felt so much better with the skin of his feet connecting with the ground. *I have to get used to wearing clothes again.*

Reynard's earlier taunts had not been far off the mark. Gabriel's swordsmanship was rusty, unequal to Reynard's in this most pressing of moments. Gabriel felt ungainly, awkward, a great lumbering hulk. His old speed in swordplay, his greatest advantage against a larger opponent, had withered like a sickly limb left unused. Even managing the disposal of his human limbs gave Gabriel difficulty.

He wanted to throw his sword away and go after Reynard with tooth and claw. As a wolf, Gabriel had still always been a man, but if he let himself hurt Reynard in the way he wanted to, then he risked losing all he had recently fought so hard to regain. He risked losing all he yet hoped to have.

Yet he didn't know how much longer he could hold out against Reynard's swordsmanship. He didn't know how much longer he could fight these animal urges—or how much longer he *wanted* to. Gabriel knew enough about blood magic, and his own curse, to know that if he killed a human being with his teeth, if he swallowed human blood he'd spilled, no matter what his shape, man or wolf, he would be a monster forever.

He *had* to control himself. He was a knight. He had to prove he could be a man. Winning wasn't winning if he killed Reynard as a wolf would kill.

Blinking sweat from his eyes, Gabriel swiped wildly at Reynard's head. The big knight retreated, and Gabriel staggered as he lunged again in pursuit. He thrust for Reynard's gut, and the other man knocked Gabriel's blade away.

Reynard stepped swiftly in, seizing his throat. Gabriel choked, chest burning, and clawed at the fingers cutting off his air. Reynard's skin opened beneath his nails in long, deep gashes. The other man growled and shoved him away.

Gabriel gulped in great breaths of air, filling his lungs. With a grunt, Reynard slashed, cutting at Gabriel's stomach while his guard was down. Gabriel howled, pressing a limb to the burning pain.

"*No.*" King Thomas leapt to his feet.

Reynard brandished his bloodstained sword.

Gabriel dropped heavily to the ground, a hand held to his gut. Waves of anguish stung his body, and sticky blood coated his trembling fingers. Stepping forward, Reynard kicked Gabriel in the belly.

Gabriel's vision blacked around the edges, his head swimming. He rolled away, shaking.

Reynard advanced, big boots stomping the grass down. The large knight seized Gabriel's sweat-dampened hair, nearly tugging a chunk out by the roots.

Gabriel had barely wobbled to a shaky standing position before Reynard thrust him away. Dizzy and off balance, Gabriel threw himself at the other knight again. Too close to use his sword effectively, he laid into Reynard freely with his knee and the hilt of his sword.

With a huff of pain, Reynard's seized Gabriel's wrist. Twisting ruthlessly, the other knight brought Gabriel crashing to the ground. Grunting, Reynard pinned Gabriel's sword hand roughly with his foot and kicked Gabriel's weapon away.

"Now what's to do, Sir Mutt?" Reynard laughed, mean and low. "You might have bested me with your teeth and claws, you know. Better as a wolf than a man, eh?"

Vision blurring, head swimming, Gabriel whipped his dagger out and stabbed Reynard in the calf.

Roaring, Reynard stumbled off and groped with his free hand, trying to draw the blade out. Gabriel kicked Reynard's legs out from under him and leapt upon him. Gabriel rolled in the grass, banging into Reynard, taking blows that left him breathless and gasping and trading ruthless hits back that bloodied Reynard's mouth and set the other knight gasping.

Reynard got a hard hit in on Gabriel's wounded stomach. As his vision swam, Gabriel fell sideways off him. The big knight rolled over and, with a sharp bark of pain, pulled Gabriel's knife from his own calf. Gabriel didn't let Reynard collect himself. He started punching the other man about the face at once. The crunch of bone against bone was brutally satisfying, and Gabriel wanted more. He pummeled the other man over and over and over, reveling in the feel of flesh turning to pulp under his fists, skin splitting open, blood staining his nails and hands as he rent Reynard to pieces. Gabriel growled with pleasure. This was just how he should kill Reynard. Slowly.

As Gabriel delivered punch after punch, something glinted just under the edge of his vision, stinging his eyes, distracting him. He paused and rocked back to sit on his heels. Face raw and swelling, Reynard groaned but didn't move.

Gently, Gabriel cupped the shining thing around his own neck in his palm, glancing down at the little golden rose. *Kathryn's bauble.*

Kathryn.

What will she think if you beat Reynard to death? I wanted this, but she wouldn't.

You knew that when you challenged him. Don't fool yourself. It's the wolf in you. Reynard's just another rival who needs to be taken down, another hunting dog whose throat needs to be ripped out.

You didn't have a choice who you were as a wolf. Now you do, and look what you've chosen. You're a worse beast than Reynard.

No. Gabriel recoiled from the ruin of Reynard's face. He gaped at his cut and bloodied hands, flipping them over, staring at them in surprise. Rasping for breath, Gabriel looked into Reynard's hard, dark irises as the flesh around them bled and swelled.

"Kill me, then," Reynard choked out through his broken face.

Gabriel narrowed his eyes and clenched his fists. Something inside him wound tight, ready to snap. His arm shook with tension as he drew back for another blow. Reynard's battered lips tipped up in a gruesome grimace of a smile. There was satisfaction in his face.

Gabriel stared at Reynard and slowly let his arm fall back to his side. With a groan of effort, Gabriel stood, clutching at his bleeding gut. He wiped blood from his mouth with the back of his dirty sleeve and fetched up Reynard's discarded dagger where the other man had dropped it. Gabriel stuck the blade into the belt of his torn, bloodied jerkin.

"What are you doing?" Reynard tried to sit up, then grunted in pain and collapsed backward.

"I'm done with revenge, Reynard. It's over. Enjoy your banishment. If I see you again I will kill you." Gabriel staggered away to receive the congratulations of his king and the spectators.

Reynard threw himself on Gabriel's legs. Gabriel crashed to the ground. The air pushed from his lungs, and his gut was on fire from his wound. Reynard, his battered face a grisly pulp, his dark eyes flaming now with hatred, clawed for the dagger in Gabriel's belt.

Gabriel grabbed Reynard's wrists and strained against this last frantic attack. Gabriel's stomach broiled with pain, warm blood soaking the shirt to his skin. Gritting his teeth, Gabriel brought up his legs to kick Reynard away and drew the dagger from his own belt.

Reynard crawled back, foam flecking his mouth, his teeth bared in a wordless snarl. Gabriel wrestled against the knight's bulky arms. Breathing hard, heart hammering, Gabriel arced the dagger up and brought it down, burying the blade deeply in Reynard's neck. The big knight gurgled and gagged, pawing futilely at his throat.

Nauseated, hot blood dripping onto his face from Reynard's neck, Gabriel released the dagger's handle with a little push, which sent the dying Reynard falling back. His body landed with a *thump* on the torn-up, bloodstained grass.

For a long moment, Gabriel lay on his back in the trampled turf, too weak and wounded to move. His skin crawled and his insides squirmed with disgust at the nastiness of the fight. Stinking of Reynard's blood and his own, feeling soul-soiled and dirty, Gabriel pinched his eyes closed. Tears leaked out between his eyelids, sliding down his filthy cheeks to drip into his ears.

"Gabriel." The voice seemed very far away. "*Gabriel.*"

The stricken note in his uncle's voice at last penetrated Gabriel's awareness, and he opened his eyes. Gingerly and by very gentle degrees, Gabriel creaked to his feet. Hugging an arm to his slashed stomach, he limped to his uncle and dipped achingly to one knee, trying not to tumble forward in a faint. Gabriel cleared his throat. "I trust, my king, I have proven my claim to the Dorré estates."

King Thomas's eyes shone with wetness. "Your lands are yours again, Gabriel fitz Michael, irrevocably and irrefutably." The king pulled Gabriel to his feet and raised their joined hands aloft in triumph. "I present your lord, the Duke of Dorré, now and forever."

A cheer went up among the men-at-arms. They clanked their swords against their shields in salute. As the jubilations began, Gabriel looked about him in wonder and gratitude. *I am the Duke of Dorré. I'm me again.*

Time to retrieve my duchess. He took one step, then blinked, black spotting the edges of his vision. Gabriel wavered gracefully on the spot, like a leaf trembling on the end of its twig. This lasted for a long moment. Then the valiant and victorious, honorable and glorious, brave and noble Gabriel fitz Michael, son of kings, heir to the throne of Lyond, the worthy Duke of Dorré...fainted.

Chapter Twenty-One

Beatrice really was quite close to tearing her hair out. She had been at the damned convent of Bourlonge far longer than she cared to remember. Sitting and waiting and furiously writing to her idiot brother. The longer Beatrice remained, the less likely she would leave again. She had to get *out*.

The damned abbess kept trying to talk to her as well, preach to her about the benefits of a spiritual life. Beatrice had to admit she was tempted. An ambitious, clever woman could certainly climb her way over all the other pious, biddable little nuns to a position of great authority in the temple. With her abilities, Beatrice could even make abbess someday—if she wanted. The idea did appeal, but then, so did being a duchess. She needed to talk to her brother and find out if she really was as irredeemable for marriage as he now believed her to be.

The *other* thing that made Beatrice grit her teeth was that all the precious little nuns were hiding something from her.

After about a week of enduring strange behavior from the sisters, Beatrice discovered one room they kept taking turns in, spending hours there at a time. Another day, one of the local foresters came back leading a horse, and the event caused a great stir of elation among the sisters—as much as nuns could be said to be observably joyous.

The next day, as Beatrice lay in her chamber, debating whether to rise or not, she caught the sound of a man speaking in low tones with a woman, whose voice she immediately recognized as belonging to the abbess.

Beatrice leapt up. Cracking her door open ever so slightly, she could just barely discern what they said.

"You need not fear for her anymore," the abbess said quietly to the man. "She is awake and knows herself. She will suffer no lasting hurt from her misadventures in the forest, and now you can trust her into our care to help her mend the rest of the way."

"Is she to stay here for good, or—"

"That choice is yet before her," the abbess said gently. "When she is well enough to travel, she will certainly let you know what her intentions are."

"How will I ever be able to thank you and the sisters for all you've done for my daughter?"

The abbess, of course, piously waved this away. "All was done in service to good. Kind Fate smile on your journey, Lord Stephen."

"And Kind Fate go always with you, Your Reverence." The man bowed to the abbess and went to his horse, which Beatrice, who now leaned all the way out of her door, recognized as the one the forester had brought in days ago.

The mysterious Lord Stephen rode off in the early-morning light, and Beatrice hurried back into her room, in case the abbess should turn and see her.

Beatrice would have to discover what this whispered conference was about. The gentleman seemingly had a daughter quartered here, and *not* one of the sisters, either. Beatrice had believed herself to be the only noble guest in residence at the convent. She was wrong, and now nothing would suit her but to find out the identity of this other woman.

She snooped about the secret chamber all day, but to no avail. The nuns were vigilant about closing the door behind them when they left the room. If Beatrice questioned them, they would say one of the sisters had fallen ill and they were taking turns in caring for her.

Later, the abbess came by and told Beatrice with the utmost delicacy that her brother, Reynard, and his wife were dead, the one having succumbed to her illness, the other killed in a duel by the newly reinstated Duke of Dorré, one Gabriel fitz Michael, nephew to the king. The abbess was respectful and gentle when breaking the news, but Beatrice could tell this was *not* ill news to the abbess.

Beatrice cried a little over her brother that afternoon in the solitude of her own room. Not so much for her brother himself—he'd always been vile to her—but perhaps for the *idea* of him. Certainly she cried for the loss of her security. She was quite alone in the world now.

His wife, Lady Alisoun, mattered not at all. She was a stone-cold bitch in life, and now she was just stone cold. That news mattered little to Beatrice.

The spiritual life was swiftly becoming Beatrice's *only* option.

———◄O►———

By the end of that week, Beatrice still had no idea who or what lay in the secret bedroom. The invalid's identity was probably not all that important, but at heart Beatrice remained an irredeemable gossip. It pained her that scandal and intrigue brewed around her, yet nothing she was able to do could unravel the truth. She went to bed every evening with her fists clenched on the covers and woke the next morning with the same acute burning of dissatisfaction in her gut.

After Beatrice broke her fast the next morning, the subprioress came to speak to her. "Lady Beatrice, a young maiden arrived last night to stay as a guest. She also is contemplating a monastic life. I thought the two of you might be good company for each other while you each sort out what is best to be done with your futures. If you would be so kind, she is helping Sister Ursula in the vegetable patch."

"Of course, sister." Beatrice nodded demurely. Rubbing her hands in expectation, she went to see this "new arrival," which, Beatrice had no doubt, was the invalid who had actually been secreted away within the convent these two weeks past.

"Her name is Kathryn," the subprioress called after Beatrice.

Beatrice all but ran to the dingy little vegetable patch.

Kathryn wore a plain brown gown, given to her by the sisters. It had probably been one of the gifts to the poor from a novice entering the order. She perched on her knees next to a fresh-faced young nun, and the two of them were up to their elbows in dirt, happily digging away in the garden.

"The subprioress recommended me to find you, m'dear," Beatrice said sweetly. "She thought you might like a companion. Someone to show you the ropes on your first day at Bourlonge."

The little witch, Kathryn, flinched and, hands shaking, looked up at Beatrice.

Beatrice couldn't help the exclamation that burst from her. "What happened to *you?*"

Kathryn flushed. Fading bruises and healing cuts covered the girl's face, and her eye particularly showed signs of an old bruise just turning yellow at the edges.

Beatrice sat on a nearby bench. She smiled at the confused Sister Ursula. "We are friends of old, dear sister. Will you leave us in solitude to reminisce?"

Darting a glance at Kathryn, who nodded reluctantly, the nun wiped her hands on her apron and wandered off.

Beatrice clasped her hands. "Well? What happened?"

Kathryn glared at Beatrice. "Men are allowed to do what they will to women. Your brother believes so, anyway."

"Yes, he does." Beatrice swallowed, an unaccustomed burst of sympathy tugging at her heart. She clenched her jaw and pushed it away, forcing her voice to go honey sweet. "Well, Little Kathryn, here all alone, are you?"

Face set, Kathryn sat back on her heels. "What do you want?"

"Retribution for what you did to me."

"I did not do anything *to* you." Kathryn turned back to her vegetable patch. "I did not force you to trade your body in exchange for social consequence. Nor did I make you tell wretched lies to the queen. Nor did I have anything to do with the king and queen's decision to banish you from the court. *I* did nothing to *you.*"

Beatrice snorted. "I could have triumphed over that she-devil, Aliénor. King Thomas would have been forced to help me to a good husband if nothing else. But you came and wrecked everything, you little—" Beatrice advanced on her.

Kathryn held her off with a small spade. "Watch yourself, Beatrice. Lay a hand on me within the enclave, and there's nowhere on earth that will take you."

Beatrice sat back on her rump and scowled.

Kathryn's brows pinched together, her eyes soft and sad. "You've made your own fate, Beatrice. Now live with it."

Beatrice glowered at the girl and stomped off to the rectory to brood.

———◦———

Kathryn's time at the convent had been painful and inconvenient, but she found much comfort in Abbess Marie. As soon as Kathryn felt up to it, she had poured out all of her story to the abbess's sympathetic ears. Marie did remark as she left the room that the story would make quite the fairy tale.

Reflecting on this, Kathryn had to agree, but *she* would never write such a tale. Not now.

The abbess, Kathryn's jailer and nursemaid in one, allowed her to go about the convent now her shoulder was doing better and her appalling bruises were healing. Unfortunate that her first day out and about the place she had had a scene with Beatrice forced on her, but this hardly troubled Kathryn. Beatrice, after all, could do nothing within the rectory, and Kathryn had been enjoying herself all morning despite the unpleasantness. She could almost forget her worries and her sorrow in the joy of being out in the world again. Almost.

The wolf had been gone two weeks, and Kathryn had received no word but what the abbess could tell her—of the disease and death of Lady Alisoun, of the wolf's return to humanity, his speech to his vassals, the duel, Reynard's death, and the duke's reputed injuries. That these wounds had been extensive enough to keep him abed for a while, Kathryn understood. And yet...

Garwaf had found his clothes again. He'd changed back. He was the Duke of Dorré once more, Gabriel fitz Michael, heir to the throne until the queen was delivered of an heir—which the abbess had confided to Kathryn would be soon enough now. The midwife had confirmed the news only yesterday, and Aliénor had wanted word sent to Marie and Kathryn.

Garwaf, or *Lord Gabriel* rather, though he would soon only be *second* in succession to the throne, had become a very important person again. His lack of communication with Kathryn also made the fact apparent that he was someone who no longer had any time for her. Not now that he was human.

Their last meeting remained vivid in her head. She thought they had come to an understanding. She remembered the speaking look in his eyes, so full of promise. Yet as the weeks passed without any word from him, it became easier to believe the promise his eyes had held was no more than a delusion of her pain-fevered mind.

Aliénor's latest letter said King Thomas and his retinue were expected to return to the castle from Dorré any day. Frankly, Kathryn couldn't wait for that happy event. Surely they would send *some* word to her, and then she could resign herself completely to a life among the sisters of Bourlonge. Kathryn had decided that to lead a quiet life of scholarship and hermitage here in this lovely haven, while it was not quite what she had dreamed of, would not be so awful. She would never take vows, of course. How could she pledge her heart to Fate when it belonged to someone else? But seclusion from the world seemed a desirable thing to her these days.

She would have reconciled herself to a monastic life already if not for Queen Aliénor. Aliénor, perhaps sensing Kathryn's disappointment, had written that *she* believed Duke Gabriel was rough-riding through the country to storm into the convent, sweep Kathryn in his arms, and carry her off to be his bride.

Had this been his plan, though, such an event should've happened already. Kathryn had written back to Aliénor and had, at least, gotten the queen to agree that if Gabriel didn't return with the king, then Kathryn had royal permission to submerge herself in life at the convent.

Over the next couple of days, Kathryn often found herself, irritatingly enough, remembering what the human Garwaf looked like from that portrait in the queen's chambers. In her most unguarded moments, Kathryn even embroidered on the vision the queen had conjured for her.

Once Kathryn realized she was doing this, however, she scolded herself soundly and recited in her mind the most gruesome tales of gore she could remember to distract herself. The strategy even worked sometimes. Sometimes she *did* manage to turn her thoughts away from the wolf she had lost forever and the man she would never know now.

———◦———

Queen Aliénor, true to her promise, rode out in company with her ladies-in-waiting and several men-at-arms to visit the convent of Bourlonge to reclaim her horse and see Kathryn. The queen stayed the day with Kathryn, and they laughed together like times of old. Aliénor showed great restraint in asking Kathryn to return with her to court only once.

Kathryn bit her lip. "My queen, I *can't*."

Perhaps noticing Kathryn's fragile state, the queen shifted topics. "The midwife says I'm a few months along."

Kathryn touched the queen's thickening belly with a grin. "I'm not surprised."

Aliénor beamed. Kathryn smiled back, a little sad but happy for her friend. The queen clasped Kathryn's hand. "My king hasn't even returned yet. He's the most abominable correspondent—only writing to tell me Gabriel is wounded and he cannot leave his nephew's side yet. When Gabriel is well, King Thomas will return. They *both* will."

Kathryn nodded but quickly changed the subject to something less painful.

The queen departed the next morning, taking with her Gaenor, the sweet mare she had lent Kathryn all those weeks ago.

As she watched Aliénor and the others ride away, Kathryn sighed. An oppressive tide of loneliness swept over her from head to foot. The day after the queen's visit, she couldn't bear company. She hid in the vegetable garden with one of the novices as her chaperone and rooted and weeded and got filthy trying to take her mind off things.

Gabriel's wounds had not been severe, but he had lost far too much blood for comfort. For nearly a week, he remained in a dreadful fever, half out of his wits most of the time. The only signs of lucidity he showed were when he spoke of Kathryn.

Eventually, the fever broke, and Gabriel began to mend.

"Well, my lad," Llewellyn said at the end of the second week, "your wound is healing just fine. Your fever's gone. You've managed to sort out the most immediate needs of the estate while bedridden. You may be fit to travel." Gabriel tried to leap from bed at once, but Llewellyn held him down with a firm hand on his shoulder. "*Tomorrow.*" Taking no chances, the magician dosed his patient with poppy juice to keep Gabriel still for the night.

Nothing would do next morning, though, but for Gabriel to mount up as soon as the sky had lightened. His uncle hastily made preparations and rode off with his retinue straggling behind as he tried to keep up with Gabriel's eager pace.

The cavalcade arrived at the convent of Bourlonge on the second day of their journey. Gabriel rode in at the gate, warily casting his gaze about to see whether she was there. She was not waiting, and he staggered almost from a physical blow. His eyes, his arms, his heart ached for Kathryn.

The abbess stood ready to greet him. As soon as he had dismounted, she hugged him tight to her chest, weeping a little. He smiled kindly as he held her away from him. "Where is she, Aunt?"

The abbess smiled in understanding, eyes still watery. "The vegetable patch. Sister Ursula will guide you."

When the king and Llewellyn started to follow him, Gabriel waved them away. "May I go alone?"

Abashed, the two went to take refreshment with the abbess and wait.

———◦———

Kathryn knelt in the garden, covered in dirt and very hot. She wiped a hand across her sweat-dampened brow, smearing a long mark of dirt across her face. Uncaring, she sat back on her heels to think about Garwaf. She missed him so very much.

In acknowledging that she missed him, she surrendered at last and allowed herself to be lost in memories of him: Llewellyn's workshop, shopping at the market together, the quiet of the rose garden, chasing each other and laughing in the king's orchard...

———◦———

Gabriel and his holy guide turned a corner, and all he saw was a young novice bent over her work. He turned to the sister who had escorted him there, his throat clogging with fear. "She's not a novice, surely. Lady Kathryn, I mean, she hasn't—"

Sister Ursula shook her head, an amused gleam in her eye. "That is one of our novices. Lady Kathryn is just *there*." She pointed.

He whipped his head around, and at last he saw that same lithe silhouette, still wearing a plain brown gown of the secular world and *not* the habit of a nun. Reluctantly, he tore his gaze from her back and looked to his monastic escort. "With your leave, I'll continue alone."

Sister Ursula hesitated, but then, with a quick nod, she left.

———◦———

Kathryn swatted a gnat off her face, no doubt leaving yet another daub of dirt on her cheek. She whistled under her breath, content with sunshine and fond recollections of her lost love, which she would always have to comfort her in her solitude.

"Excuse me...Lady Kathryn?"

She whirled, startled by the soft male voice behind her. As Kathryn stared at the visitor, aghast, her breath strangled in her throat.

She gazed with dazzled eyes at the dark young man who stood above her. Dusty from the road, he carried his traveling jerkin clutched in one hand. He was tall and well-muscled, and his deep black hair fell in beautiful waves to frame his face. His jaw and fine cheekbones were dark shadowed with a normally well-kept beard, now spotted in places by a few patches of errant stubble. His lips were wide and shapely, and his nose would have been noble and aquiline but for the crook in the middle where it had been broken. He had a few long scratches on his cheek, and some yellowing bruises, but other than that, he was most obviously a young man glowing with happiness and in the prime of his life.

The white scar on his face looked familiar but oddly out of place where it puckered over a *human* eye and cheek. The wind whipped up and pulled back his shirt from his shoulder to show the thin white lines of a wound newly healed and scarred over.

Kathryn pinched her eyes closed. *The dog bite.* She snapped her eyes open again, and the golden pendant caught the light in its rosy petals, dangling on the same chain as a heavy cross of Fate.

She steeled herself and gulped in a breath. Without even looking, without any of these outward signs, she would have known this man. With her eyes closed, blinded forever, deaf, dumb, or dead, still she would have known him. Something inside her simply couldn't help but thrum and sing out in his presence—wolf, man, or otherwise. For all that, there remained one thing more. One last test she had to try before she could let her heart break. She clenched her jaw and looked into his eyes.

As his dark gaze held her in its thrall, caressing her, cradling her, promising everything—even though it was impossible—her own eyes prickled with tears.

She wanted to look away, to break the contact and run from him. Instead, she found herself all but falling toward him, her arms reaching out, her feet tangling in her skirts as she rushed forward.

He lifted his hands, long hands calloused with a lifetime of work, battle, and running unshod through forests, but still shapely and gentle. He caught her arms, and she felt a shiver pass through him. "Kathryn."

She swallowed, the lump in her throat all but choking her, and eased back to get another look at him. Kathryn had realized she felt rather more strongly for the wolf than she had wanted to believe. Now, to find herself head over heels in love with a werewolf was something quite different. Still, no denying it. She loved him, beast or no, werewolf that he was, and she would love him in any shape, any color, any form the world might choose to make him. "*Gabriel.*" She gave him a watery smile.

He voiced a small groan and held his arms wide to embrace her. She stepped happily into the circle of his embrace as if she had done so all her life. She wanted to tangle her fingers in his silky dark hair but then, remembering the garden dirt on her hands, she clenched her fingers tight so as not to soil his shirt. Even as she twined her arms more tightly around his neck, she kept her hands curled into fists.

Gabriel clasped her to him and gulped in a deep breath, his gaze intent on her mouth. Her heart fluttered in her chest. They both held their breaths, easing toward each other. Over the protesting gasp of the novice chaperone, Gabriel touched his lips to Kathryn's.

He kissed her rather thoroughly, and for quite a long time too, making her all warm and tingly inside, and totally insensible to the rest of the world. For her part, she threw her arms around him, pressing her body tight to her garwaf, her duke, her one true love.

Chapter Twenty-Two

Eventually Gabriel and Kathryn were persuaded by the offended novice to break apart. Only then did Kathryn take herself off to the washbasin to clean her hands, laughing all the while. When she came back, Gabriel held one hand out to her and, with wonder in her eyes, for the first time but certainly not the last, she shyly curled her fingers around his.

The novice escorted them to the receiving room to reunite with King Thomas and Llewellyn, but those worthies had already stepped out. Gabriel ordered the young novice to go find them *at once*, and the flustered girl ran out of the room to obey.

Kathryn started to scold her duke for such high-handed behavior but, on realizing they were quite alone for the moment, she subsided, her cheeks flushing. The first thing they did, of course, was kiss each other again. Kathryn found this activity quite enjoyable and thought she was rather getting the hang of kissing.

———◦———

A short time later, Gabriel had his lady cradled in the crook of his good arm. He looked down at Kathryn's sweet face and tucked an errant tendril of golden-brown hair behind her ear.

She traced the line of his jaw, brushing his stubbled cheeks gently with her knuckles. Her gaze fluttered up to meet his. "Well, Sir Wolf, what now?"

"Now..." He drew a deep breath, burying his face in her hair so he would not have to watch her reaction for this next bit. "You marry me."

"I'm to become your lady?"

He nodded against her hair, which smelled of roses and fresh earth and the promise of tomorrow. "If you'll have me." He leaned back to study her face. "I'm still a werewolf and always shall be. There will be at least a few nights out of every month when you will have a wolf for a husband."

Kathryn seemed to think deeply about this for a moment, and then she smirked at him, one dimple bobbing a haughty curtsy at him from her cheek. "Well, I always have several days a month where I'm not the most enjoyable person to live with too. I daresay it evens up." He laughed at her and leaned in to kiss her, but she pulled away, suddenly serious. "But, love, I'm only a poor baron's daughter. Shouldn't you explore your options before you settle for me?"

Gabriel wrestled her into his lap, comfortably crushing her in his arms. "Idiot girl, I played that game once before and ended up with a lying harpy for a wife." He paused. "May she find her peace." He shook his head. "Do you think I want to play that game again when I have the best catch in the kingdom curled so deliciously in my lap already?"

She frowned still. He cupped her cheek and tilted her face so she would have to look at him. "Kathryn, I had a grand lady before, but now I should far prefer a true lady. And so you are. You are my one true lady. The only woman I could ever have to be a real wife to me. If you won't have me, then I'll just have to join a monastery. Or maybe I could be Llewellyn's apprentice."

"I am your true lady?"

He held her tightly, emotion roughening his voice. "You are my miracle, my salvation and, indeed, my true lady. I should be lost without you if you ever left me."

"Well," she said with a brusque tone as she settled herself securely into his lap and arranged his arms about her. "In that case, I had better not leave." She brushed his lips with her own. "After all, can't have *you* go to waste. You're such a fine morsel of manhood—"

Gabriel kissed her.

"Werewolfishness—"

He gently touched his lips against hers.

"*Mmm*—"

He pulled her to him in a lingering embrace.

———◦———

Meanwhile, the king, the abbess, and the magician returned to the receiving room to break the solitude of the couple. The poor little novice had missed these worthies at every turn, and so they were still in ignorance as to the whereabouts of the young couple.

"I thought Gabriel went out to the garden to find Kathryn and bring her back to see us," the abbess said testily as they walked along a corridor.

"Yes," King Thomas said. "We can't exactly announce a royal engagement without the couple."

Llewellyn, however, had nothing to say and had fallen behind as he stood just out of sight of the entrance to the small receiving room, the sound of quiet voices murmuring in contented tones having reached his ears.

The king and his sister turned to start asking him questions, but the magician motioned them to silence and cocked his head toward the room. Furtively, King Thomas and Abbess Marie stole up beside him and joined in on the spying.

Quiet murmurs passed back and forth for a moment before the voices ceased altogether. "*Oy*," Gabriel's booming tones barked out to the eavesdroppers. "Bugger off."

It seemed one didn't spend two years as a wolf without developing an impressive sense of hearing.

King Thomas and Llewellyn burst out laughing. After indulging in a moment of offended piety, the abbess was also unable to control herself, and Marie howled with laughter too.

Eventually the disturbed lovers were persuaded to admit the others into the antechamber. The couple was chastely arranged beside one another, forced to content themselves for the moment with merely holding each other's hand.

King Thomas grinned. "Have you come to an arrangement between you, then?"

Gabriel grinned wolfishly and kissed Kathryn's hand. "Meet the future Duchess of Dorré."

A general round of hand shaking, back slapping, and much kissing of the bride-to-be commenced before everyone could settle down and remember what they were about.

"Is Kathryn to stay here until the wedding or remove back to court?" the king asked.

Kathryn bit her lip. "I am grateful for all the abbess has done for me, and my stay here has been a pleasure, but I miss the queen and my friends at court."

"And you don't wish to be parted from Gabriel while the wedding arrangements are made," Llewellyn said.

"And I don't wish to be parted from Gabriel while the wedding arrangements are made." Kathryn's dimple pierced her cheek.

The king stroked his chin. "The only difficulty I can think of is that you need a lady chaperone back to the castle. After all the intrigue we went through to spare your reputation, we can hardly have you riding back without a female escort in company with so many men."

"I will go with her." Beatrice stepped from behind the half-open door.

***

Oddly enough, the arrangement worked out quite well. Kathryn and Beatrice didn't actually need to interact for things to be seemly. The truce also accomplished what it needed to, in that Kathryn's reputation remained as spotless as ever when she, in company with her fiancé and his uncle, rode into the royal castle the very next day. In exchange for her return to court, Beatrice would not repeat any of the juicy gossip she had discovered.

Beatrice had a room in the women's chambers again, but she did not share her chamber with anyone, and no one expected her to perform any of the duties of the ladies-in-waiting. This suited everyone admirably—Beatrice, apparently, most of all.

Lord Stephen returned to court when news of his daughter's extraordinary betrothal reached his ears. He stayed at the castle for some time and then, though no one was quite sure how, announced to his daughter and son-in-law to-be that he, too, would soon marry. "She is an estimable lady, Kathryn, to be sure. I've asked the Lady Beatrice of Troumper to be my baroness." Lord Stephen smiled brightly at his shocked daughter.

Kathryn opened her mouth to tell him all about Beatrice, about Beatrice and the king, about Beatrice and everyone else with a codpiece in the royal court, but Gabriel stomped on her foot to quiet her.

Lord Stephen continued, oblivious, "The castle at Réméré has been very lonely without you these past months. The place needs a mistress, and I'm sure my dear lady is capable enough to set all to rights. She is kind and so considerate of my gout. I'm quite taken with her."

Kathryn left the interview with her father with extremely addled wits, and when she finally decided to confront Beatrice, her soon-to-be stepmama, the change that had come over the former termagant amazed her.

"Oh, *dear* Kathryn," Beatrice said, "your father is quite the sweetest man I've ever met. I pray you won't spoil this for both of us by carrying tales to him of my old life. I'm quite reformed, I assure you, and I want nothing more in this world than to be a good wife to Lord Stephen." Beatrice smiled angelically, patted Kathryn's cheek with infuriating condescension, and glided away to sew her wedding dress.

Kathryn left this interview even *more* addled. When she told Gabriel, he held her in the crook of his shoulder and explained his thoughts on the matter. "The convent didn't appeal. She has no male relations to care for her. I suppose Beatrice's options are rather limited. Better to be a poor baron's wife and have the rule of him than to be an old spinster sitting by a fire somewhere unwanted and alone."

Gabriel was right. The more Kathryn thought about her father's marriage, the more she realized Beatrice might be the making of Lord Stephen, and he the making of her. Their marriage was, oddly enough, really all for the best.

———◦———

Kathryn remained far too busy taking daily delight in Gabriel, the man who couldn't become her husband quickly enough, to care much about the affairs of court. The both of them were very busy, but now that they were both back at court, the morning walks, more properly chaperoned, of course, continued.

Kathryn spent the first week of mornings drinking in with awe and gratitude every word that fell from Gabriel's lips. They talked of everything, shared everything that had, because of circumstances, been left unsaid between them. Every day was a revelation of how much more they could be in love, and every day they were proportionately grateful events had fallen out so well for them.

Kathryn and Gabriel's marriage took place several weeks after their engagement—to allow enough time for planning and to make sure the wedding night was not on the eve of a full moon. It seemed everyone in the kingdom was invited, and the great hall of the king's castle filled fairly to bursting with all the dignitaries and nobles come to see the beast marry his beauty.

Under the kind sermon of Abbess Marie, Kathryn accepted Gabriel's ring, and together they exchanged vows, ignoring all the pomp and consequence of the event. Aliénor's complaints about the silly, oversized frock she was forced to wear to accommodate her growing belly, and the king's whining about a split seam across his shoulder, both fell on unheeding ears. When Llewellyn stumbled on a rug in the shrine and accidentally swore during the ceremony, Gabriel ignored him to keep his attention focused on Kathryn. The dubious sobs issuing from Kathryn's soon-to-be stepmama and the snores of her father were likewise disregarded. And the two lovers barely noticed when Marie accidentally skipped a page of sermon as the sheets of vellum stuck together. Kathryn tripped on her own train, but her gaze never wavered on her way down the aisle to Gabriel. Gabriel sneezed before he pronounced his vows, but the action barely registered. To both of them, the day was about their love, about joining their lives together, and as such, that was all Kathryn and Gabriel concerned themselves with.

"Those whom Fate has united let no man try to part," Marie intoned with convincing solemnity. She ruined this pretense the next moment, though, when she leaned in confidingly to the newlyweds and murmured, "Well, kiss each other, you great silly fools."

Gabriel pulled Kathryn to him, and they melted into each other. The crowd watching rose to their feet in appreciative delight. The newlyweds broke apart after a short time and beamed at the wildly approving wedding guests.

Gabriel hugged Kathryn to his heart as they faced the cheering crowd. "Any regrets, love?"

"Just one," Kathryn said quietly.

He turned to her, scrutinizing her face, his brows pinched together. "What?"

Her dimple peeped at him from her cheek. "That I let Aliénor convince me to have this idiotic train on my wedding dress."

Gabriel grinned and kissed his bride again.

———————— ◆ ————————

So it was that they were happy and united at last. Though Gabriel still turned into a wolf, he now had a warm bed to spend the night in and never again banished himself to the forest for his change—unless, of course, his uncle fancied a spot of hunting.

Kathryn and Gabriel would have their small fights and misunderstandings, hard times and good. But they would be together now, always and forever, living, for the most part, happily ever after.

That is all anyone can ask for, and all they wanted anyway.

Acknowledgments

Many thanks to:

Valerie, my first and best reader, the Queen of the Comma and Paperdoll Maker Extraordinaire.

Mom, even though she likes him better as a wolf.

Biag, who helped to make the final confrontation more than just "Insert fight scene."

Phoenix Sullivan, who helped me get my blurb in shipshape.

Simone Sadie for yet another gorgeous piece of art, and Najla Qamber for the beautiful cover design.

Eleanor, Henry, and Marie, whose histories and personalities I have mangled for my own nefarious ends.

Once again, many, many thanks to Chris Juzwiak, for the inspiration, for his encouragement, for teaching me French swear words, and for being one of the best teachers I've ever had.

Update for 2023: Thank you to my husband, my kids, and my mom for all their love and support.

Also By Eli Donovan

Sweet Feminist Fairy Tale Retellings
The Fairy Tales of Lyond Series:
The Beauty's Beast
Enchanting the King
The Apprentice Sorceress
The Changeling Child
*

Science Fiction with Romantic Elements (and time travel!)
Time Traitors
Time Traitor Files: Agent Nakamura
*

Standalone SF Romance with some heat
Jacen
Zandro

About the Author

Eli Donovan is an author who grew up reading too many Robin McKinley books and knows all the words to every Disney song. Eli lives in Southern California with a husband, kids, and one grumpy elderly cat.

Eli Donovan Website: www.elidonovan.wordpress.com

www.ingramcontent.com/pod-product-compliance
Lightning Source LLC
Chambersburg PA
CBHW060325260626
47160CB00007B/2683